The
Cast Stone

The
Cast Stone

Harold Johnson

thistledown press

Thistledown Press Ltd.
118 - 20th Street West
Saskatoon, Saskatchewan, S7M 0W6
www.thistledownpress.com

Library and Archives Canada Cataloguing in Publication
The cast stone / Harold Johnson.

ISBN 978-1-897235-89-8

I. Title.

PS8569.O328C38 2011   C813'.6   C2011-905348-9

Cover: photographic detail of *Gag* by Kate McGwire
Cover and book design by Jackie Forrie
Printed and bound in Canada

Canada Council   Conseil des Arts   SASKATCHEWAN   Canadian   Patrimoine
for the Arts   du Canada   ARTS BOARD   Heritage   canadien

Thistledown Press gratefully acknowledges the financial assistance of the Canada
Council for the Arts, the Saskatchewan Arts Board, and the Government of Canada
through the Canada Book Fund for its publishing program.

The
Cast Stone

THE EARLY SUN FLASHED OFF THE ALUMINUM gunwale, a silent flare amid thousands of sparkles where brilliance smashed into rippled water. The boat rocked gently to the rhythm of the man's pull on the net. He stood in the bow, feet set apart and pulled hand over hand, a steady draw that moved the boat incrementally forward, stopping now to kneel for a moment as he untangled a pickerel, pulled the net mesh from the sharp teeth, the head free. He clawed the remainder of the mesh over the thick-skinned body and dropped the prize-sized fish into a plastic tub, stood, and resumed lifting the net.

The pickerel changed the man's thoughts. His eyes lifted from the net that slanted into the water in front of him and found the blue green hills off the western shore, where the scars of industrial logging blotched brown smears against the boreal, smears that leached mud and silt into the streams where pickerel spawn. His thoughts followed the silt flow down the ancient hills into the once rich lake, swam through the weed beds and rushes back to the boat that floated on beige water and the mostly empty net.

He turned his head to look toward the northeast for a moment. There, where the horizon was flatter, where muskeg began at the shoreline and spread back for kilometres of wetland, of moss and stunted spruce and tamarack, the death of the fish began there. Acid: sulphuric and nitric, built up, absorbed from the wind, held there during the dry periods and winter and pulsed out during the spring flood, when snow melted and filled the bog and overflowed into the lake. The acid concentrations poured into the water at the same time that the pickerel found the small streams to lay and fertilize eggs.

The pickerel disappeared. Their death was sudden. Fisher people scratched their heads, stood on the shore and stared at the water. The government biologists scratched their heads, took water samples, and went back to their offices to write reports that never completely answered the question. As lake after lake died, fishers began to understand that the dominant northwest wind was bringing acid from the tar sands refineries. It wasn't just killing the lakes, it was killing the trees. The pine were turning red, the birch were not producing leaves. They stood barren and dry and over the years the memory of their lushness began to fade.

With the last of the net into the boat, the rock anchors and white plastic jugs that served as buoys stowed in the belly between the seats, Ben Robe released the clasp and lowered the motor's leg into the water. He thought for a second of using the electric start, decided against it, and pulled on the starter cord. The four-stroke engine purred into life. The electric start was there for when Ben was old. Today he decided at sixty-seven he was still too young to use it.

The boat clipped the water, resonated dull metallic thumps with each wave, a sound that betrayed the boat's heavier than normal construction. Ben gave silent thanks for the fish as he rode, one hand on the tiller, throttle open three-quarters across the lake, gave thanks for the new day, for the sun, for the sky, for the water, for his good health. Dread thoughts found him and he pushed them away, accepted the day as it was, a good day, a day of sunshine and wind. He followed the east shore of Moccasin Lake for a distance then cut across the large open end towards the reserve at the south.

A speck in the distance grew into a bird, a small bird flying straight toward him, something unusual. The bird did not belong out on the water. Here gulls swooped and swirled or followed the boat, chased for a moment, hung in the air on slender wings then slid away. Eagles sometimes waited high in a dead tree near the shore until the boat drew too close for comfort before they dropped, spread their wide black wings and powered away with forceful thrusts that lifted and carried them over the trees and out of sight. Cormorants formed packs and hunted fish. Long lines of large black birds chased fish across the surface of the lake, hundreds of silent hunters worked together to drive a school, lifted off the water to land again in front of the wave of feeding birds, a constant feed, lift, land, and eat.

The little brown bird did not belong out here. It did not fit. It belonged in the willows close to his cabin. Shy and quiet, patient in the summer heat, it was a bird that moved slowly and never for any distance, a seed eater.

Ben watched it beat the air, fight the wind with rapid wing strokes and struggle straight for him. Straight and purposefully, its short wings never intended for long flights, it should not have been here on the water. It was out of place; a message, a warning, an abnormality to pay attention to. The bird belonged at the cabin. *Someone is coming to visit.* The thought came unbeckoned seemingly from nowhere, the way intuition always defies logic. Ben opened the throttle full and the boat responded, lifted a little higher in the water and clipped the waves a little quicker.

When the fish were prepared, and the cabin was cleaned, and the dishes done and a pot of tea was set on the table beside a new box of cookies opened on one end, the clear plastic wrap torn back in invitation, Rosie knocked at the door. Another abnormality, Rosie never knocked.

"Why are you beating on my door? Have you got something against it?"

"Just bein' polite, I didn't want to interrupt. Never know what you're doin' in here by yourself." Rosie noticed the clean swept floor and kicked off her shoes; she had seen the cookies and was heading straight for them.

"How's your diabetes this morning?"

"You are a mean son-of-a-bitch, Ben. *Mean!*" She pushed the word through her teeth, curled her lips back in a snarl to stifle the smile that was trying to betray her feigned anger.

"Help yourself."

"Oh, you are a mean bastard Ben. Put them away." Rosie opened a cupboard, moved aside a heavy black mug with Z99 Radio blazoned all over it and selected her favourite thin, white china cup, the one with the little blue and purple flowers. Before she poured the tea, she folded back the plastic wrap on the package of cookies and put them in the wooden breadbox on the counter, the box with the lid that could shut.

She settled heavily into a chair, rose slightly to slide it back from the table for a little more room, then lowered her weight fully before she leaned a shoulder against the log wall. "You always make a good cup of tea."

"Did you want some sugar for that?"

"Fuck you, I'm tryin' to be nice. Sometimes I wonder if the only reason you came back was to give me a hard time."

Ben couldn't hold the laugh back; it oozed out, a little rolling chuckle. "Give you a hard time?" His eyebrows raised above his deep grey eyes. The forked lines around the edges showed lighter than the wind and sun-darkened face. "Give you a hard time." He repeated the words because of their ridiculousness.

His laugh spread itself thinly through the cabin, wrapped around Rosie and melted her pretension of anger. She jiggled, set down her cup of tea before it spilled, and let her mirth mingle with his. Her higher pitch laugh played with his deep quiet rumble, the laughs twisted together and became one sound that reverberated gently around the room and chased away anything of remorse or shadow.

This was the reason Ben had returned to the community on the shore of the lake. He had said it was for the quiet, for the return to nature, for tranquility, but in reality it was for the company of laughter, to share, to belong. Here in the cabin he built with his own hands, where the logs soaked up the water from broken blisters, where he was warm and dry, fed and belonged, where memories had roots. Here with Rosie, the little girl from his childhood, the little girl that used to follow him, shyly. Rosie who stood in the shadow, with cotton flowered dress and moccasins. Little shy Rosie, smiled and looked away when he glanced at her, then followed at a distance, a kit fox pretending to hunt but still too full of play.

"Yeah, give me a hard time." Rosie again feigned sternness. "I came here try'n to be nice and you give me a hard time." "Okay, Rosie. I'll apologize. I shouldn't pick on you. But I was just getting you first before you jumped me like usual."

"Maybe you should lend me twenty bucks for being mean."

"Is that what you came over for? To borrow a twenty?"

"Well, yeah, but since you were mean to me, you should just give me twenty instead of lending it."

"I suppose." It really didn't matter to Ben whether he loaned or gave Rosie a bit of money in the middle of the month. In the three years that he had been home she had never repaid a loan or reciprocated a gift. Not that Rosie lacked in generosity or gratitude. The little welfare that she received did not leave any cash over to match the greatness of her heart.

"I sometimes wonder Ben, whether you have a stash somewhere." Rosie stuffed the twenty into a pocket. "You can stretch a pension cheque further than anyone else."

"I don't play bingo." Ben responded quickly.

"And you don't drink. But even so, you seem to always have money when everyone else has run out."

The accusation had more power than Rosie knew. It forced Ben to keep a steady face, forced him to calculate his response, his words, his actions. He chose not to respond and let silence do its work. It did. Rosie finished her tea, rinsed her cup, and put it in the cupboard. Never let it be said that a man washed dishes for her.

⁓

Lester tried to read the words on the bus ticket, but the letters were nonsense. He closed his left eye and some of the reversed letters reverted to normal. The C and the L he remembered, yeah, the M was there. The ticket should say he was going to Moccasin Lake. He handed it to the man in the grey uniform, hoped he was the bus driver and not someone else. The man looked at the ticket and handed it back. Unsure but unwilling to allow anyone to see that he was unsure; Lester entered the bus. No one stopped him. He sat in a tall back seat with his small pack on his lap, his cheek against the cool glass, and watched the people move around the bus depot, watched for trouble. He saw no sign of anything that might be out of place, not that he knew what normal was out here. He wondered whether his ability to know when trouble was coming would work here in this world. Would he know when to shrink into a wall, find a corner, and become invisible.

The bus filled. Lester watched faces. Men he understood. Knew their way of walking, their mood. Women he could not read at all. They walked strangely, sounded strange. The bus continued to fill and pressurize. He turned back to the window, to the bright green building and black asphalt parking lot.

"Is it okay to sit here?" she asked.

"Yeah, I guess. Yeah. Sure." I sound like an idiot he thought.

The driver closed the door and it did not clang and echo the way prison doors sound.

She was sitting close. Lester could smell her. The smell of diesel fuel and turpentine filled his nostrils. The base of her perfume overwhelmed the scent she had so carefully chosen. Or rather it was lost on Lester, or Lester had lost the ability to smell that particular aroma and only the turpentine that the scent was mixed with filled the thin air between them. Lester turned away, his cheek against the tinted glass and tried to breathe.

The bus rolled out of the little prairie city, crossed the arch of a long bridge across an ancient river, turned through an overpass, and headed due north. Lester watched the new prairie, the land turned by the rush of homesteaders a century before. People who hated trees and pushed the forest line two hundred miles further than the old buffalo hunters' wintering sites. They were easy to hate. Wealthy farmers with big tractors bright red or John Deere green and fancy pickups on the way to town, fat wives and fat children.

The land changed and so did the traffic; now there were more logging trucks. They still hated trees, slashed them down and hauled them to the mill to make paper to wipe their fat arses with. Lester wished he could breathe, wished the woman would get off the bus at one of the tiny dying farm towns where the bus stopped, unloading parcels from its undercarriage. But she sat there in her stink, eating some kind of health food bar, nibbled on it, one tiny bit of oatmeal at a time and flipped the pages of a picture magazine, stared long at photos of celebrities on glossy paper.

Abruptly the prairie came to an end. The bus rounded a corner and began up a long incline and the last farmhouse and bright red barn disappeared behind a stand of spruce. From here to the Arctic Circle was boreal forest; trees, lakes, rivers, muskeg and Indians. Lester was home. Twenty-four years, eight times three is twenty-four, three manslaughters, consecutive, a bargain. Not one minute off the sentence, every damn second of the judge's pronouncement. They had to let him out, couldn't keep him any longer. Fuck the parole board and early release, Lester Bigeye was free. They couldn't send him back. He was completely out. Not on parole. The last eight years had been tough. Ever since that fat cow had said: "Lester Bigeye, your application for parole has been declined. This board finds that you are an unsuitable candidate due to your inability to take responsibility for your actions." Bullshit, bullshit, bullshit."

They filled him with hope before every Parole Board hearing and took that hope away from him every time. Now he was beyond their reach. Lester was home and the trees were still there, beautiful poplars in full, dark mid-summer leaf, and tall spruce with spread boughs like a jingle dress dancer's skirts. The roadside flashed past and Lester caught sight of wildflowers. Flowers that he had forgotten. Brown-eyed Susans and lilies. There were still a few wild roses out. Summer was still young.

Moccasin Lake Reserve was where it was supposed to be; where the sign said it would be, at the end of eight miles of gravel road off the main paved highway that headed north to the mining towns, but it was nothing like the place Lester left. New metal-sided buildings stood over the places he remembered. The band hall was gone and something that might be a skating rink stood in its place. There was a chain link fence around where the schoolyard had been. The new building with steel poles placed architecturally above the entrance to look like a teepee had replaced the old school that he had attended. Then Lester saw the lake, blue and green with white streamers of foam and he knew that he was home.

The house by the lake, up the short, sandy road, amid tall spindly black spruce wasn't there. Lester was not expecting to find his car, the burgundy 1972 Monte Carlo, but he hoped the house would still be there. The house was gone. The car sat flat on the ground without wheels, glassless. Its windows long past the targets of kids with slingshots just for the wonderful tinkle sound glass makes when a stone passes through it. Poplars grew up through where the hood had been removed. Someone had taken the engine, Lester's pride — a Chevy big block that roared and spun gravel. He smelled the mould of rotted seats when he put his head through the gaping driver's window. The tape deck was still there, under the dash, an eight track add on. Someone must have needed door parts; the inside of the passenger door lay across the front seat. Lester thought he remembered electric windows. Something caught his eye and he forced the door to open, to creak against rust and time. He knelt and reached under the seat.

Canadian Club whisky, a twenty-sixer, right where he left it, and still a quarter full. He remembered putting it there, remembered the smooth feel of the neck of the bottle in his hand as he stashed it. He remembered slamming the car door and the solid weight of the 30:30 rifle, the chill of the cold lever action against his knuckles and the steps toward the house.

Ben stood in the doorway, one hand on the frame and looked out at the parallel indentations of sand that led to where his truck sat. They couldn't be called a driveway, just the marks of driving over the same ground again and again from the gravel road to the log house with its narrow deck all along the front. The logs had begun to yellow nicely, the way pine does, its own sap and pitch acting like an expensive treatment. Or maybe it captured sunlight and held it in its stickiness, glued the sun to the logs.

The cabin was square and solid with a low-pitched green metal roof. "Guaranteed for fifty years." The lumberyard attendant had tapped the pile of metal with his toe. "A little bit more expensive, but probably worth it."

"Fifty years sounds about right. I don't imagine it will be me who changes it. I'll be a hundred and fourteen." And they'd loaded the sheets onto the back of Ben's truck.

The little brown bird was back in the willow clump. It sounded a melodic "*tchi tchi, tchi, whooi, whooi, tchi, tchi.*"

"You didn't fly all the way out there to tell me that Rosie was coming to borrow a twenty." Ben stepped gently away from the door. The song sparrow shifted positions in the clump of willow and gave another version of its song.

Ben scraped a heavy white plastic deck chair out a bit from the wall so that he could recline it, and waited. The sun sat high, just over the pine tree, a little east of south, still on the morning side of noon. The pine stood solidly in the middle of its circle of brown needles and the parallel ruts of the driveway curved around it and crawled up behind the truck. The shade of the pine dappled the dark red of the heavy-built, four-year-old Toyota extended cab.

Ben had purchased the truck precisely because it was used. A new truck stands out. He thought about the morning he had stopped in a gravel pit to rub it down with grit to remove the shine laboriously applied by the dealer's hired help. It was a solid dependable vehicle. It didn't need to shine and attract attention. The truck was much like the boat he had purchased that same morning, solid, dependable, the way Rosie would describe Ben.

The song sparrow sang again. Ben mimicked its song. "Someone, someone, someone is coming for tea, tea, tea." The little bird walked sideways along a branch, out of the shadow to where the sun caught its feathers and brightened its drab colours. "You sure have a nice song for such a plain-looking bird." It responded to the compliment and gave Ben the long version of the song with a few quick trick changes. He sat back into the curvature of the deck chair and waited for whoever might be coming for tea.

There were things to do. There were always things to do. There might be three or four new weeds in his garden since yesterday. The gate at the corner of the pole fence was beginning to sag slightly and scrape against the ground. Maybe he should paint that fence around the square garden. Black spruce poles made excellent fence rails but they were not like pine, they darkened with age. Maybe he should paint them white. But that would mean a trip to the city to buy paint and someone, someone, someone was coming, coming for tea, tea.

The sun drifted past the pine and Ben noted the movement of the tree's shadow as it crawled slowly from his right to left across the grassy space. His mind drifted with the shadow and he let it spill back over time. He remembered his early days on this reserve, school, sports and people. He remembered his first metamorphosis. Not a physical change, a spiritual rebirth where all that he believed in came crashing down with the death of his father. Then there was the slow rebuilding of a personality, different than before, but only visible to him. That was the beginning of manhood. There were other times in his life when his universe had collapsed, when a strong belief in something was proven false. There was a poem from when he was twenty something:

Adrift in a sea of chaos
I gather my reality about me
And build a raft thereof.

What he had tried to say was that he had core beliefs that never changed. When his larger belief system collapsed, he returned to that core, that centre, that basic definition of Ben. After a series of metamorphoses he realized that there was very little in which a solid belief could be justified. Most of science, virtually all academia and political discourse was unstable and could collapse in a moment. That realization had been his moment of freedom, his emergence. He rose from the dark and walked in an ephemeral world open to change, open to contradiction.

The pine shadow crept across the planks of the deck and touched his foot. A yellow dog sniffed its way down one rut of the driveway, moving slowly the way dogs do in summer. Ben watched its cautious approach, lethargic in the heat. She would be the progeny of the dogs Dolphus and Zachius brought back. That's the story of where the good sleigh dogs came from. It was said that the brothers had paddled north with a canoe full of trade goods and returned in the middle of winter with two dog teams and sleighs filled with fur. Those dozen dogs were the great, great grandparents of every dog on the reserve. He noted that the yellow dog looked pregnant, a bit big in the belly, nipples beginning to show through the fur. She would be looking for a place to make a den, a home, someplace safe to give birth.

The sun sat high over Ben, shone down through the gap in the forest canopy that opened above the small clean space around the cabin. A little wind would be nice now, something to move the still air that was beginning to heat up. He removed his thin jacket, folded it over the arm of the chair, and bathed in the warmth. Old bones like warm sunshine. Not that Ben would admit that he was old, but he was getting there. Time now to slow down, to take in all those elements that he had rushed past, time to sit and absorb. Maybe, just maybe, he would find some way to give back, to make up for the things he had taken. Everything has a price, a cost, an affect that comes from every choice. Put out good things and good things come back. The more you give the more you get; the more you take the less you can keep. He remembered all that he had taken and wondered when balance would assert itself and something would come and take away from him.

The shadow of the pine moved away and began to point more easterly. Five children on three bicycles wove noisily down the gravel road. The sun's heat drove them to the lake and the water. Two larger girls, eleven, twelve maybe, each peddled a bike with a younger child balanced on the cross bar. A smaller square boy with a long towel over his shoulders that was in danger of catching in the chain and sprocket, peddled as fast as he talked. He was one of those children that had not learned that internal dialogue should be kept internal. He voiced every thought, unconcerned whether any one was listening. The two older girls were not listening; they carried on their own conversation. The sounds of tires on gravel and the voices of the children dimmed as they travelled on down the road past Ben's home.

He went back to his thoughts from before he caught the pickerel this morning, President Obama shaking hands with Hugo Chavez. Yes, that was the last time he had hope. The world looked as if it might heal itself. But then . . . Oh well, best not to think about it too much. What was, was. It had been so long; so long since the famous handshake. And hope. What the hell was hope anyway? Such a pitiful word.

The afternoon settled into summer silence, too hot even for mosquitoes. The sun eased across the westerly part of its zenith and began its course to the horizon. Ben stayed in his chair. He sat forward slightly and looked for the song sparrow. It wasn't in the willows. He sat back and waited, wondered what he would have for supper, or rather how he would cook the fish, or which fish. If the person who was coming were white he would fry the pickerel. White people seem to like that kind of food. If the visitor was an Indian, he would cook the big whitefish.

～

Lester found his way back to his car as the sun touched the horizon. He had not really tried to find his relatives today. How do you return to your family and say, "Hi, I'm Lester, remember me? I'm the guy who shot my father, my mother, and my wife." He had walked around some, kept mostly out of sight, not skulking, just avoiding where people gathered, like at the gas station and store or around the band office. He found the old trails were still active, the paths through the trees, the short way to somewhere. The change to the reserve in twenty-four years was incredible. Who could have guessed that the Canadian government would be so embarrassed that they would build houses for Indians that were more than the shacks that Lester left? A quarter of a century is time enough for change, but for Lester who had been away from any change at all, confined to the constants of concrete and steel and wire reinforced glass, the reserve was unrecognizable.

He sat in the back of the old Monte Carlo and sipped slowly and steadily from the bottle. Was the whisky better after twenty-four years of aging under the seat of a car? Lester could not answer, he had no comparisons to say better or worse than. It was different than jailhouse brew, but he could not say it was better. The light changed to copper, tinted the treetops, softened the colours and eased the day to a close. The whisky had the effect that Lester sought; he closed his eyes and let himself drift away.

~

Ben fried the pickerel. Monica laughed and joked and got in the way as she tried to help in the preparations. "Where do you keep your potato peeler?"

"In the knife block."

"I don't see it."

"It's called a knife, it's the one with the handle sticking out."

They managed to get through the preparation of a very late supper and enjoyed the simplicity of crisp fried fish, boiled potatoes, and canned tomatoes.

"What took you so long to get here today?" Ben eased back from the table and placed his fork across his empty tomato-stained plate.

"What do you mean?"

"I was expecting you earlier."

"Stopped to shop in Saskatoon." Monica gave Ben her puzzled look. He let her stay puzzled. He had his answer. He had sat all afternoon in the sun while she shopped.

Monica sat up straight, rested her thin arms on the table, "What do you mean, you were expecting me? Has someone been here?"

"No, no one."

"Then why were you expecting me?"

"A little bird came and told me you were coming." Ben poured himself the cup of tea that he had waited for all afternoon. It did not matter if he knew anything or not. He was satisfied. He was fed, he was dry, and he was warm. The tea held a hint of the wild mint he picked that morning along the shore.

"As long as it wasn't Homeland Security." Monica wiped her mouth with the square of paper towel she had placed beside her plate. "Have you kept up with the Resistance? Her voice changed pitch. It was sharper now. The visit, the customary extended 'how do you do?' was finished and now it was time for business, for work.

"Only what I get on CBC."

"And that's all bullshit."

"Are you telling me that we haven't had three thousand bombs dropped in Canada since the annexation?"

"Annexation! Annexation, fuckin' invasion. CBC may as well be NBC for all the shit they put out." Her anger pulled at her face, lengthened it.

Ben shrugged.

Monica leaned back, "I know, I know, they put out what they can. But, it pisses me off that the people don't hear what's really going on."

"Is the bomb count wrong?" Ben's question wasn't rhetorical.

"Who knows, probably. Does the bomb count include cluster bombs? Does it include Bolts from Heaven? They've dropped at least a dozen. Tore the shit out of the boys in Lac La Biche. What gets me the most is that garbage about balanced reporting; I mean what was that righteousness stuff about? The Christian right isn't balanced, hasn't been since Bush. And we all know that isn't what it's all about. It's about Fort Mac, it's about oil. They invaded us because Prime Minister Thoreau threatened to cut off all trade with the Americans. San Francisco was just an excuse. Everyone knows that it's about oil. Terrorists from Canada, immorality and drugs and atheism and all that other crap are just excuses, and the world allows it."

"I'm not defending the invasion, annexation, but the bombing of San Francisco changed a lot of things."

"I'm not convinced that bomb came through Canada. I think they don't have a clue how it got there, and used it as an excuse. I wouldn't doubt they did it themselves. Think about it. The Christians didn't like what was happening in Frisco; they called it sin city and hated it as much as Islam did."

"That's too far for me. Nobody sacrifices that much."

Monica sat back "I don't know. I don't know." She used a stray strand of dark brown hair across her forehead as an opportunity to run her hand over her head, to soothe her thoughts. "Frisco changed things. But, how did anyone get a dirty bomb across the border. Ever since 9/11 there have been radiation detectors at every border crossing. I'm just not convinced that those eight were the ones that did it. And now we'll never know. Nobody can re-examine them."

"Quick trials and quick executions have a way of putting an end to questions."

"James Henderson was talking at the university awhile ago and he said we were back in the last century, that all of the gains in human rights have been erased. His argument was that we have to start all over again and redevelop a body of law stronger than the old UN Charter or our Charter of Rights and Freedoms, a body of law developed without interference by special interest. You should've been there Ben. The entire theatre sat there with their mouths open. I was wishing someone like you were there to push his buttons; get him to see the other side, to see the people in the equation."

"James is doing what James knows. It took courage for him to stand up."

"He wasn't standing up against the Americans. Never once said directly that the bastards needed to be put back into their place. His argument was that law needed to be redeveloped. He was quite conciliatory."

"As he should be. Calling people bastards doesn't do much."

"Have you read Warren Churchill's piece about American Bastardism?"

"No, What's he saying now?" Ben stacked Monica's plate on top of his, gathered the knives and forks and carried them to the sink.

"Oh, it was a wonderful piece about how the Americans are truly bastards in the literal sense. The world does not recognize the marriage of their parents, that the left was not free to marry the right, the Democrat–Republican marriage was never consecrated, thus American politics is illegitimate." Monica poured herself another cup of tea.

Ben stood for a while looking out the window above the sink at the night's blackness, at the silhouette of the pine with a few stars in its crown. He looked skyward to see more of the stars but the house's eaves stopped his view. "Like I said, it doesn't help." He turned back to Monica. "We can swear at them all we want; they're still here."

"Churchill does inspire however; everything becomes important now. Every act of resistance adds to the body of resistance. Someday the world is going to stand up to the Americans. That's why we need you Ben. Your work on supremacy is far more important now than it was when you were writing about colonialism. You know your students are at the head of the resistance. It was you who inspired them; Jeff Moosehunter, Roland Natawayes, Art Livelong, Betsy Chance. They're all part of it. Betsy was at Lac La Biche when it got hit."

"Is she all right?"

"Shook, really shook. She wasn't hit, not physically anyway. But it changed her. She's jumpy, can't stand noise. I saw her at Batoche, looking over her shoulder all the time, thinks she's being followed. But, she hasn't weakened; she's still strong the way that Betsy always was strong, a proud Ojibway woman."

"She'd correct you and say a proud Anishinabe woman. You know this was never our fight, this American–Canadian thing. Canada promised in the Treaties that we would never be asked to go to war for them."

~

Lester's head hurt and he put it back down on the seat of the Monte Carlo. His nose was plugged and his eyes felt itchy. This was more than a hangover; maybe something in the whisky, maybe old whisky caused this. He opened his eyes again in the early light at the sound of an approaching car. He watched the lone white woman drive past, wondered who she might be: social worker, public health nurse, schoolteacher — probably a schoolteacher to be up and around this early in the morning. Dawn light bronzed the land, softened the features of the trees, coated them until they appeared to have been dipped in a vat of boiling copper and set out again to stand guard along the side of the road.

The smell of mould filled him as he tossed about on the back seat of the car. Here was the answer to his symptoms. Whisky would never betray him but mould he knew about. It had been in the farm annex when he spent time in minimum security. That was black mould, the mould that killed people, and prisoners were assigned bleach and scrub brushes to get rid of it. Lester needed a better place to live. His old Monte Carlo no longer held the power and prestige of its and Lester's youth.

~

"Are you going to lift your net this morning?" Rosie wanted to know how much time she had to visit.

"I pulled it out yesterday; I have enough fish for awhile." Ben stirred a half teaspoonful of sugar into his black coffee. Rosie was going to want to know who his guest had been. Ben decided to make her work for the information and only answer direct questions, see how long it took for Rosie to hint around before she came right out and asked.

"Did you have a good sleep?"

"Very good."

"Hmm." Rosie did not much like coffee at the best of times, and she really did not like Ben's morning coffee. It was way too strong for her tastes. She only accepted a cupful to be polite; now she was stuck with it. She put the cup down, held it for a moment between her hands, then eased it away, slid it across the wood of the table as she talked, moved the bitter black to greater and greater distance.

"I had my children between eighteen and twenty-four, all in a rush, four kids in six years. Then they were my life for the next twenty years. Then all of a sudden I'm forty and all alone. My baby goes to live with her sister in the city and I have a new life to figure out. I'm alone and I have time to think again. And do you know what I think about for the next twenty years?"

"No." Ben shook his head.

"I wondered what happened to the pictures."

"What pictures?"

"The pictures of Father Lambert. What other pictures?" Rosie waited for an answer.

Ben did not have an answer; he sat back and took the time he needed. Three years he had been home. Rosie came over almost every day; she drank tea, nibbled cookies, told stories and retold stories, offered to sew buttons back on, made him moccasins and a beautiful pair of gauntlets covered with otter fur and she never asked, or talked about that summer. He had relaxed, maybe she would never ask, but now there it was; the question.

"There are no pictures, never were; I stole the camera from the school, but there was no film."

"You bluffed him?" Her face changed, serious Rosie dissolved into everyday Rosie. "You bluffed a priest with an empty camera." She shook her head in disbelief. "You always had that, that something." Rosie did not have the words to describe Ben's inherent sense of absolute justice, his determination, his sense of self and place that overwhelmed less aware people.

"I'm sorry, Rosie."

"No. No don't ever say that. If you apologize then you did something wrong and I can blame you, and I don't ever want to blame you. It wasn't you. All you did was ask me to put on my little sister's red dress and go play in front of the church. He did the rest. When you came with the camera you saved me from him. It wasn't your fault for what he done."

"I'm sorry, Rosie, I'm sorry because I didn't think you would get there so quick. By the time I broke into the school and got the camera and got back, well . . . "

"But you did get back, and he saw you with the camera, and he never touched me or any other kid on this reserve again. I don't blame you Ben. I'm proud of you. You took on a priest and beat him. You forced him off the reserve and now I find out the camera was empty. Well, in a way that's a good thing. Nobody will ever see my shame."

~

Ambrose Whitecalf never went to university along with the others, his brothers, his classmates. Red dutifully finished grade twelve, honoured his parent's wishes, attended the graduation ceremony that was for them, not him. He didn't care. It wasn't important. It simply marked the end of an era. Graduation was the signal of freedom, freedom to go back to the land, to enjoy the earth.

Red was law-abiding. But it was his law that he abided. Red's law wasn't much different than that written in criminal codes. The principles were the same. Respect others, take care of your family, don't interfere. Red's law imposed upon him a duty to help anyone who asked. He had no desire to change the world, not even to push the Americans back across the old border. They were part of a world that had no impact on him; they didn't matter. Their rules and regulations and imposed security were meaningless in the forest.

Their economy was not Red's economy. He cut a bit of firewood for people who still burned firewood, took the bit of money they gave, sold a bit of fish and a bit of moose meat occasionally. Sometimes in good years he sold some of the rabbits he snared to people who remembered eating rabbit but were too busy trying to earn a living to take the time to go to the forest, cut a few young tender pine and scatter them around until the rabbits came to feast. He pitied and loved those people, the ones who remembered how it was, the ones who smiled at their memories as they reached for the stringy meat that would go into their soup. They paid with big, happy smiles, not caring that the price per pound, if calculated, would bring the price of rabbit above that of beef. They weren't buying meat; they were buying memories.

It was gasoline that forced Red into the economy, gasoline for the chainsaw, for the truck, for the boat to go lift the net. If Red did not have to buy gasoline, his life could be a whole lot simpler. Everything he needed for a good life was in the forest; food, heat, shelter. Gasoline was his prison, his captor.

Red was completely unsophisticated and loved it. The problems and complications of modern society did not touch him, did not enter into his analysis of any given morning. He woke, made a pot of coffee for himself and a kettle for Lorraine's tea when she got up. His day began with a prayer, usually outside, a simple "Thank you for today, Grandfather."

Then Red would look around to see what needed doing or what the day was best suited for.

He was getting good at predicting weather, watching the sky for those subtle changes, those markers that he recognized — low clouds in an arc above the eastern horizon always meant that the weather would be warming. Sky colour held meaning beyond the red sky at night, red sky in morning cliché. There were also shades of blue, variations near the sun or moon and an encyclopaedia of cloud forms.

Today, Red decided, would be a good day to stay close to home, help Lorraine with the little things around the house, knowing that by noon she would be chasing him out, sending him somewhere. "Go help Moses fix his fence." Or, "Dianne phoned, she needs someone to look at her car. It's making a funny sound."

$$\sim$$

Rosie sat on the heavy plank steps that led up to Ben's door. "The light is good here," she told herself as she sewed beads to leather and created an eight-sided star for the back of a pair of gloves. The truth was that the light at her house, a hundred steps further from the lake, was as intense. But if you challenged her on it, she would argue with you and no matter what proofs you offered, you would eventually lose the argument worn down by the strength of her conviction. She would never admit to you or to anyone that she was there because she was lonely and the feeling of Ben's spirit moved around his cabin and comforted her.

A whimper from under the steps drew Rosie away from her beadwork to kneel in the grass, bend way over, and look under the heavy lumber frame. The yellow dog lay curled around six puppies tumbling with each other for a teat, all mouth and sucking, eyes closed. "You picked a good spot to have your babies." The yellow dog raised her head at the words. "Seems everyone knows Ben will look after them." The yellow dog licked the puppy closest to her tongue. "Thirsty work giving birth, isn't it. Bet you'd like some water." Rosie found a bowl she was sure Ben wouldn't mind sharing. On the way out she grabbed the left-over fried fish. Sleigh dogs and fish, something about that combination just seemed natural somehow.

Rosie sat back on the steps — a fed, watered, contented mother lay in the shade somewhere beneath her — and wondered absently where Ben might have gone. To the city perhaps, more than likely the city she agreed with herself. He would not have gone north for any reason without taking his boat. She wet the thread by drawing it through her mouth to stiffen it so that it was easier to control and returned to firmly attaching the string of beads to their precise location on the leather.

Now if she were her grandmother, she would not sit here and wonder, she would fly away and find out exactly where Ben had gone and how he was making out. Rosie had never seen her grandmother, old Jeannie, do any of the things she was purported to have done. She had only scraps of conversations and whispers that told of the old woman telling her children, including Rosie's mother, "I'm going to check on your uncles on the trapline. Don't be scared. If it looks like I'm in trouble, just pass my shoes over me and I will come back." And the old woman would go to sleep and dream and toss and turn and talk and if she became quiet, her children would pass her shoes over her and she would wake up and tell them how their uncles were doing. "Delbert killed a moose." or "Walter fell through the ice, but his dogs helped get him out. He's okay now."

Ben had a secret, Rosie knew. He had a secret and it had a hold of him and wouldn't let him be, it was like a limp or an ache, and it was always in the way and needed to be cared for like a sore thumb. But Ben had a big secret and it had started to bend him over with its weight. If he wanted to share it with Rosie, she would help him to carry it. She had carried the secret of the priest all her life and it hadn't crippled her; it had made her strong.

But Ben's secret was something newer, something he brought with him to the reserve, something from outside, from the white world. Probably had to do with money. Rosie looked around. The aluminum boat on the trailer parked in the shade of the large pines must have cost Ben a fair price, and the motor, well those don't come cheap, not new ones anyway, and this house. Rosie turned around and looked at the log structure behind her. He must have spent money on it. Those were new windows set in wooden frames, and the door was solid, not one of those cheap doors like the contractors put on reserve houses. Yeah, Ben had spent a fair amount on his house. It might not look like it unless you looked close. Everything was plain, simple and the best quality. And if you added in the truck, well, Ben had spent a big pile of money since he moved back.

So Ben had money, big deal. He was a retired professor after all. So why did he go to lengths to act like he didn't? Maybe he was embarrassed by it. Maybe he didn't want to embarrass her with it. It didn't matter. Funny thing about money — you put people and money together and strange things happen.

She slipped the long thin bead needle through a sequence of different coloured beads, raised the needle and shook the pretty little bulbs of glass down the thread to where her solid left thumb waited to hold them firmly in place while she sewed them onto their designated spot.

If Rosie could travel like Old Jeanie, she would go find Ben and tell him — tell him what? That she was sitting on his steps while he was away because she wanted to be where he had walked, on boards he had nailed. She was sixty-four years old and acting like she was fourteen. What would Ben want with her? She wasn't pretty. Not anymore. She wasn't one of the educated, sophisticated. She was competently literate but wasn't versed in literature. She preferred to read Stephen King and wasn't in the least interested in the William Faulkner novel that lay open on Ben's bedside table.

Something shifted in the shadow of the pines off toward Rosie's left. She watched for it with her peripheral vision rather than turn her head and search boldly. The figure moved again. It was not skulking, just moving slowly between her house and Ben's. She did not recognize the man at first, now that he was obvious and she could openly look at him. His hair was too short for the reserve where the fashion ranged from slightly longer to long. His was very close cropped. There was a familiarity about the face, as hard as it was. Somewhere beneath the mask of sternness lived someone she once knew. He came out of the shadows, walked up, and now stood in front of Rosie.

"Well, drop kick me Jesus. How you doin', Rosie?" the humour in the words did not make it to the voice so the statement sounded bizarre.

"End over end, not to the left or the right, straight through the heart of those righteous uprights." Rosie completed the football cult song. Her light laugh brought out the missing humour. "I'm not bad." She put down her beadwork. "How's Lester?"

"I'm standin' here."

"I can see that."

"I mean, they never broke me, I'm still on my feet."

"I can see that."

"I made it. I made it home again." Lester put one foot up on the first step, so that he stood at a slight angle to Rosie, so that he could deflect any possible attack.

Rosie sat squarely in front of Ben's door, protective. "So what brought you back here?"

"It's home, I guess. Nowhere else for me to go."

"I was just wondering 'cause you don't have any family here anymore."

"Don't have family anywhere I guess." Lester looked around, then looked back up towards Rosie again. "I guess you're about all the family I got Rose." He closed his mouth firmly at the end of her name and stood there, with his mouth clamped shut so that his chin protruded. He looked strong, standing there with his hands tucked neatly away in his hip pockets, one foot on the step and his chin forward. Strong, and resolved, not begging. "Here I am; take it or leave it," his body language spoke.

At that particular angle with the light filtered by pine, Rosie saw the resemblance between Lester and his mother. It was in the oval of the face and the proportions of cheekbone, chin, and brow.

"Have you eaten?" Rosie began gathering up her sewing. She would take him into her home. She was all the family that he had left and a cousin could never be turned away hungry, no matter what kind of a cousin he had been.

She was thinking about her Aunt Ester as she fried up the last few pieces of chicken. Ester had only been a few years older than Rosie, a young aunt, young enough that there were a few occasions that they had played together. Aunt Ester sitting with her little niece and putting dolls to bed. When they were a bit older but still young enough to be just playing, Rosie remembered Ester at parties, dances and laughter.

Then Lester was born and Rosie saw less and less of Ester. Then came Rosie's children and she saw even less of her young aunt and her hard working husband and their house on the other side of the village. She had seen Lester occasionally as he grew up.

She glanced his way. He looked almost swallowed by the large over-soft couch as he tried to figure out the remote control for the television. Rosie liked that couch. It fit her. It clearly did not fit Lester.

Where did he fit? Anywhere? She wondered how he had fit in at the penitentiary. Maybe that was the place for people like Lester. Maybe, who knows? Maybe he changed. Maybe in all that time locked away he had gotten over being mean. Somehow Rosie doubted it, not the power of an institution to affect change, but that anything could ever be done to take the meanness out of Lester. He seemed to have been born that way. Rosie remembered comments that followed him around the community and now resurfaced in her mind a quarter-century later. The voice of an old man, an Elder spoke clearly in her memory again. "He didn't get that way from either of his parents. He brought that with him when he came here."

Rosie scraped the chicken from the splattering grease, careful not to leave anything stuck to the pan. The trick to brown chicken is in the turning. Rosie took pride in her ability to cook. It was something that she did well even, as was often, with very little to work with.

It made Rosie hungry to watch Lester eat. She left him at the kitchen table and took a cup of tea into the living room and visited with her friend the television. There wasn't enough chicken for both of them. Oh well, it wouldn't hurt her any to miss a meal now and then. She could call it dieting. She was happy that at this time of the day there were fewer food commercials, not like Saturday mornings when junk food lured children.

She suddenly wanted her children, any of her children, to be with her on the couch, to cuddle together against the danger. Yes, Rosie allowed herself to admit that she was afraid of Lester, had always been a little afraid of Lester. Even when he was a child, she had watched him closer than the children he played with, and never let any of her children play alone with him.

There were rumours that he tortured little animals, kittens and puppies and a squirrel that he knocked from a tree with a slingshot and kept alive until old Cecil found him and killed the squirrel out of pity. The stories had drifted through the community and followed Lester as he grew up.

"Norma went out with him; he said he was taking her to a movie in town. She won't do that again."

"You know how Wesley is, he wouldn't fight back if he was being murdered. Why would someone pick on a guy like that?"

But, everyone is entitled to change right? Why couldn't Lester have changed? He was human. Maybe he learned something in prison. It was possible. Rosie changed channels, pointed the remote and clicked. Crime scene investigation was not something she wanted to watch at this moment. People can change, unless they're born that way.

He had put his dirty plate on the counter by the sink. Rosie quickly scraped off the bones and remains into a small plastic pail, something for the dog, hated to waste. Her hunger grabbed her again when she saw how much meat he had left on the bones. She was tempted to clean them off, nibble that morsel that hung loose, crunch the gristle from the end. Chicken bones should be clean. But she didn't want him to see, didn't want to embarrass him.

She finished her night routine; she had never gone to bed with a dirty dish in her house. The thought of it might wake her in the middle of the night and torture her. She did something however, that she had never done before and double-checked that the door to her bedroom was tightly shut before she put on her nightgown.

~

The sun shimmered on the black pavement, created illusions of cleanliness, of smoothness. Ben let the truck find its way around the curve, his hand easy on the wheel, relaxed. Summer exploded in colour where prairie met parkland, where farmland stopped pushing against the boreal. Aspen blended with large white spruce together in a canopy that protected the forest floor from direct sunlight. In the shade places, currants, and highbush cranberries grew in tangles. Where sunlight splotched the floor, broad spreading sarsaparilla protected the earth and buried its roots in the loam and lichens. Farmland ended in abrupt straight lines against walls of trees, a final fatal attempt at agriculture abandoned to scentless camomile and thistles. The fence lines that never did keep the deer from the fields sagged in droops of rusted barbed wire where some of the staples still held the strands to leaning posts rotted at ground level.

South, Ben cringed. Why in hell was he going back. He had a good life. He had everything that he needed. No one bothered him, no one asked him for more than he was ready to give. Time had become his friend, rather than his master. Mornings like this should be for good brewed coffee and bird song. He contemplated turning around, but Monica had asked. A promise is a promise, is a promise. Ben's word was more powerful than his wants. He clicked on the cruise control, set it to a hundred and nine, breathed in and let his shoulders relax as he breathed out.

Moccasin Lake pulled at his mind, or perhaps he was repulsed by the rush of glass and steel on asphalt. Rosie's actions yesterday perplexed him. He had expected her to behave like an old gossip, rush to his cabin as soon as Monica's car left to find out all that was to be found out. She had not even asked. Perhaps she was unaware? No, she had moved the silk scarf Monica carelessly left on the arm of the chair, picked it up, checked its authenticity by gently touching it against her cheek, nylon feels different up close, and laid it carefully aside before sitting.

Ben's ability to predict had developed over the years to the point now where he was confident in his gift. Rosie disrupted that confidence. She had not behaved in the manner he expected. That was it, wasn't it? She had not acted the way he, Ben, expected. His gift was secure. He had not used it. The gift was something outside of Ben. It was different from rationality, closer to intuition. His prediction of Rosie's behaviour was premised upon his ego, upon his sense of importance and superiority. He had assumed that Rosie would behave badly out of jealousy. A good lesson in humility, the most necessary ingredient of the gift.

He was going south, again. He touched the control and CBC radio entered the cab of the truck.

" . . . *is a ticking bomb. President Wright went on to say that the US policy in Canada served the needs of the continent.*

France again demanded that the US withdraw all troops from Canada and Mexico and restore local government, however it did not repeat its threat to withdraw from NATO."

"Chavez speaking only for Mercosaur, again warned the US to stay above Panama."

"To analyze yesterday's developments CBC spoke with Professor James Henderson of the Frazer Institute." A previously taped voice that produced well-enunciated though quick words came on. Designed for media, Ben thought, as Professor Henderson rattled.

"The overall change to Canadian society has been minimal if we consider the possible paths that Canada could have taken following San Francisco. We would have either had to develop our own security at a cost that would have nearly bankrupted the country given the state of our armed forces, or remain open to sneak attacks. If the United States had not assumed the responsibility for our security, we would have been forced to impose the same or possibly more stringent measures. Given the impoverishment of Canada's armed forces prior to the annexation, it is reasonable to imagine that in order to maintain security, Canada would have had to implement measures to compensate for the inability to adequately patrol, and enforce. Homeland Security has the manpower, equipment, and technology to ensure we are not open to sneak attacks, without undue physical intervention. The rights of Canadians living under Homeland Security are actually less infringed — if infringed at all — than if we were to have implemented our own necessarily less-adequate systems to protect Canadians from destruction."

Ben turned off the radio. Hugo Chavez was shaking hands with President Obama in his mind again. He remembered those days of hope and dismissed them. Hope, what a desperate word.

He rode in silence for a few minutes, listened to the tires hum against the pavement and turned the radio back on.

" . . . that's absolutely not true." The voice of a woman came through the speakers. "This suggestion that the US annexed Canada only because of oil has huge holes in it. First of all, in today's world, security is more important than transportation or industry. Neither would be of any use without freedom from sneak attacks. And," her voice rose an octave, "and, the suggestion flies in the face of the fact that Venezuela produces nearly as much oil as we do. If the issue was truly only about oil, Chavez would not be in power. He would not be free to spread hatred and would not have the resources to polarize the Americas into north–south blocks."

Ben turned the radio off again.

"Of course Wright never invaded Venezuela. He might take it, but he could never keep it." He spoke to the steel and glass. "Afghanistan showed them that." The morning sun warmed his left shoulder through the window. The warmth melted his irritation, eased it away. Best not to get caught up in it. It's just a distraction. The important things are being ignored in all the hype, he reminded himself as he adjusted the airflow controls, considered the air conditioner control, decided against it. Better to have fresh air even if it was warm. Next winter he would appreciate a little warmth.

He gently pushed against the CD that protruded above the radio. The player pulled the disc into itself and a male voice sang over an acoustic guitar. *On a slow road home . . . Can't dance in lumber jack boots, Can't sing with a mouth full.* Ben listened to the song nodding his head. "You got it, Jay. You understand."

~

Ben recited Monica's instructions to himself, "Four miles south of Aberdeen, go east at the alkali lake, a little ways up the road the house is behind a row of spruce on the right," and finally turned the truck onto a lane that led up a hill. Behind the row of spruce that stood bough to bough, out of place on the prairie, a two-story farmhouse, swallowed in their shade, spoke of neatness and care. The entire farmyard was an example of the owner's personality of part thrift and part perfectionist. The grain bins to the south of the yard stood aluminum sentinels in parade, rank laser straight. The west of the yard was taken by an over-large brilliant-white barn with red trim, its doors open to the light and air.

A man in blue jeans and short-sleeved shirt that ended above tanned, muscled arms walked out in front of the truck and waved Ben toward the Quonset.

"Park her in there." He pointed.

"Abe Friesen." He put his hand out as Ben climbed from the truck inside the galvanized metal half-cylinder building. "Best to keep the vehicles out of sight." He shook Ben's hand, two strong pumps. "You must be Ben Robe. Monica said I wouldn't mistake you. Well come along, everyone is staying up at the barn; there's beds up there and we'll do our business there or in the shop."

Ben looked around the Quonset as they walked toward the sunlight of the open sliding doors. He recognized Monica's car near the end of the row, dwarfed beside the out-of-place Chevy suburban truck. Someone has money for gas, Ben thought, as he followed Abe past the other smaller vehicles toward the light.

"Hey, Ben, glad you made it." Monica wrapped her thin arms around him and kissed his cheek. "Let me introduce you around. You've obviously met Abe. This is his place. He's our Amnesty connection. This is Ruben." She led Ben to a stout, reddish-coloured man whose face was offset by his bright green John Deere hat.

Ben let Monica lead him around the loft of the barn and introduce him to Roger Cardinal, Stan Jolly with a pony tail, Philip Maurice, Joan Lightning, pretty, with a gentle hand shake, Billy Two Horses, the very elderly Rose Bishop who sat in the comfort of a stuffed arm chair befitting her age, Leslie Iron . . . the names and faces blurred as Monica continued introductions to the thirty-odd people in the loft of the cleanly-swept barn.

"Make sure you help yourself to the food. Coffee is Brazilian dark roast thanks to Faye. She'll be on later today with updates from South America."

"You might not remember me, I was in your class in '06." Ben tried to remember, but the face in front of him did not register. Neither did the name, Roland Nataways. Ben did his best not to offend, with a smile and a shake of his head. "Don't matter," Roland continued. "I did learn a lot in that class. Looking forward to your talk this afternoon." Roland's tanned face framed by long black hair smiled back. But the smile was strained, forced as though through a history of pain.

"*Everybody.*" Abe's voice reverberated through the loft. "*Everybody*, were going to be starting in a few minutes, if we can get you to start taking your seats. Are you ready Joyce? You're up first." He turned slightly toward the grey blonde woman to his left. "Ready Abe." She brushed her cotton dress with a quick motion to remove a stray crumb of zucchini bread as she stood, gathered a thin bundle of notes from a packsack and headed toward the end of the loft where the large wooden doors stood open to the morning sun and the prairie sloped away to the horizon.

"Welcome to the first gathering of the coalition of thinkers." Joyce began as soon as most people were seated. The remainder quickly filled their coffee mugs, grabbed fruit or biscuits, or breads from the table at the back and hustled to the rows of mostly metal folding chairs interspersed with wooden kitchen or an assortment of plastic lawn chairs. The few cushioned arm chairs were all taken.

"First up, I'd like to thank Abe Friesen for risking his home for this gathering, and to remind people not to be outside in groups of more than four or five. If you are outside during a break, remember to come back in and allow someone else to enjoy the sunshine and air."

A chair scraped beside Ben and he did not hear Joyce's next words. He glimpsed the stylized NS tattoo on the smooth-dressed man's right hand as he manipulated a full coffee mug, trying not to spill. He nodded to Ben as Joyce continued. "The food at the back is courtesy of the Mennonite Central Committee. Who would ever have thought that MCC would make the list."

Ben turned at the sound of a woman loudly clearing her throat coming away from the food table. She smiled broadly, raised one hand in the air and balanced a bottle of juice and small plate of pastries.

Joyce continued: "Two weeks ago Wright added them to the list of dangerous organizations. Not the Evil list, they're not full-fledged terrorists, but they are on the watch list. Congratulations MCC. You must be doing things right. I would also like to thank Native Syndicate for the security. So very important. They've assured me that the buildings have been swept and it was their workers who put up the screen." Ben glanced up at the mesh wire tacked to the ceiling. Someone hoped that it would interfere with surveillance. "Everyone should know not to have brought cell phones or platforms. If you have, please remove the batteries. Abe has put his property at risk by allowing us here, let's not put him at any greater risk."

Joyce looked down at the notepad in her hand. The yellow lined paper matched the sunny dress she wore, matched her brightness, a compliment to the youth of her spirit despite the age lines that crossed a face devoid of makeup. "Stan Rediron is here, he'll be up this afternoon, along with Ben Robe as we hear from the academics. This morning is dedicated to reports. Native Syndicate's own Richard Ross is here personally with updates. And a very special guest, we finally get to see the face behind the words. 'That Jack' is here." The screen on the ceiling vibrated with the sound of applause and foot stamping.

"*Easy, easy!*" Joyce raised her voice to cut through echoing din, used both her hands, the notepad in her left flapped pages as she waved down the volume. The applause cut itself short as people realized the risk.

"Finally." NS tattoo grinned at Ben. Ben shrugged. "That Jack," NS tattoo nodded toward Joyce. Ben shrugged again.

"You don't know That Jack?"

"No"

"Wait. You, sir, are in for an awakening."

NS tattoo stood to speak when Joyce introduced him as Richard Ross, president of Native Syndicate.

"I know a lot of you. I know a lot of faces here and I'm looking for That Jack." Richard stood in the spot vacated by Joyce and exaggeratedly twisted his head back and forth. "Patience, I guess, patience. The Elders say to be patient. I'll have to wait like everyone one else to find out. Whoever you are, Native Syndicate thanks you. If it weren't for you we would never know what was going on." Richard stood with his hands behind his back, his feet firmly flat on the floor, a military stance, straight. It was a stance that suited his long arms and lean build. "Native Syndicate knows business. That's where we started and that's where we are. The new world order is the old world order. Was a time NS was just another street gang, on the margins, doing business, taking care of our own. Today nobody can call us a street gang. We are more than the streets; we are more than the jail house. We are the first line of defence. The machine needs grease and NS knows about grease. If we stop the grease, the wheels will stop turning. To that end we have hit targets in Alberta, and recently took a truck of yellowcake. Now that is terror. That is absolute terror. It doesn't matter that we ever use it. We don't have to use it. We just have to have it and they know we have it, and they are terrified."

Ben cringed. A thought rushed at him: *An angry dog is never as dangerous as a dog that is afraid. Cornered animals fight the hardest. Even a spruce grouse will attack if it is afraid.*

~

Ben looked around the loft. It was unpainted, bare wood angled rafters held what looked to be tongue-and-groove planks faded uniformly with age. The loft had appeared neat when Ben entered up the stairway, now he noticed it was more than that, it was immaculate. He looked back to the stairway landing where the floor should be worn. It was, but not to any depth. Someone had used a polishing stone to smooth the floor to an even depth. This was not a barn loft, a place to store bales of feed for the animals below, it was a meeting room. There were no stories left, nothing hanging from the rafters that would tell of usage; a bit of horse tackle that would tell of a day's ride, a pitch fork or a set of tongs that would tell of a day's work, the stories had been erased. Even the nails that might have held the stories had been removed from the wood of the rafters that longed to tell their own unedited version of events.

There was some applause at the end of Richard's talk. Ben did not clap; he couldn't bring himself to endorse that level of violence and anger. The tall, straight woman who Joyce introduced as Mary Wiens, co-chair of the Mennonite Central Committee was another who had not applauded, who tried to keep a neutral face, but the pain had seeped through the pores of her very scrubbed forehead and deepened the shallow lines around her blue-green eyes.

"And it's thanks to Mary and her team that we have the wonderful food." Joyce stepped easily away, leaving Mary at the front of the loft waiting for the gentle applause to subside.

"Thank you," she unconsciously brushed the lapels of her short jacket, let her hands fall to the folds of her matching long skirt. "Thank you." There was no hint of nervousness in her strong voice. "Mennonite Central Committee is dedicated to peace. To that end we have spoken against Wright's agenda. If peace is counter to the principles of freedom and righteousness, then MCC and its members belong on the list. We have been accused of assisting listed people and organizations. If giving food to the hungry and shelter to the homeless is a crime, then MCC is happily a criminal organization.

The room stirred.

"But, I don't believe that it was those activities that resulted in the listing of MCC. We had among our membership and on the executive, people who believed that living in a free and righteous society was a worthwhile objective. I was among them. As things changed, MCC participated with Homeland

Security's Freedom and Righteousness Division. We were at the table, we prayed with them, we actively participated in planning for a new democracy. The ideals were high — an end to corruption, efficient government, clean streets, a strong stand against crime, and an end to drugs and dependencies — all worthwhile objectives. We even closed our eyes to some of the means employed to achieve those objectives believing that they were intermediate and immediately necessary means.

Mary paused, not for affect. It was just a good place to take a breath. Someone cleared their throat in the otherwise silent loft, breaking the tension that had begun to build. Mary continued, "The listing of MCC had nothing to do with our activities. We were applauded at Freedom and Righteousness meetings for our humanitarianism. We were listed one day after MCC made a presentation advocating the return of control over education to our communities. It has been the goal of Mennonites since before the first immigrations in the last century to live in our own communities and to have our own schools.

"In fact it was the promise of control over education that enticed Mennonites to immigrate in the first place. When we were betrayed, when the government took education away from us, many of our brothers and sisters left Saskatchewan for Mexico.

"We now have communities in all three American Divisions." A movement of feet and straightening of bodies rustled the loft. "I mean countries, sorry for the slip. I might have spent too much time at Freedom and Righteousness, I am beginning to sound like them.

"But the point is, it wasn't until we began to demand our own schools, our own historical demand, that we were listed."

Be glad you didn't have to go to residential school. The thought surprised Ben as he leaned into a rafter.

Mary recovered from her slip and launched into a strong denunciation of the shift in government policy. "Freedom and Righteousness has an education agenda, an agenda that includes God, uniforms, bright shiny silent children, and no teachers' unions."

Monica offered, "Do you want to get some air? Let's go outside for a minute."

Ben wasn't comfortable walking out in the middle of a talk, but followed her anyway.

The sun stood a little before noon, high in the large blue prairie sky; its heat held a bit of sting to it as Ben and Monica stepped from the barn shadow into its direct blast.

"How about over there?" Monica pointed toward a yard swing; wooden, freshly painted, white, bright white, even though it stood in the shade of large Manitoba maples.

"That caustic sun is another reason to never stand out in the open."

"It's warm," Ben agreed. "Do you really worry about satellites, or are you just caught up in the hype?"

"No, no it's not just hype for me. It really makes me nervous out there. Ever since Lac La Biche." Monica leaned forward on the bench. Ben leaned back and gently pushed with his feet. The twin benches of the yard swing eased into motion. "Did you ever see any pictures of that?"

"No." Ben shook his head.

"Doesn't matter. They couldn't do it justice. The hole is fifty feet deep. It's not like a bomb. The dirt isn't thrown out. It's gone, vaporized, what's left is turned into glass. The house was gone, the people were gone, everything. Imagine being here one second, the next second you're not. So simple, so efficient, drop a tungsten rod from outer space, the rest is gravity and friction. By the time it hits the earth it isn't even metal anymore. It's vapour, and that's what our friends are now, vapour, nothing to bury, nothing to say good-bye to."

"Even in a bunker." Ben kept pushing and relaxing, the swing to- and fro-ed.

"There was no fucking bunker. They dropped that thing because they could, or they just wanted to play with their fucking toys. I don't know. Maybe the bastards believe their Bolts From Heaven are the equivalent of biblical brimstones. .*Shit*." She leaned back hard into the bench and jerked the smooth sway of the swing. "They weren't in a bunker. They were meeting in a house, just a house; they weren't even in the basement. Betsy said she went out to pick up KFC. She was telling me that she was a little pissed that they sent her, a woman. That's what she was thinking as she walked back, that she was being discriminated against because she was a woman, when she thought she saw a falling star during the day." Monica relaxed, the swing flowed and ebbed.

"There were no bunkers; there were no terrorists. They picketed the highway to Fort McMurray. They walked in front of semi-trucks with signs that said "Yankee Go Home.""

"What about the burning trucks, the roadside bombs?"

"That wasn't us. I don't know who was doing that. Maybe the bastards themselves."

"That's too hard to believe, that they're killing their own presumably to justify attacking innocent people. It's too much of a stretch. Sorry, Monica, even if it's true, it's too much."

"It's easier to believe the media is it?"

The swing stopped, stood silent. Ben and Monica both leaned back into their respective benches, distance between them. The moment stretched out, waiting for Ben's answer. He dodged the question.

"There was nothing else going on? Just peaceful picketing? Nothing else?"

"Not the violence that was reported. No burning trucks. Oh, there might have been a few flat tires, sugar in the fuel tanks, things like that. We don't have the money for explosives. N75 is expensive."

"You'll have to excuse my ignorance. But what is N75."

"Synthetic nitroglycerine. N75 is seventy-five times more powerful than the old traditional stuff."

"Seventy-five times the power of nitroglycerine, that boggles the mind." Ben started the swing moving again. "And where would you get it from?"

"From them." Monica pushed a little to contribute to the swing.

"From them?"

"Of course. The world's biggest armaments dealer, who else? Want an assault rifle, a detonator, poison gas, whatever — you buy it from the masters of war."

"You just go up to Homeland Security and put in an order, or what?"

"It's about that easy, except you need a lot of money. The people dealing are probably HS during the day, at night they look after themselves. Steal a bit of technology and put it on the street. Take a nice little bundle home to retire on, part of the benefits package."

"You've got to be kidding."

"No I'm not. The only people making N75 anywhere in the world are the Americans. If you want it, you have to buy it from them." Monica looked away toward the distant dry field of wheat struggling in the baked earth to grow. "How much?"

"How much what?"

"How much do you have to pay for N75?"

"Oh that, last I heard you could get a kilo for about ten thousand Ameros."

"Expensive."

"Depends what you're buying it for, and hey, when you consider its power it's really seventy-five kilos, right."

On the way back to the barn Monica took Ben's hand. He cringed, not outwardly, as he let her hold his calloused fist; he was twenty-five years older than her. Even a short ten years ago would have been different. But now, now he was nearly to the end wasn't he? It would be good for him to have company into these years. But what about her? She would be left alone again. Better she found someone else. Someone a little closer to her age.

～

When they re-entered the loft Joan Lightning had replaced Mary Wiens in front of the open doors.

"Those stacks either have to come down or they have to find some way of removing all the sulphur. They represent the greatest ecological disturbance ever experienced in Canada." The sun behind her highlighted the silver in Joan's otherwise long loose black hair. "The price you are paying for your cheap gas, and some of you might not think your gas is cheap at over five Ameros a litre, but it is — the price you are paying does not come close to the cost to the environment. Tons of sulphur and nitrogen are pumped into the atmosphere every day through those stacks, tons that precipitate out over what we used to call Saskatchewan and Manitoba all the way to Labrador. We once had viable fisheries in the north. Well, viable for the families who fished, maybe not so viable when we had to sell through government-run marketing agencies, but viable for many families.

Joan spoke quickly, though not out of any nervousness. She spoke at the speed her mind worked, the way her mind worked, all in a tumble, a rush. Her hands flashed around her body, indicating directions, wind patterns, and precipitation "When sulphur connects with moisture, and there is still moisture coming over the mountains, it might not seem like it on days like today, but there is still moisture up there. The sulphur connects with H_2O, add a little heat and we have H_2SO_4, sulphuric acid. It's not so much what comes out the exhaust pipe of your car as you burn their product, though that's still a problem, it's what comes out the stacks at Fort McMurray. Those refineries, and I don't care that they cost billions of Ameros each, I don't care that Wright makes a big deal out of their investments in the North Division, I don't care about the employment lies — Fort Mac is automated to the point where there aren't that many jobs anyway. With the unions broken, those jobs don't pay more than subsistence.

"I don't believe I am about to say this." Joan touched her face, ran dry fingers across her cheek, "I have spent my life caring about the Earth, about peaceful co-existence; I have never advocated violence. But when I see the pine trees all turning red, when I see withered birch, when I see mushroom pickers walking for miles looking for what used to be abundant, when I see fishers hang up their nets because there is nothing left to catch or going out on snow machines to spread lime on their lakes trying to counter the acidity, when we have winters without enough ice to go out on the lakes, then I have to side with the people who are fighting to stop the oil companies. Every day that production is stopped is a day when tons of sulphur are not pumped out onto the land.

"Keep it up, you guys, keep up the fight, keep hindering them." Her hands were clenched into fists. "It might not seem like it, but every truck that you slow down, every person that you take out of production, everything that you do that slows them down has a very real effect on the land. Some days it might seem like we're losing. When we look at the McKenzie River and see the sheen of oil all the way to the Arctic, it might seem like it is too late, When we see the bare rocks of the Precambrian Shield, without even moss, let alone trees, you might think it's too late. But we have to do something, anything." Joan's hands stopped, she stood outlined in the sunlight of the doors, solid, straight, her dark eyes stared ahead into the group, looked into their eyes, tried to look into their hearts. "Anything," she concluded.

Ben took his coffee to the big doors that were open to the prairie, and just stood there and looked to a hazy horizon and let his thoughts flow outward across a parched earth. What was he going to say to this group? His lecture notes on supremacy were leftovers from a university and a life from before this rampant insanity.

A car rolled off the grid road and through the wire gate into the yard, crunched gravel in the drive and into the open space between the barn and the house. It was one of those newer models, with the oversize wheels that always made Ben think of Red River carts. He stepped back out of view as Abe crossed the yard to speak to the driver.

Roland Nataways stood where Ben had intended to go.

"Hey, Professor"

"Roland, right?" Ben stepped around him into the shade.

"Yeah, Roland, from your seminar class in '09."

"Right. So how are you, Roland?"

"Good, good," he shuffled until his back touched the wall.

"So what've you been doing recently?"

"Not much now, used to do a lot of work for NGOs, or Near Government Organizations as I liked to call them. First Nation stuff, even worked with the Metis for awhile, development work."

"Not anymore?" Ben liked this young man. He wasn't that young, in his thirties probably. It was hard to tell. The face was of a person who had stood too close to suffering and the pain etched itself into lines.

"Not anymore. Not much you can do when they erase your bank accounts. The last place was an organization trying to feed city kids. I guess we weren't Christian enough or something. The virus not only took out the organization's accounts but nearly everybody who worked there. Some of us tried to keep going. I was hunting in the river valleys and bringing in deer meat. But after a while I just couldn't afford it. Not just the gas, ammunition was getting crazy even then. That's what I'm talking about next."
"The price of ammunition?"

"No, I did two-and-a-half years in Dakota Max for a break, enter and theft. I broke into a gun shop trying to get ammunition. Tell you something, Prof. It was some of your ideas about supremacy that got me through. I forced myself to remember that the reason they were treating me as lesser was because they needed to, that someone else was treating them as lesser. I wanted to thank you for that."

What to say? Ben had no response. He nodded. Stood in front of someone he did not remember speaking to about an abstract subject and found his words returned to him in concrete, as solid as the prison walls of Dakota Max.

When it was Roland's turn to speak, he did not begin with his experiences in the ten-thousand inmate privately run prison. Instead he started by asking if anyone had heard the news this morning. People stirred, but no one answered.

"Well, Wright announced that Canada is a ticking bomb." He paused, "Rhetoric? Not at all. The words were chosen and deliberate. Ticking bomb is a justification for torture. Of course it's never called torture. It's called aggressive interview. In American law, if you know that there is a ticking bomb, and you know that your prisoner knows when and where the bomb will explode, you can legally torture him in order to save lives. That is the first criteria in Homeland Security directive sixty-six. The second criteria is that only enough pain is inflicted that the prisoner responds. Other criteria in the directive include that the interviewer is supervised and decisions about the amount of pain, type of interview, and duration are decided separately. The directive also requires that a trained doctor be present. Note, that the directive does not stipulate the training, nor that the doctor be licensed. Most medical associations refuse to license anyone specializing in pain administration. You would think that any real doctor, someone dedicated to the alleviation of suffering, would refuse to participate, especially since they would have to give up their licence. But, with the amount these guys are getting paid there is no shortage. Nearly double your wage, and work less than half the amount of time. It's a gold mine.

So we have in one room the prisoner, the supervisor, the interviewers, and a medic and a book of guidelines. This is all designed to make torture as humane as possible. Only the amount of pain necessary is administered, taking into consideration the health of the prisoner, the prisoner's tolerance levels, and the permanence of the affects. Very clinical." Roland's own words were clinical, precise. He spoke as though he was reciting, without feeling. "What it does, what all this procedure does is remove any emotion on the part of the interviewers. As long as they are within the guidelines, anything goes.

"Pain can be physical or psychological. Degradation is allowed in the guidelines, except that they cannot use the prisoner's religion, race, or nationality. Women cannot be degraded on the basis of being a woman. No homosexual forms of interview are allowed. The Christian right disallowed that after the prisoner abuse at Abu Ghraib prison in Iraq. Neither can a person's age be used to administer degradation. These prisoner's rights are interpreted by the supervisor. The first target to maximize both physical and psychological pain is always, always the prisoner's testicles."

Roland took his hands from his pockets, put them behind his back, hesitated then let them fall to his sides, limp.

"When Wright said that Canada was a ticking bomb, he put every Canadian prisoner into the interview room. The first criterion has been met. It's estimated that forty percent of the population of Dakota Max is Canadian. The interview wing of that place is going to be busy.

"For those of you who don't know, Dakota Max is owned and operated by Greatwest Electric. It is a privately run, for-profit prison. It does not pretend to be a correctional facility. There are no programs. The prisoners are not there to learn to correct their ways. Prisoners in Dakota Max are there to suffer for their crimes. Period. There is no such thing as a private cell. Prisoners are in ranges of one hundred. These are open rooms with twenty-five foot walls. The roof is made to open outwards. Once a day for an hour the roof opens, rain or shine, and the prisoners get their mandatory one hour of fresh air; bake, boil, or bath."

Roland smiled, a little upturn at the corners of his mouth that only tightened the hard lines of his bony face. He ran his hand across the leg of his pants, maybe to remove the sweat from his palm.

"Food is supplied by whatever fast food company bids the lowest — breakfast, dinner, and supper, wrapped in tinfoil and tissue." The tiny smile faded.

"It's quite the place. Prisoners and guards never interact. Control is accomplished with knockout gas. Seal the range, pump in the gas and all the prisoners go to sleep. End of riot. But what is a riot? Guidelines again. A riot is any major disturbance. Couple of guys get in a fight, in comes the gas. Somebody gets sick. Either the prisoners themselves take him to the door, or they go to sleep so that the guards can enter the range safely. Someone throwing up can be a major disturbance.

"Of course there are calculations that need to be made. Too much gas and prisoners die, too little gas and some will not go to sleep. The guidelines allow for a death rate of less than one percent. Some people have suggested that they over use the gas to keep the population down. I don't think so. Greatwest Electric is paid by the person; purposely killing prisoners is poor business."

He shifted slightly, so that the sun at his back completely shadowed his face. He was too far away for Ben to read his emotions. His words were flat.

"The beds are moulded into the floor. Can't hide a shiv under the mattress, there is no mattress. One personal affects locker moulded into the headboard, room enough for a toothbrush, a pocket book, maybe, definitely room for a Bible. Razors aren't allowed, nor haircuts; after awhile everyone begins to look pretty shaggy. The guards however are all very clean-shaven, helps to differentiate.

"So that's the ranges, pretty bare. Entertainment is each other. Next to the ranges are the interview facilities, and finally the exit. With Greatwest Electric in charge, of course the exit is the chair, no fatal injection, or gas chambers at Dakota Max. It's full current. Nothing cheap or chintzy about the exit."

Roland was about to step away from the spot where the sunlight washed the loft floor when Monica stood quickly. "Roland, a question please. You said that you didn't think that GE used gas purposely to make room for new prisoners, but isn't it true that DM is chronically overcrowded? That gas is used routinely? You were there. You are our best source of information. We've heard rumours that DM is mostly filled with Canadians, but the official reports suggest that DM only has about a forty percent Canadian population. You, yourself said that it's estimated that the Canadian population there is about forty percent. What's the real count?"

"Yeah, I was there." Roland's voice was softer. He was not listing facts now. The words came from a place deeper than the top of his mind. "That's why I don't think it's intentional. I did two-and-a-half years. I was only sentenced to two. The judge was Canadian, Roberts, right over there in Saskatoon. He had to give me a two-year sentence instead of two years less a day where I would be sent to a provincial jail. The charge involved weapons. I did two and a half because Greatwest Electric gets paid by prisoner days. It was accounting that kept me there. Purposely killing prisoners is not good business. It doesn't pay."

"But you were gassed?" Monica continued to stand.

"More than once."

"We know that. How many times? How many did you see killed?"

Roland inhaled, he opened his mouth but no words came out when he exhaled. He raised his hands palms up. "I don't know. I lost count. Gas is colourless, odourless. You're talking to your buddy and your tongue gets numb and you wake up on the floor with a real bad hangover. You don't know how long you've been gone, hours or maybe days and some people are missing. Sometimes you wake up in a different range, or you wake up and your buddy is gone. Maybe he never woke up, you hope he's in another range, you even hope he's gone for an interview."

"But you have seen people killed by gas."

"Yeah, a few."

"How many? In two-and-a-half years, how many?"

"Eight, eight that didn't wake up, that were still in the range. But I don't know if they were brought back or not. We carried them to the door, stepped back behind the yellow line, and they came and got them. I hope some of them were revived, but I don't know. I really don't know."

"How many Canadians? What's the real count? Or do you know?"

"To be absolutely honest, I don't know. It's possible I was only in ranges of Canadians. Maybe they kept Canadian and American populations separate. In the ranges I was in, the population was eighty, ninety percent Canadian."

A woman in a dark denim jacket raised an arm in the air. "Were you tortured?"

Roland took an unconscious quarter step back as though hit in his centre by the question. Looked straight ahead, his voice flat. "I was interviewed."

"What did they do to you?" the woman's voice held a hint of intrigue.

"That's not something I want to talk about." Roland spoke direct, clear, purposefully blunt.

"But, do you know why you were," the woman paused, "interviewed?"

"Ticking bomb. I was involved in a weapons offence. Maybe I knew something about the resistance. I can tell you that I told them every damn thing I knew. Everything, every name of every person I ever knew, everyone who ever spoke badly of Americans, every conceivable plot that I could imagine."

The memory stirred a strong emotion. Roland paused; he seemed to be struggling with it. His face contorted slightly; he opened his mouth but no words came . . .

"Okay everyone, lunch." Abe stepped from where he leaned against the soft-coloured wood rafters into the patch of light and stood beside Roland. "Thank you, Roland." He shook his hand gently.

Ben sat quietly during the break, enjoyed the fresh tomato in the sandwich of homemade bread. That tomato must have been picked not more than yesterday; it tasted of earth and water and vine.

"You have a nice place here." Monica washed down her sandwich with a bottle of cranberry juice.

"You're not the only one who thinks so," Abe responded. "Had a fellow in here this morning determined he was going to buy it even if it wasn't for sale. Had to threaten him before he would leave."

"So, how much was he offering?"

"Started at two, by the time I was pushing him into his car he was up to four."

"Four, four what, four million?" Monica's cranberry juice held suspended half way between the table and her mouth.

"Yup, four million for a quarter section, an old barn, house and Quonset. I only paid a hundred and a quarter for it thirty years ago."

"So what's the big jump in real estate. I thought the market was collapsed."

"In the big cities houses are almost worthless, but that's because everyone who can afford to is trying to move out into the country."

"Frisco." Monica got it. That was the answer.

"Frisco." Abe agreed. "So the people in Vancouver, Toronto, Montreal, move out to Saskatoon, Regina, even Prince Albert. People in the small cities move out into the country."

"But, four million Ameros. You could live a long time on that." The cranberry juice made it to her lips.

"Not as good as I live here. What's four million? Doesn't mean anything. If the price of land doubled again and it was eight million, I'd just end up using it to buy another place. If I sold out to that guy this morning, I'd just spend it all this afternoon pushing someone else out of their home. Naw, it wasn't much of a deal."

"Or you could buy yourself a condominium in Toronto."

"Yeah. Right." Abe bit into his sandwich.

~

"*Waweyatsin*." Ben pushed the word out, imitated his grandmother's voice, clear, concise, tinted with a little smile. "Good for you, you deserved that, now learn from it," she had said.

"*Waweyatsin*," he repeated because the word meant everything he wanted to say to these people seated, fed, legs outstretched, still holding bottles of water, relaxed after their meal. "Now you know what it feels like." The sun through the open doors warmed his back, grandfather was behind him, he could speak from here. "Canada's assertion of superiority over Aboriginal Peoples lasted for centuries. The Americans have only been here for a few years. Get used to it. They are not going home. No matter how much you cry, no matter if you say it's not fair, they lied to us; they are not going away. Make all the rational arguments you want — this is our land, our home, you have no right to come and take it away from us, you are a bastard nation, supremacy knows no logic. The supremacists are here because they thoroughly believe that it is for your own good. And, maybe it is. Maybe Canada has to learn what it feels like, what it feels like to be dominated, to be moved off the land, to be re-educated. We tried to tell you for decades, but you wouldn't listen. Way back at the Treaty signing, some of our ancestors tried to explain to you that you had no right to take, that you had to ask. But you wouldn't listen, so *Waweyatsin*. Good for you. This is what happens to you when you act like you're better than someone. Someone or something will come and put you in your place."

The room stirred, legs crossed, backs straightened, legs uncrossed, arms folded, unfolded.

"Don't worry about it. Learn from it. The same thing is going to happen to the Americans: someone is going to come along and put them in their place. Doesn't matter that they have the world's biggest army, doesn't matter that they have robot soldiers, or half-robot soldiers, doesn't matter they can kill you from outer space, that they have lasers that can fry you, or Bolts From Heaven to kill you in your hole. They're still humans. They only believe they are God.

"That is what supremacy is about, that's where it came from, from people who thought they were more Godly, the chosen ones. They were given a flaming sword by their God to beat down the other. And, with that flaming sword they became part of their God, the hand of God, doing God's work, bringing light to the darkness. Little Gods."

Ben had not intended to start speaking so strongly. The notes in his shirt pocket, scribbled on a single sheet of paper, folded into a tiny square, held an outline of an academic lecture on the premise of colonization. He had wanted to talk about Albert Memmi and *The Colonizer and the Colonized*, how that book had started a revolution in academia. Albert wasn't wrong. He had written about what he saw, what he felt, his truth; he had put a name to the oppressor, the colonialist. Then when people around the world began to see that Albert's truth was their truth, the academics followed with their papers and journals until the discussion had become dominated with the dichotomy of colonization. But, even though the academics had imagined such things as a postcolonial period, nothing ever really changed. Colonial discourse never captured the heart of the phenomenon. People still died of hunger, of AIDS, from bombs, and loneliness.

Ben had wanted to tell these people, this gathering of children of colonists sprinkled with children of the people of the land, that colonial discourse was about the symptoms of a doctrine of supremacy, that supremacy needed analysis. But his grandma spoke instead. He heard her laughing and the sound of that almost forgotten tinkle filled him and he laughed. He stood in front of the people and let his laugh rumble; it came up from his belly and out into the loft. It spread. Magic. Someone tittered. Someone else chuckled. Then the loft rattled with the laughter of everyone. It was funny that Canada experienced its own oppression, ironic and irony needed to be laughed at, to be laughed away.

~

On the quarter section of land to the south of Abe's place, Ruben Weebe looked at the silent cell phone in his hand. The phone had died in the middle of his conversation with his daughter in Saskatoon. It squealed for a full second, sharp and shrill in his ear, then died. He put the phone in his shirt pocket and tried the landline, the old-fashioned phone. It was silent, dead. The screen on the computer in the den was blank. "Ruth, Ruth." Ruben walked through the house calling his wife. She was in their bedroom, putting clothes into the closet. "Ruth, something's up." She looked to Ruben's face for the answer, ignored his words. The face said urgent and she followed him out of the house, to the shelterbelt where the caragana grew thick, to the spot they had decided upon, created, a spot with a hollow where two people could hide. Ruth sat silent and hugged Chico, a spaniel who squirmed but kept silent as though he too knew something was coming.

~

Ed Trembley leaned against last year's straw bale, enjoyed the sun in his face, on his shirt, heating his legs through the denim. He read from a little blue book that he had read many times, started over at the first page. He spoke the words to the sky.

"*The people of Venezuela, exercising their powers of creation and invoking the protection of God, the historical example of our Liberator Simon Bolivar, and the heroism and sacrifice of our aboriginal ancestors and the forerunners and founders of a free and sovereign nation."*

The remainder of the page he read louder, as though an oath, *"To the supreme end of reshaping the Republic to establish a democratic, participatory and self-reliant, multiethnic and multicultural society in a just, federal, and decentralized State that embodies the values of freedom, independence, peace, solidarity, the common good, the nation's territorial integrity, comity, and the rule of law for this and future generations, guarantees the right to life, work, learning, education, social justice, and equality; without discrimination or subordination of any kind; promotes peaceful cooperation among nations and furthers and strengthens Latin American integration in accordance with the principles of non-intervention and national self-determination of the people, the universal and indivisible guarantee of human rights, the democratization of imitational society, nuclear disarmament, ecological balance and environmental resources as the common and inalienable heritage of humanity; exercising their innate power through their representatives comprising the National Constituent Assembly, by their freely cast vote and in a democratic Referendum, hereby ordain the following:"*

Ed stopped for a breath and in the new silence heard the sound of diesel engines, then the sound of military bombproof tires on gravel. He slid down until he was lying in the short barley and looked toward the grid road that ran straight and bare across the earth from horizon to this rise of land where he smelled the dryness of the soil inches from his face. He did not need the binoculars; the convoy of Hummers raised a cloud of ashen dust that sped toward him and toward the people in the loft at Abe's place.

He kicked the straw away from the blocks of industrial Styrofoam, poured the plastic bottle filled with a mixture of diesel fuel and gasoline, struck a lighter to the fuel, waited a long second and another, until he was sure that the flame had taken, then ran; ran hard for the river to the east, to the valley where the river wandered between steep banks and willow and aspen grew thick and would hide a person from the sky. The burning foam billowed a greasy black finger of smoke upward behind him as he ran crouched. His knapsack with the little blue book, a little food, water, a mirror, and an industrial laser bounced on his back.

"*Out! Out!*" Abe yelled into the loft. People scrambled, all laughter died at the sight of the black smoke in the distance climbing into the sky.

"I'll drive," Monica almost shouted as she and Ben ran up to his truck.

Abe stood at the gate and designated the vehicles leaving the yard, spreading them to the four directions. "Go north and at the first intersection take the west road."

~

"So, how's your day going?" The ferryman leaned into the passenger side window of the truck, rested his elbows on the door.

"So far, so good," Ben answered.

The flat-bottomed ferry angled in the current of the South Saskatchewan River, followed the cable strung shore to shore. Its diesel engine rumbled and tugged against the cable, drew it into the little house and expelled it again out the other side, drawing the six-car ferry toward the far bank of aspen and the winding lane of gravel that ended abruptly where the heavy wooden planks marked the landing. Monica stared straight ahead, watched that landing draw incrementally closer.

"Would it be all right to get out and walk around a bit?" Ben asked.

"Oh, hell, yeah, everyone does. People just love to see water." The ferryman stepped back so that Ben could open the door. "Takes about seven minutes to get across," he added as he turned to talk to the driver of the older Ford pickup.

Ben walked over to the ferry edge to watch the flow of beige water slip away down the river valley. He stood looking out downstream, felt the moisture rise from the water, and wondered about the others. Was anyone still there when whoever was coming arrived?

A lone gull tilted wings and glided beside the ferry, flashed white in the sun as it banked away and turned to follow the river. There's a shortage of birds, Ben thought.

Even though he was only a few kilometres from the university, Ben had never been here before. The river rippled far below its high-water marks. Willow and a coarse grass that he did not know had begun to grow on the dark mud flats abandoned by the shrunken river. But, it was green. The valley was lush in contrast to the burnt prairie it cut through. Comforting to see trees, green trees. Ben wanted to be home, the lake still blue, and evergreens.

Monica wanted to be anywhere but here, exposed, dependent, trapped. Any minute and Homeland Security would appear on that far landing that was taking forever to arrive and they had no way out. Jump into the river and swim back? If she had to. Could Ben make it? Probably not. Too old for that. But, maybe. Ben was strong. Built like a bear. Her mind tumbled as it raced.

Off the ferry the truck spun gravel as Monica turned sharply to the right, away from the main road onto a track that led into the aspen and willow, over a rise, down again, a curve then the truck was pointed at the steep wall of the river valley. The track ran at an unbelievable angle upwards. She pushed the four-wheel drive button and eased the truck into the climb. It pointed its hood at the cloudless sky and began the ascent.

"Hey, just a second." Ben was reaching around for his seat belt.

"Not to worry. I've done this before. Well, I haven't actually driven up here. I had a boyfriend when I was in school who used to bring me here to show off his truck. It's okay. Really. We just have to take it real slow and steady. These Toyotas are incredible here. Watch."

The engine changed tone as it began to work, a deeper sound, a grumble. It climbed the impossible bank upwards, pushed Ben back into the seat until all he could see was the blue of a hot, dry sky.

~

Ed Trembley ran hard for the green fringe at the edge of the dusty summerfallow. He found a strength that rose from somewhere, maybe from fear, felt it first in his chest, then in his legs as he increased his stride, stretched new legs and ran. The Hummer's engine grew louder behind him. The last vehicle of the convoy had turned as it passed the smouldering foam to give chase.

The river valley dropped quickly away from the prairie, a near vertical drop of a dozen metres where the cut bank had crumbled, hid at its top by a bramble of chokecherry and thistles. Ed charged through this brush, dropped suddenly and slid feet first down the steep decline. The roar of the Hummer and the sound of smashed brush behind him became the sound of an airplane over top of him. The driver of the heavy truck must have intended to run Ed over and now it was too late. The Hummer dropped grill first, slammed into the valley wall where the cliff bottom became a steep slope. It flipped end over end through the aspen, bounced incredibly high after each crash landing and ended on its roof in the swirl of the river bend.

Ed slid down the slope, caught a broken tree trunk, put his feet under himself and quickly worked his way to the vehicle. Two Homeland Security officers looked to be dead, hopefully dead. They were not breathing. Another black shirt gasped unconscious, twitched in the back seat. A fourth, opened his eyes when Ed pulled at him. Ed slammed a fist between the eyes and they shut.

The river current made canoeing tricky. The added weight of two bound black-uniformed officers in the small canoe helped to balance the craft fore and aft but made the canoe ride deeper in the water, made paddling harder. Ed followed the shoreline, less current here in the shallows, as he worked his way upstream, pushing the paddle into the mud as much as he drew strokes in dark water. Following close to the shore also meant that it was unlikely that he would be seen as he neared the city with his hostages. It was always good to have something to trade with.

⁓

"You're going out on the lake? You just got home." Rosie walked behind Ben as he attached the boat and trailer to the truck, removed tarpaulin and straps. He turned and looked directly at her. The little girl was there again, for just a second it was little Rosie.

"Do you want to come along?"

"Me?" Rosie suddenly found herself flustered.

"Yes, you. There's no one else here." Kindness filtered his words. "I wasn't talking to the puppies." The first bold pup toddled out from under the house, fell, picked itself up, and pushed forward. "Hey, you." Rosie picked it up by the scruff, cradled it in the crook of her elbow. "You're too small to go wandering around." She gently rubbed the soft pink of its belly before kneeling, bending further than her body was accustomed to and placing the puppy back in the tumble of its siblings between the outstretched legs of the yellow dog. "What you going to name her?"

"Haven't thought of it."

"If you have a dog it has to have a name."

"Then we'll call her Betsy or something."

"No, what was the name of that dog you had when you were a kid?"

"Duke," Ben answered quickly through a flash of memories.

"Yeah, him." Rosie remembered

"Can't name a female dog Duke."

"Then Duchess. She's kinda royal, don't you think?"

"Seems fitting to name a dog after monarchy, sort of irreverent. I like it."

"Good start, but you've got six more under there."

"Wait and see what they turn out to be first. They'll tell us what their names are."

"Got to be careful what you name a dog. Give a dog a dumb name and they'll live up to it. My kids once named a dog Mischief. Good enough of a name, but it wasn't until I got them to change it to Maggie before that dog stopped getting into everything."

The lake reflected high clouds at its north end, grey against dark water. The boat skipped across shallow waves as it followed along the west shore, to the lee of the line of hills. They rode in silence for an hour. Rosie sat with her back to the wind, huddled in a large red-and-white life jacket and watched the lake flow away behind Ben at the tiller. The boat curved across from west to east then followed that shore south, back to the community, and Rosie found herself on the rickety wooden dock wondering what the purpose of the trip had been. She tried to help Ben reload the boat to the trailer, finally gave up and just stood out of the way.

"He'd only been away for a few days and he was lonely for the lake," Rosie concluded as she hoisted herself into the truck.

She stayed around all afternoon as Ben kept himself busy, not the busy of a man obsessed with doing, going, rushing, but the busy of maintaining space, putting away the net that hung on two wooden pegs on the cabin wall where it had been left to dry, folding it into a plastic tub so that it would come out easily the next time he used it. She kept up a steady stream of talk while she helped pick the dried weeds out of the net mesh. She talked for the sound. Now that her children were gone, her house silent and empty, she felt a vacuum that needed to be filled. And there was of course Lester. Ben needed to know everything about Lester, but she needed to be careful not to cross the line into idle gossip. Ben accepted Rosie's voice as background to their visit; let the words fill the space around them. The words were kind, and gentle, simple stories, everyday things that happened, remembered and brought back to life.

"And there we were with no spare tire, on a dirt road and nothing but prairie all around us. It's times like that when you really appreciate trees. Imagine four little ones, in the winter, and no way to make a fire to keep them warm."

"Yeah, I like trees."

The silence that followed did not last very long. Long enough to be noticed, but not long enough to be noteworthy.

"You like trees, but do you like children?"

"Sure, yeah sure, I like children."

"But you never had any. You went out of your way not to have any."

"Well, children didn't fit into the life I was living." He placed the last of the net into the tub, and in picking up the tub to carry it to the shed, turned his back to Rosie.

"And, what kind of life was that, Ben?" She followed him to the shed, waited just outside as he put the bin on a shelf where it was less likely that mice might make a nest in it, then followed him back around to the front of the house, and pulled up the other white plastic chair and sat looking out toward the pines.

"It was a good life. I don't regret any of it." Ben reclined his chair until it rested against the wall.

"Not even that you didn't have any children."

"Especially that I didn't have any children. Children have to pay for the wrongs of the parents, and I don't want anybody to pay for me."

The sun poured into the trees. Rosie leaned a little more into the chair, let it take her weight. The pines breathed back into the warmth of the day. She leaned forward. "We all have to pay, both you and me have had to pay, whether it was for our parents or grandparents, don't matter we had to pay. But it was still worth it."

"How about your kids, Rosie?" Ben altered the direction of the conversation.

"Good, they're all good. Elsie called the other day. Her and the baby are doing just fine. Dougie, well Dougie is doing what Dougie does best. Working, always working that one. Takes good care of his family, but someday he's going to learn, maybe the hard way, that working and money aren't everything. And Theresa, she's still the same, spends all her free time with her daughters, so much so that she isn't even looking for a man these days."

"I haven't met that one."

"Theresa?"

"Yes, Theresa, I haven't met her yet."

"Well, she won't come back to the reserve for whatever reason. When she wants me to come visit she sends me a bus ticket. Sure would be nice to get the girls up here where they can really play and away from that city. But she says that with her work she doesn't have time. I don't know, I think they get vacations." Rosie rattled on and Ben reclined a bit more and listened to her tell him about her favourite subjects, her children and grandchildren, and she didn't ask him again why he did not have any of his own.

~

Lester Bigeye waited.

~

"Your father?" Monica looked at the young man, his dark hair and grey eyes were too familiar. "Your father?"

"My birth certificate says 'father unknown'."

Monica watched him over the rim of a paper cup of dark fresh-roasted coffee. She liked it this way, with that slight taste of paper. She liked the Broadway Roastery where they sat outside in late-morning shade across the old concrete bridge where Broadway Avenue began its journey south. The trees at the edge of the parking area were beginning to catch some of the rising sunlight. Early, she thought; it was too early in the day for such a conversation. To early, too soon in her busy life to speak about it. Her son had phoned her and asked to meet. Twenty years. Twenty years it had taken him. At the eighteen-year mark she had wondered. Would he come looking? Was he still alive? But the war had come and she had other thoughts to occupy her. Now he was asking for his father.

What right did he have to question her loyalty? What right did she have not to tell him? He was asking for his dad. He wasn't begging, trying to manipulate her. He wasn't demanding, forcing. He just sat there, young, innocent and at the same time impossibly old, jumped from being a baby held by the nurse as Monica sat in the Royal University Hospital bed and signed the forms clipped to the board in front of her. She answered the questions, except for the one that asked for the father's name, wrote "unknown" in the space, clamped her mouth shut, loyal. She would not give him up. Would not ruin a good man for her mistake.

"Benjamin, Roberto, Bird" the young man paced the words. "You gave me those names. I wondered why those names."

"Roberto was after a writer I really enjoyed back then. I thought Roberto Unger was going to change the world."

"What about Benjamin?"

The hard question.

"Your father was my professor. The reason I gave you up for adoption, well one of the reasons — I was young, a student,

student poor." Monica tried to find words, exact words to walk the line between truth and honesty. The rush of traffic on the street beyond the line of trees didn't help. "He would have been fired if anyone found out he slept with a student." The wind out of the north swirled around the building, chilled the morning, chilled Monica. She zipped her light nylon jacket a little higher. Maybe they should have sat inside, it's always safer inside. It was his idea to sit out here, exposed.

"So you named me after my father. Was it his idea to give me up for adoption."

"*No!* No, I never even told him I was pregnant. I've never told him. He doesn't know." She caught herself, "I never said that I named you after him."

"But you just did." Benji smiled to himself. "It's okay, Mom. Strange to call you Mom. But it's okay, it's all right. It feels right." He fumbled for words among his tumble of emotion. "It doesn't matter that you were sleeping with your professor, nothing wrong with that."

"I wasn't sleeping with my professor." Monica spoke firmly. It had to be made clear. "We made a single mistake, once. It only happened once. And I never told him."

~

"Can I borrow your phone?" Lester stood in Ben's doorway, narrow in the frame of the solid door.

"Sure, what's wrong with Rosie's?"

"Cut off. She didn't pay the bill."

"Oh."

He wasn't listening in on Lester's conversation, he was trying to read his book. He was trying to concentrate on the complex structure of, *As I Lay Dying*, appreciating that a writer could have the courage to write a five-word chapter.

My mother is a fish. Lester spoke loud enough to interrupt his concentration. Unwelcome words into a hard plastic device pulled Ben away from the 1920s America into the now.

"I want to talk to the chief then.

"Somebody at the band office has to be able to help me."

Ben was forced to listen to one side of the conversation.

"Somebody has to pay for my meds. I can't. I thought you guys were there to make sure our Treaty rights were respected.

"That's bullshit. Tell them that the Treaties promise a medicine chest. They can't do that.

"You don't understand. I need those meds.

"But, I need them.

"*Shit!*" the phone snapped shut. "Shit." Lester put the phone on the desk. "Shit. At least in jail I didn't have to pay for them." He walked heavily to the door and out into the day that waited for him; not a good day.

～

"It's just the AIDS drugs that they refuse to pay for. I still get mine covered," Rosie explained later as she poured her afternoon cup of tea.

"Homophobia."

"Yeah, seems like they want to let all the queers and faggots die of natural causes as quickly as possible."

"Lester's gay?"

"Naw, well, I don't know. He got infected in jail, maybe he is. Or maybe he was, who knows. He got AIDS in jail that's all I know, maybe from a man, maybe from a needle. Doesn't matter. He can't afford to buy his own meds and he doesn't believe in Indian medicine."

"Worried?"

"Not for myself. Doesn't matter if he dies in my house or in a hospital. I'm not worried about catching it if that's what you mean. But I am worried about Lester, what's he going to do now? Not that he does a hell of a lot anyway. Just sits around the house like he's still in jail waiting to get out. I guess if you spend a lifetime waiting for something, when that something happens, when they let you out of jail, all you know how to do is wait. So Lester waits. He's still waiting."

"Any idea what for?"

"Like I said, it seems like he is just so used to waiting that the waiting is what's important and not what he's waiting for. Lester probably doesn't even know; maybe now he's waiting to die."

"How much is your phone bill?" Waiting for Lester to die was too much; he did not want to think about it.

"Never mind. It's awright."

"What do you mean it's all right? Rosie you need a phone." Ben drained the last of the warm tea, placed the cup firmly back on the table.

"Don't worry about it." She waved a dismissive hand. "Got it covered." She raised an eyebrow showing Ben the twinkle in her eye.

"Tell me."

Rosie looked into her teacup because it was some place to look away from Ben's questioning gaze, took her time answering, enjoyed the delay. "It's being taken care of."

Ben waited, knew better. Rosie would tell him. Rosie wanted to tell him, wanted to tell him and drag it out as long as possible.

"My daughter can't phone me."

"Uh-huh."

"So, if she can't phone me. Then what?"

"I'll bite, then you can't talk to your granddaughter."

"You're getting closer, but no cigar."

Ben shrugged.

"If she can't phone me then what?"

"Then she — " Ben was caught in Rosie's little game — "then she sends you money for your phone bill."

"No silly. Then she comes to visit."

"Okay." Ben did not sound convinced.

"Really. I figured this out long time ago. I think my mother used to use it on us, and I know my grandmother, Old Jeanie, could do things like that. Sometimes I get lonely for just one of my kids, and a day or so later that kid either phones me or comes home.

I remember when I lived with Delbert, locked away down there on the prairie. It was like I was his prisoner. Once in a while I would suddenly need to come home. Just a real strong need to come home and see my mom. I'd make Delbert bring me back, or I would take the car, use all our money for gas. He never understood. Used to drive him nuts. Anyway, when I got back, there would be nothing wrong. My mom would be here. Happy to see me, play with my kids, all smiles. But, she never said anything."

"And, you couldn't phone?"

"My mom refused to have a phone in her house. No, when that feeling came over me, there was nothing I could do but come home. Remember when we were kids, out sliding or playing and our parents would stand outside when it was time to come home and yell our names?"

"Uh-huh." Ben remembered. "Well you went home right away. You didn't take one more slide down the hill when you heard your mom calling. You just went home."

"Yeah, I remember." It was a good memory. Children playing on snow in moonlight. "You could hear her yelling a mile away. *Roseeeee. Roseeeee..*"

"Yeah, like that. I think they trained us to come. Do you think she could really yell loud enough for us to hear her from the hill? Try it."

"Well it was quieter back then."

Rosie smiled at Ben.

"Really, there weren't so many cars and things."

Rosie kept smiling.

"I guess not eh."

"No, there was something else going on. Anywhere we were, we could hear our mothers calling us. Well, I'm using that on my daughter. Right now she's packing my granddaughter in her car and by tonight I'm going to be bouncing that little girl on my knee. Just wait and see."

∼

Ed Trembley looked into Corporal Rick Fisher's face, didn't like what he saw there and slammed a fist into it. "Fuck you." He had nothing else to say. "Fuckin' black shirt," was the best he could do here in the basement away from the light, away from the sky, away from wind, and rain, away from people and living things. His hate churned his stomach, acid rose and filled his mouth, bitter and sour. Rick's lip bled bright in the fluorescent sheen of the workroom light, dripped down the side of his chin. He wiped his face against his shoulder and tried to glare back at Ed. He did not have the strength for a powerful glare and the look came off an indifferent "I don't care," rather than "Fuck you back."

It might have saved him from another punch in the face. Ed stood back, kicked Rick in the thigh, once, not hard.

"Listen prick. If your buddies fuck with Abe, I'm going to fuck with you the same way." Kicked him again, harder. Ed's fear eased back into the place that anger had filled. If they tortured Abe Friesen, would he talk? Of course he would. Everyone did. How much did Friesen know? Why the fuck did he stay there? Why didn't he run like hell the way everyone else did? Scatter, spread out, hide, mingle, let the masses absorb him. They couldn't watch everywhere at once.

Ed left his tied prisoners in the dark, no sense wasting electricity on the likes of them, and went again upstairs to sit by the window and watch the street, to pace to the back porch and search the alley, watch and pace and watch.

~

Benji felt safe again as he drove out of the city that was not a city at all but only a very large prairie town. He was mildly surprised by the extent of paved roads as he took the four-lane north. He had half expected to need a four-by-four.

He caught a glimpse of himself in the rear view mirror as he adjusted it, held it at that angle for a moment and looked, really looked. A narrow face stared back, a thin delicate bone structure covered with healthy, gently tanned skin. The hazel eyes below the high forehead peered quizzically back at him. Who is this man? They seemed to be asking. Who are you?

I am the son of my father, Benji answered the reflection. Do I look like him? Are those my father's eyes? Am I the younger version? He turned the mirror and the highway unrolled behind the truck.

His adoptive parents were old from the time he could remember, too old to play out on the street with, too old to wrestle with, too old to have their own children, and too old to participate in the life of the one they'd borrowed. He made up stories for himself about his real parents, exciting stories, and put in the good parts from his favourite books. Old James and Joyce helped with that, they gave Benji all the books he wanted with time and space to read in the quiet Toronto two-story stone house seven blocks from the library.

Today Benji would meet the fairy tale hero. Would he tell him? Would he say "I am your son come for my inheritance; teach me your art, teach me your science"? Or would he play the practiced role. "I am a gem merchant, see my emeralds and my rubies. How they sparkle." Would he dazzle his father's eyes, eyes that must be hazel like his own, blind him with colours and lead him away from his horde. Take his money and slip away? Into the den of the old dragon and out with a bag of treasure, the rite of passage. Would he then be able to walk free of the legend, write his own saga, become his own fairy tale hero?

Benji checked the map again. Highway 11 to Prince Albert, then Highway 2, north past the National Park, then east to Moccasin Lake I.R. What does I.R. stand for? Is it like R.M. rural municipality as they say out here, or maybe it's something like County Seat. It didn't really matter whether Ben Robe lived in an Intergalactic Region or not. Today the son would come and get his inheritance. I.R. equals Inheritance Restored.

~

The sun marked a bright circle on the whiskeyjack-grey sky, poured its heat through the high empty clouds and stuck Rosie's blouse to her back. The day stood still and damp. A boat ride would be nice today; maybe Ben would go out and set a net or just go for a ride. She hung a dripping sheet on the clothesline, straightened it so that it would dry without wrinkles and pinned it in case the wind she hoped for would come. She stood for a moment and looked, at the line of sagging laundry, at the sky that promised her it would not rain. Not that rain would be so bad. The laundry could stay out for another day or so, nothing urgent there; when it dried she would fold it and take it inside — inside a house that was too hot to sit in for long, too hot to run the clothes dryer.

Lester was in there in front of the television. The heat didn't seem to bother him in his sprawl on the couch. It was his couch now, blanket and pillow, duffle bag under the end table. It used to be Rosie's favourite place, tea and cupcakes and gentle entertainment. Now it was coffee and a full ashtray and the violence of professional sports — even golf seemed tinged with anger when Lester watched it.

Rosie left the laundry basket on the steps to the back door and was going to see what Ben was up to. She walked around to the front of the house to where the path through the trees began. Lester could make his own lunch. He'd make a mess, and Rosie would clean it up. But that could wait until evening when the house cooled down. Rosie had never in her life gone to bed with dirty dishes left out. Learned from her mother, "Spirit things come in your house at night and eat off your dirty plates." It disgusted her to wake up in the morning to find dishes on the counter from Lester's late-night meals.

The black Jeep Cherokee turned onto the track that led from the road to the front of Rosie's little house, too quick — it bounced at the big pine root that ran out under the north track. Not someone from around here; Rosie waited. The truck rolled, slower now, up to the front of the white-sided house. The driver rolled down the window with a buzz of electricity. She waited; too unseemly for a Native woman to talk to a man through an open window, cross her arms and rest her elbows on the door and wiggle her bum in the air. She sat instead on the front step and exercised a little of her deep learned patience.

The man was young and had not earned patience yet; a young man with a salon haircut, and shoes, brown leather; slacks and short-sleeved shirt that matched; black and tan.

"Hello." He stood not so tall in front of her.

"Hello yourself."

"I'm looking for a Mr. Ben Robe." Benji shuffled his feet, tried to find a more casual stance, couldn't, and stood exposed like a schoolboy in front of the master, or a penitent in front of the priest.

Rosie recognized the young man, though she had never before seen him. She smiled inwardly and the smile found its expression on her face.

"A Mr. Ben Robe, are there more of them?"

"I'm sorry?"

"It's okay. So what you want with Ben?"

"You know him?"

Rosie nodded. "Oh yeah, some days I know him better than I want to."

"He lives near here?"

"Right through there." Rosie pointed with her mouth to the beginning of the path through the trees. "Come on, I'll take you there." She stood up quickly. She wanted to be there when these two met.

Ben's son was here, her daughter would not be too far behind.

～

Leroy was eleven months older than Elroy. Their mother must have been too tired to have much imagination left over when she named the second son, still angry that the myth, you can't get pregnant when you're breast feeding, wasn't true. People who knew the boys occasionally mixed up which one was older, Leroy was born January tenth and Elroy celebrated his birthday a month earlier on December ninth, other people thought the boys were twins. Twelve siblings knew the boys' correct ages, but even their mother Agnes occasionally mixed them up. She mixed up the names and ages of all of her children, and had to recite their names in chronological order to find the one she wanted. "Rudy, Barbara, Martha, Elizabeth, Leroy, Elroy, Mary, William, Jonas, Stewart, John, Peter." Never in Agnes's life had she blamed the church for inflicting the denial of birth control on her, and had dutifully attended, a ladder of children behind her, every Sunday.

Tomorrow, Elroy would be in that church for the last time. Tonight he lay in his finest, white buttoned-up shirt, hands folded, head on a satin pillow, eyes closed, his long bright white hair shiny in the fluorescent light. He looked to be almost smiling. "Peaceful" people remarked when they looked into the casket. "He looks so peaceful." It gave them comfort that Elroy's suffering was over.

Leroy was at the wake. He sat with his friends at a table near the exit doors of the school gymnasium, close to outside where he slipped every once in a while for a cigarette. Later in the night when the crowd thinned out he would exercise Elder's privilege and smoke inside. It would piss Elroy off if he knew. Elroy had never smoked, probably because Leroy had started first.

The competition between the boys had begun as soon as they laid eyes on each other. There were some here tonight who remembered when Leroy and Elroy played hockey, never on the same team, each pushing to excel over the other. If Elroy scored a goal, Leroy would be nearly manic to get one as well, skates shattering ice, driving for the net. The boys played hard, elbows and shoulder checks, and sometimes, but not often, a teammate might think that he could drop the gloves against the opposing brother, only to find that brotherhood was far more powerful than team spirit. Fight with one brother, you had to fight both, regardless of which team they were on.

Ben sat across the gymnasium from Leroy at the same table as Rosie and Elsie and little Rachel whom Rosie had on her lap. Benji was there, not knowing what to make of the situation. This was completely foreign to him, not only that an entire community would attend a wake, but that they were all Indians, and he was half-Indian too. He didn't know how to behave, didn't know the protocol. This should be a solemn occasion, the death of an Elder, but people were teasing and laughing as though it were nearly a celebration. All of the stories he heard were either ribald or otherwise twisted to evoke laughter.

There was the story of how Elroy had beaten Leroy in a poker game and went home wearing Leroy's jacket and driving his truck. Time blended and someone else — Benji could not remember the person's name, had trouble remembering all the names of all the people he was introduced to, all the new relatives — this someone, this relative, told of another famous poker game.

"In them days they used to play for muskrat pelts, I guess. In the spring when trapping was over they used to come down here to the Hudson's Bay post from all over as soon as the ice was off the lake. This is way, way back — thirties, forties, maybe. My dad said they used to play anywhere. Someone would spread a tarp on the ground," the unknown relative spread his hands to show Benji, "and a trapper could either win big or lose a whole winter worth of work. Anyway, this one game it was old Kooch Primeau, I barely remember him, he was old when I was a kid and that was a long time ago, and he was losing. He took out his false teeth and threw them out there. And they say old Duncan Bird, he was chief here after that, he took out his glass eye," the unknown relative made a plucking motion, "and threw it on the pile and said 'I see you.'"

When the laughing died down, when the last person had repeated, "I see you," Ben explained to Benji. "Old Duncan Bird was my mother's grandfather, so your great-great grandfather."

"You're related to just about everyone here." Rosie adjusted Rachel in her arms, tried to find some way to ease Benji's tension.

"Be careful who you try to snag." Elsie liked Benji. He was a good-looking young man.

"As if. He knows better than to try to snag at a wake — if he wants a woman he'll come back at pow-wow time." Rosie was really reminding her daughter of propriety.

"Am I related to — ?" Benji even had trouble remembering Elroy's name. He indicated the casket in the centre of the gymnasium with a nod in its direction.

"Sort of, I guess. Leroy and Elroy were my dad's cousins I think." Ben was not sure.

"No, The Moosehunter family came here from the west side," Rosie remembered. "Your family has been here since Treaty; they came later. Your dad and Elroy and Leroy used to go work together in the logging camps, but they weren't related."

"So I'm not related to him." Benji wondered what he was doing at a wake for a stranger.

"Well, sort of. Leroy married a Bird woman. She's been dead now for so long I can't remember her name, but she was your Granny's cousin." Rosie had a good memory for lineage.

Benji guessed from the white casket with the red C logo blazoned on the open lid. "He was a Montreal Canadiens fan."

"No, that's Leroy getting his last lick at his brother. Elroy had to cheer for the Maple Leafs because Leroy cheered for Montreal. Everybody knew that." Even Ben knew of the famous rivalry. "It was Leroy that got to pick the casket."

Rosie warned. "Leroy thinks he got the last laugh at his brother. But Elroy's still around, Leroy better watch out. Tricks from the Otherside can be cruel sometimes."

~

Before the midnight meal was served, Ben was asked to go sit with the Elders.

"How come not you?" Elsie asked Rosie.

"Oh, that's just Leroy, wants to talk politics with the men. He sees me here with my granddaughter. Knows I'm with family, and hey, he paid me a compliment. I'm not old enough to sit with them." Rosie smiled at her daughter. There was no insult, none intended, none taken. Rosie lifted the little girl under the arms until she stood on Rosie's lap looking at her, looked long into her granddaughter's face, at the way she held up her head, felt the strength in the legs as the baby tried to stand against her thighs. "I can't place you little one. You look like someone from long ago but I don't remember who."

"She looks like her father."

The silence that followed was broken by Benji. "Where is her father?"

A longer silence was broken by Elsie. "He was with the Pats,"

Benji offered a bewildered look.

"PPCLI" Elsie responded.

The look deepened.

"Princess Patricia Canadian Light Infantry, defending Toronto."

"You're a widow." Benji didn't know what else to say. He felt a tinge of guilt. The man died defending his city, died defending him, defending the school where they had gathered and waited, cringed at the shriek of sirens.

"I never think of myself that way. Bert never even got to see his daughter." Elsie read his guilt. Offered a gentle explanation to ease what she thought was concern. "He was home on leave, we got together, I got pregnant, then the Americans came. I hardly knew him. But I am thankful to him. He left me a bit of himself, a gift."

~

The food served at the Elder's table ran over the paper plate in front of Ben, deer meat stewed in its own juices until it fell apart, pan fried pickerel, baked bannock, fried bannock, a little scoop of dry pounded meat placed carefully on the edge of the plate where it wouldn't get soaked by the juices from the deer meat; it should be dry, eaten with fingers and dipped in butter, and of course, every wake needs potato salad, lots of potato salad.

"Bet you didn't eat like this at that university, eh Ben?" Roderick nodded toward Ben's plate as Ben tried to keep the blueberries thickened with cornstarch from running off, with a flimsy plastic fork.

"Can't say I did." Ben decided to just eat what was there instead of trying to dam the flow that was defeating him.

The talk during the meal was general, "Who shot the deer?"

"It was Red who shot the deer, of course."

"That Jemima sure can cook."

"You bet, taught by her mother, still knows how to make pounded meat, don't see much of this anymore."

Then when the plates were nearly empty, a few bits of bannock remaining, too much for old men to eat who didn't work hard all day anymore, a young woman served hot tea from an overlarge black enamel tea pot, black tea that smelled of the handful of muskeg leaves thrown in 'just for the Elders', poured into white Styrofoam cups.

Leroy stirred a second plastic spoonful of sugar into the tea. "So, Ben," he leaned back into the hard chair, stretched old muscles, "What you make of this Treaty process that's goin' on?"

"Haven't followed it too close, I'm a bit out of the loop." Ben talked around the bit of baked bannock dipped in the blueberries he had saved for the last.

Roderick said something that he had repeated all his life, something his father had repeated to him: "Can't change the treaties; doesn't matter what, we can't change the Treaties."

"Treaties were with Canada. There is no more Canada." Leroy set the agenda for the coming discussion.

Roderick remained adamant. "Treaties were with the Queen. Queen is white. I take it Treaties were with white people, Canadian or American shouldn't matter."

"AFN don't seem to think so. They're negotiating as we speak," Leroy invited.

"Who said AFN could speak for us."

Ben joined, "That's the thing, isn't it. Who negotiates for us? If we are a Nation, if we really are Moccasin Lake Cree Nation, then we should be the ones who are at the table."

Roderick stood firm, "There shouldn't be a table. We've been saying now for as long as I can remember, Treaties are sacred. If that really means something, then we have to act like it and not run to suck up to whoever has the power right now."

Leroy moved the discussion forward, "There's talk of moving all the Cree onto one reserve, a big reserve like they got down in the States, instead of all these little ones."

"Can you imagine, eh, living beside Plains Cree and Swampy Cree — and where would everybody hunt? Won't work."

"But think about it." Ben was into the discussion. "Just think, if we had a big enough of a land base for us all, if we joined together, we might be a Nation. The reason we have tiny little reserves is because when we were negotiating Treaty, Commissioner Morris didn't want us to have big reserves. He wanted to break us up so that we would be weak and less of a threat to Canada. The reason we have small reserves here is because Canada had a weak military. They were afraid of us."

"That's not how I heard it." Leroy couldn't stay out of the discussion. "The way I heard is that the old chiefs selected their own reserves. Now here William Charles was chief at the time of Treaty and he selected this place for the reserve. Some of the people wanted to be over to the west where the national park is now, but William chose the biggest lake because it would have the most fish."

"Yeah, that's how I heard it too." Roderick agreed. "From what I been able to piece together, my family have lived here as far back as anyone remembers. Always lived here beside this lake. Used to be, we lived up by Thunder Mountain on the west shore, but when the reserve was made we moved here to the south end. But you know what will happen if they make one big reserve. They'll move all the Indians from the South up here. Government always wanted to do that, put the Indians on empty land."

Leroy's hand paused, held the cup of tea half way to his mouth: "Not anymore, I don't think. They might move us down there on the prairie so they can take the resources from here. Americans need lumber and paper and especially our water. No, my bet is if they move us, they'll march us down there to the empty prairie; we'll walk another trail of tears."

Roderick disagreed, "Naw, they been taking the resources from here all along. Used to be they could just buy it and our government would sell it to them cheap. Didn't matter that we were here or not. Just look at all the highways in this country. They all run north–south. That's not so that we could get around. That's so that they could get the resources out of the North and sell them to the Americans. Won't be anything different now."

"Well, Thoreau sure as hell didn't sell us out, did he?" Leroy shot back.

"All the ones before him did, didn't they? And look what happened when he shot off his mouth." Roderick was beginning to have fun.

Leroy the Liberal had to defend Thoreau, had no choice at all now. He would have to stay a Liberal because Elroy died a Conservative. Roderick knew well the ferocity of his cousins' politics. He had mediated between and around them for decades, knew of the rivalry and the campaigning, and who put up more posters for their party and who attended more rallies, and speeches, and who was the best prime minister and who was running the country into ruin.

"People blame him for bringing on the invasion, but you got to remember he stood up, them spineless Conservatives had us in so many wars defending the bastards that the world was beginning to think we were the same country. That's probably why nobody's helping us now. Sure Thoreau was a radical, that's why we elected him, remember. It took a Liberal to stand up to the Americans."

"Well the way I remember it, Liberals weren't much better before Thoreau; they gave away as much as the others."

"What about Trudeau? What about Chretien? You can't say they gave in to the Americans. Compare them to Harper or even Mulroney, remember him? Now that's going back maybe a little too far for you. But do you remember free trade, remember what that did?" Leroy was on a roll. How dare anyone knock the Liberals.

"I always thought that Thoreau was a populist," Ben joined in. "He won that election because of anti-American sentiment. People didn't vote for the Liberal party as much as they voted on a single issue — 'get back at the Americans'. He didn't really have much when he threatened to close the border. The border was closed. They had already built their fences and towers, Black Hawk helicopters, cameras, all that."

"It wasn't a single issue." Leroy defended. "We were going to do something about global warming remember. The big oil companies were screaming and spending money on that election. Every spare dime they had went against Thoreau. We had a plan for greenhouse gases that was the most aggressive in the entire world. Canada was going to become a showcase for the planet. We were going to prove that you could do something. Canada was about to shine again after years of following the Americans. We were going to stand out in the world again." The old fist, knuckles scarred, rested on the table, not pounding, not yet. "The world was beginning to think that Canada was America, and after Afghanistan, and how we acted under the Conservatives over Iran, it's no wonder."

"I gotta agree with you on that." Roderick hesitated while a young man cleared away the stained paper plates. "It was getting so that the rest of the world saw us all as one, and that used to worry me. If we were too close to the Americans, their enemies became our enemies, and the Americans were good at making enemies."

"You bet," Leroy spoke in a rush. "We were set to change that when they annexed us. We never got the chance."

Ben held his ground. "I wonder if Thoreau really would have followed through with his threats. He won the election on the promise to do something, but he was in power for two years and was still only making noises."

"Thoreau was only one man," Leroy defended. "It takes a whole nation to make change, especially the big changes we were trying to effect."

"Well, Ben might not have believed Thoreau, but Wright sure did." Roderick sided.

Ben put his study of obscure history to use. "I don't know, the Americans always intended or at least contemplated taking over Canada; Thoreau's noise only offered an excuse. In the nineteen thirties the Americans had detailed plans for invading Canada."

Roderick also remembered history. "1812, was the first, eh."

"Then the Fenians." Leroy knew history too.

Ben set the record straight. "1775 was the first one. That was the Quebec invasion. The next was 1812. Some historians have suggested that the reason for the American Revolutionary war was not because of the tax on tea as popular history would have you believe but was rather started by the Americans as an excuse to invade Canada — annexation, expansionism seems to have been part of the American ideal since its inception. They thought it was going to be easy, in fact Jefferson said it was 'just a matter of marching'."

"What about the Fenians?" Leroy wanted to know.

Roderick held up an old hand. "Before you go there, I thought the American Revolution was about taxes and conscription. You're saying it wasn't?"

"I'm not saying anything. I just said that some Canadian historians have written that the American Revolutionary war against Britain was started by the Americans as an excuse to invade Canada."

Roderick thought about it. Let it settle in. "Makes sense." He concluded.

"The Fenians." Leroy still wanted to know.

"1866 to about 1871." Ben exercised his memory. "The Fenians were Irish revolutionaries who wanted to cut Britain off from its colony. There were about a half dozen raids into Canada over that time period. The Americans looked the other way. President Andrew Jackson was supposed to have said, "We'll recognize the established facts," meaning of course that if the Fenians were successful, America would recognize the annexation."

"That's right." Leroy rested his hands on the table.

Ben continued his history lesson. "There was also a lot of talk after the American Civil War about another invasion of Canada. After the North beat the South they were looking at us. Some people say they would have invaded if the American people had any stomach left for war." He paused for a taste of his tea, something to wet his dry throat. "Of course the famous 1870 Wolseley expedition sent out to Manitoba was not only about Riel and the Metis. John A. MacDonald was reacting to American newspapers in the West calling for an invasion of Canada."

"If we're counting attacks we can't forget the Cyprus Hills massacre," Roderick added.

Leroy asked. "What was that one again?"

"Remember, the American wolf hunters who attacked the Nakoda at Cyprus Hills, accused them of stealing horses?"

"Oh, yeah, that was an American whiskey fort, wasn't it?" Leroy remembered.

Ben put his cup down. "If we're talking about American commercial activity in Canada, I'd say we have to consider all the big corporations that have taken over."

"Now that was an invasion." Roderick leaned forward. "One thing I really learned when I was chief was that if an American company wanted something, the Canadian and Saskatchewan governments went out of their way to make sure they got it. If a First Nation wanted something we had to wait. Weyerhaeuser, the American pulp and paper giant, wanted all the trees in this territory. We were trying to save some — know who the governments sided with?"

Leroy nodded, "It was always like that. But it got worse under Hopper. It was him who made an agreement with them to use each other's armed forces in case of civil disasters. He invited the American army in. We almost lost Canada in '08 without a fight. Hopper was ready to give it away."

"You know they always planned on an invasion." Ben spoke softly. "In about 1928, maybe '30, they had plans to invade. They were going to take Halifax first to block British support, then attack Winnipeg to cut the rail system. Most of the attack was aimed at Ontario and Quebec. Even when the plans were declassified in 1974, nobody in Canada made much of a fuss about it. A few people went to the American archives in Washington to look at the plans, a few articles appeared, but it was mostly written off as a hoax or something. Nobody really cared."

"Yeah, and look what happened. All the warnings were there and nobody did anything." Roderick leaned back.

Leroy defended: "Well, Thoreau was going to do something."

A silence followed as the three Elders remembered how it had been. Ben looked back at the table where Rosie, Elsie, and Benji continued to sit. Benji seemed to be in conversation with Elsie; Rosie still held her granddaughter, wasn't going to let her go.

Ben wondered if Benji felt deserted. *Well, he came to find out about me — Rosie is a part of me that he needs to know.*

The gymnasium buzzed with conversation, occasionally a laugh rattled across it. People ate, visited, remembered, relished the memories, the good times and those memories washed away the sorrow, the loss of a respected Elder.

Ben had never really considered himself an Elder before tonight, but here he was, sitting at the Elder's table with the very old Leroy, and Roderick who had always been older, but now was clearly old.

"It don't do Thoreau much good now." Roderick interrupted Ben's thoughts. "Governor Johnson sure as hell isn't going to legislate against the oil companies."

"Governor, my ass." The old fist hit the table. "Canada is led by a prime minister, and Thoreau is our prime minister until he's defeated in a fair election. Just because Johnson was appointed don't give him any authority. You can bet Canada will resist until there isn't a breath left to fight with."

Ben came back to the conversation. "That's the problem. The Americans aren't going to go away. We're stuck with them. Like the Borg used to say in the old Star Trek movies:

'Resistance is futile.' We can resist, like we resisted Canada when they were stomping on us. Didn't do a lot of good. They still stomped on us. Now the Americans are stomping on Canada. We have a new supreme master to live with. We'd better learn how. Did you hear the other day about those kids that crucified themselves at the border? A dozen of them nailed to crosses. It didn't change anything. Hungry for three days, sore hands, a little media attention, but they'll be forgotten soon enough."

"They weren't hurting so bad," Roderick paid attention to news. "Morphine; they were all higher than kites on morphine, didn't feel a thing. And the nails they used, weren't even real nails. Did you see them, they showed them on CBC, ground down to the size of needles."

"It wasn't so much how they did it," Leroy liked what the kids had done. "It was that they did it. It wasn't against the government so much as it was a shot at the Christians; a shot at the new Zion. Those are the crazies we have to watch out for, the ones going around preaching the end of times and that America was prophesied in the Bible as the Promised Land. That's what's behind all this you know. Got nothing whatsoever to do with security or oil or water or nothing. It's them crazies and their millions showing up for revivals and screaming their salvation. They're the ones that are war crazy. Those kids did something. They might have been on morphine, maybe they ground down the nails. So what that they didn't nail their feet. They did something about the real enemy. They embarrassed the Christians, reminded them about Christ for a minute and got them out of the Old Testament."

"I have to agree with you, Leroy," Ben nodded toward the older man, a man in his nineties with vigour and strength.

"It's that 'One People, One Country, One God' stuff that's worrying. Now that's supremacy, pure and simple supremacy."

Roderick entered with a little more excitement now: "That's where it comes from, from the Supreme Being stuff. All those Christians believe in a supreme single God. That's their culture. It's all about hierarchy, every bit of it."

"It's certainly cultural. But it's not limited to Christians. Muslims and Hebrews believe in a supreme God too." Ben needed to be balanced. An argument that was too one sided, could not persuade. "It goes back to Plato and his theory of Gold, Silver, and Bronze people. Organized society has tried to follow his formula ever since, and spread the idea to the rest of the world during the era of expansion. Not only to the Americas — this idea of supremacy was used in Africa and Asia. It never diminished. When the academics started to speak of a postcolonial period in the last century as though colonialism had ended, we had the International Monetary Fund and the World Bank forcefully spreading the economic dogma of the Super Powers, America, and the European Union, on the third world. Colonialism never ended. It just changed forms. If we want to understand this symptom we have to examine the cause, and I've been saying for decades that the cause is supremacist ideology"

Roderick liked what Ben was saying. "It's like Indian Affairs. Oh, they were polite and dedicated, but couldn't get it through their skulls that we wanted to do something different. They genuinely could not understand anything but top down."

"How many terms were you chief?" Leroy couldn't remember.

"Three." Roderick held up three fingers. "Two terms in the nineties and again from '06 to '09. That's when I hung it up.

We couldn't do anything. You can't change people's minds who only have one way of thinking."

"And how do you change people's thinking?" Ben asked rhetorically.

"You don't," Roderick answered. "All we can do is live our lives the best we can. Walk in a good way and maybe people will see us walking in a good way and want to walk with us. Can't force anyone to change, never could. It never works."

Ben responded with a hint of sarcasm: "I think assimilation worked pretty well for Canada."

"No it didn't. All those policies did was wreck our people, we never did become them. When they stripped our culture we didn't adopt theirs. That's still what all the grief is about, people trying to find where they belong. So from about the nineties onward there was that movement back to our spirituality. So much for assimilation."

Leroy stayed out of the discussion. It wasn't pure politics and he wasn't really interested.

"But you got to admit that supremacy was what was behind the policy. They believed they were superior and were doing it for our own good."

"And we learned it from them. We started to become, as you say, supremacists ourselves. Indians got to be just as good as white people at believing they were better than others. We had our hierarchies too. AFN, FSIN, Chief and Council. I even got sucked into it. They elected me chief, thought I really was a chief for a while, forgot that I was only *okimakan* and not *okimaw*."

Ben nodded to Roderick, "*Ahie*" he agreed.

"You too, Ben. You got yourself a good education, stayed in that big university. You must have felt pretty important."

Ben's first response was to deny the allegation, deny that he ever put himself above the people, but he knew that to verbalize the denial wouldn't be completely true. He kept silent.

"It's okay, we all got caught up in it. Now we're old, had our ups and downs. Some of us took real shit-kickings before we figured it out. When we started to act like we were better than someone else, something always came along and put us in our place. When you're an Indian, you learn it fast."

"*Ahie.*" Ben understood. Maybe for the first time, understood why things went the way that they did. Why he really wasn't teaching anymore. It might not have had anything to do with his age or his desire to come home. Maybe those powerful forces that keep balance in the universe decided Ben needed to get balanced again. "*Ahie,*" he nodded again to his Elder Roderick.

~

Rosie watched Benji, saw his discomfort, saw him sit too straight, saw the mechanics of his movements. This young man was completely out his element and it showed — it showed in his voice, in his questions, or lack of questions; it was there in his silence, in his perfect politeness.

She had watched, stood aside, not part of the reunion, only an observer. She couldn't help herself. She needed to be there when Benji met his father. She needed to see what Ben would do, how he would react — it was important to her, beyond curiosity, way beyond tidbits of possible gossip. How Ben reacted when he came face to face with his child, with his offspring, with his little alter-self, would inform Rosie of the true Ben, the real man inside the image she had created.

She had stood there under the trees, watching from a distance, smiling, maybe even smirking a little as Benji explained, tried to explain, faltered — started again. She couldn't hear the words. She imagined he said who his mother was, gave his birthday, said his name again, "Benji" or "Benjamin", or something.

She'd watched Ben's stance, watched as realization filtered through broken speech, until realization broke the stoic and the body sagged, drained of will and then Ben hugged his son and she knew, even at a distance, that Ben was crying.

She left then — quietly, soft steps away. Now she knew the true Ben and knew that he was the same Ben she had always known, only now he had another dimension. He was a father.

～

"This is what I wanted to show you." Elsie felt around on the dash of her car for a tiny note pad, found it through the open window, flipped pages at the edge of the white schoolyard floodlight, not nearly enough to read by, but she didn't need to read, she only needed enough to assist her memory. Benji stood awkwardly in the gravel parking area while Elsie read out the poem she had composed on her way north, driving with one hand and scribbling with the other.

"Who needs an army?" She read with a deeper voice than she used for conversation.

"Beaten with a Bottle
Broken Spirits Spilled
Bashed
Robbed
Rolled
Stole the Little Bit of Dirt
The Earth
Broken Spirit Lost
Stole the Ragged Bit of Shirt

Ghost Danced
Bashed
Beaten by a Bottle
Spirit Spilled
Spewed
Broken Lips Speak
the English
Beaten
Bottled
Robbed
Rolled
In Drunken Stupor
Stoned."

She looked up to try to read Benji's face. She needed him to like it, wanted him to like her for writing it, wanted him to see her as an Indian, a good Indian woman. Her mother would frown on this, trying to be noticed by a man while at a wake, disrespectful. But, she might never see him again, never see those anxious eyes, those eyes that looked through her and saw the dreams, dreams of great things, great doings.

His expression didn't tell her anything. His words did. "Read it again."

She did. Slower, punctuated, put her heart into it. Three-quarters of the way through she realized. "He doesn't get it. He was raised white."

"I like the sound of it. The rhythm." He confirmed her thoughts when she finished. "I have to think about the content for awhile, but I like it."

But did he like her, Indian woman, traditional Indian woman?

"My adopted parents weren't drinkers. I never saw a drunk person until I was in my late teens. Just never saw anybody act that way. I guess if you grow up around alcohol you might hate it. Or love it," he corrected himself. "Alcohol is a big issue these days, but I just don't see it. Always thought it was just the right-wing Christians imposing their beliefs on the world. I guess from your perspective it would be different."

"I didn't grow up in an alcoholic home either." She corrected his assumption. "Mom never allowed it in the house. She's the inspiration for the poem. It echoes her words. She always said that the whiteman used alcohol to defeat us and to keep us down. To her this neo-temperance movement is a good thing for us."

"Hey, look, a falling star." Benji pointed toward the southern sky. "Wow. I've never seen one so bright, or that colour, almost blue."

"Incredible. Did you make a wish?"

"No, you?"

"For good things." she answered, "good things to come." Good things for her and Benji.

"Are those northern lights?" Benji continued to stare at the enamel black sky and the tinge of white, almost cloud like across the eastern horizon.

"Yeah, they are. Let's go down to the lake away from these lights and maybe we can see them better. It's just down here a ways, not far." She led the way to where water lay perfectly flat and reflected stars, northern lights, and the track of speeding satellites.

"I've never seen them before. You don't get them in Toronto."

"Probably do, just can't see them." Elsie could not imagine anywhere on Earth where the spirits did not dance. She stood close to him, close enough to feel his presence, and as Benji's gaze wove back and forth across the black star-studded sky, where the lights were beginning to dance in sharp waves of green tinged with red, he began to feel her presence too.

~

The hood smelled of vomit, not Abe's. That's all right, he thought, I've smelled vomit before.

"Abraham Isaac Friesen." The voice was not strong, did not have natural strength to it, though the speaker tried to sound authoritative. Like a substitute teacher, Abe thought.

"Charged with conspiracy against peace, order, and good government." The voice continued. "What is the evidence?"

"He was captured at his residence. A reliable source reported suspicious activity there and when a squad led by Captain Ross approached the residence, warning signals were activated by co-conspirators." The voice sounded as though it was reading, flat, empty. "Several vehicles were reported fleeing the residence as the squad approached. Abraham was the lone occupant when it arrived. He was taken into custody, read his right to voluntary statement, due military process was explained. Abraham declined a voluntary statement. Upon investigation, evidence of a terrorist cell was discovered. They had occupied the loft of a barn on the premises; however, a complete search did not uncover any weapons. It is assumed that the fleeing co-conspirators removed that evidence with them."

"Heart rate eighty-four," Abe felt cold metal against his chest, he assumed it was a stethoscope. "Breathing normal." The doctor's voice held a slight southern accent, an educated Virginian, Abe guessed. He slowed down his breathing, willed his body to relax. A heart rate that high showed his anxiety, and Abe needed not to be anxious.

"I'm not convinced there is evidence of imminent danger." The substitute teacher sounded nearer.

"Upon approach to the residence, a unit was dispatched to investigate the signal fire. That unit was attacked, two officers were killed by the insurgents and two were taken captive. Their whereabouts remains unknown."

"Imminent danger is established." Teacher flipped a page.

"The subject is a healthy male, approximately fifty years of age, cardiovascular and respiratory systems are better than would be expected of a person of this age."

Virginia thinks I'm old, Abe thought.

"He appears to be in better than average physical condition. It is obvious that the subject has received military fitness training. The calluses on his hands appear similar to those observed on subjects who have recently attended terrorist training."

"Hoe and rake. I should have used herbicide in my gardens."

Whatever hit the soles of Abe's feet, bound tightly together at the ankles, was thin and very strong. The sting was a lot sharper than he expected.

"You will only speak when asked a direct question." The reader continued to sound like he was reading.

"Abraham Isaac Friesen; tell him he has the name of a good Christian."

"You have the name of a good Christian."

"Read him his charges."

"You are charged with conspiracy against peace, order, and good government."

"Read him his first option."

"You may give a voluntary statement admitting the charge. Cooperation and truthfulness will be taken into consideration when final determination of your sentence is pronounced."

"Ask him if he desires to give a voluntary statement at this time."

Abe took a deep breath through the heavy black hood, considered what he might say.

"The subject declines to make a voluntary statement." Reader sounded closer.

"Continue," Teacher answered.

Abe breathed out slowly, measured.

The first jolt of pain began somewhere near the bottom of his abdomen, shot upwards through his body and ricocheted around inside his rib cage, sudden, sharp. It left Abe gasping inside the hood. The second jolt followed the same path, lasted several gasps longer. The third jolt did not stop. The pain tore through Abe's core, filled him, as though he was suddenly flooded with sulphuric acid, burned intensely forever, beyond gasps, beyond memory, beyond thought. It erased his brain, became the moment, the only moment in history, then tapered off, gradually allowing thought to return. *Storms never last, do they baby.* The chorus of an old country song crooned in Abe's head as the pain diminished. He searched for the other words to the song, could not find them and repeated. Storms never last, do they baby. Put it to voice, a whisper "Storms never last, do they baby."

"We have a singer." Reader's voice sounded somewhere out in the audience.

"Terrorist training is confirmed." Teacher sounded relieved.

"I don't understand." A fourth voice, from further away.

"Terrorists are trained to sing, usually a battle song or one of the songs of their false religion. It is not too much different than the North American Indian singing their death chant," Teacher explained. "It makes interrogation much more difficult because the subject removes himself consciously." Teacher must have turned away. Abe could not make out the rest of his conversation. The pain ended, tapered off to nothing, empty. He smelled fresh vomit in the hood.

Wagner. Abe recognized the opening to "The Ride of the Valkries". *There must be speakers on both sides of my head. Good choice.* The volume increased until the music was all that there was. Abe put himself into the music, rode the crescendos, kept himself conscious through the surges of pain that arched his body, knew his body writhed and thumped against the metal table, but it was far away. Abe rode a winged horse out of heaven, brandished a flaming sword in the war at the end of the world, rode Wagner's music, one of Abe's favourite works.

~

"Everyone talks." Monica looked closer at Betsy. She seemed distant, further than the few feet across the back table of the Olympia Restaurant. Monica recalled when this back area was the smoking section, when she and Betsy Chance were in university together, when the discussion was about a different kind of revolution, about First Nations and the shelved Royal Commission on Aboriginal Peoples report.

"Abe will talk." Monica tried to give her voice the extra distance needed to reach Betsy.

"So what. He doesn't know anything." Betsy did not move any closer.

"He knows the names of everyone that was there."

"So."

"Don't be a bitch, Betsy."

"I'm not, as you so delicately put it, being a bitch." Betsy leaned her elbows on the table, arms folded, looked directly at Monica. "You have to learn to grow a thicker skin, sister.

Who is it that you are worried about? The important people who were there are safe. Richard? They'll never find him. Abe never met That Jack, didn't know who he was. The only people at risk are that Mennonite woman and the environmentalist, what's her name?"

"Joan Lightning."

"Yes her, and who else? They already knew about Roland. Who else might our friend Abe know about?"

"There's Ben Robe."

"Oh yes, forgot about you and him. Monica you'll have to learn to let him go. He might have been something when you were a student. Now he's nobody. Even if they catch him, so what."

"You've changed." Monica leaned back. Now she wanted distance between herself and Betsy. "You used to be a good friend."

"Don't pout. It makes your face all funny looking. Listen, Monica." Betsy's voice softened slightly. "They have Abe, and I agree with you, everybody talks. Abe is probably not having a really nice time right now. So, he tells them everything that he knows. Still, so what. We still have the advantage. They can't build enough prisons, enough torture chambers. They can't get enough guards, or interviewers. They can't lock us all up. There are too many of us. Their focus is on finding the leaders. Those are the people to worry about.

"Even if Abe tells them about Ben — let's assume that for a minute — what's going to happen? They might go up there and arrest him, they might even interview him. But he doesn't know anything. Six months, a year maybe, and they'll release him. He'll go back up north and you can slip away and go see him in his wonderful cabin on the shore of his lake, your little romance will pick up again and you can lick his wounds for him."

"Oh, you are a bitch, Betsy. You know damn well that we were only together once and nothing has happened for twenty years."

"And I know that you still dream about him." Betsy smiled mischievously.

"He's a good man."

"I know." Betsy's voice was soft now. "I know, but reality says he might get caught."

"What about those two black shirts Ed has?"

"What about them?"

"A trade."

"For who? For Abe?"

"Why not?"

"No." Betsy shook her head while she thought about it. "No, we'll trade them, but for somebody important, like Edwin or Noland."

"We don't even know if they're alive. Come on, Betsy, we know that Abe is strong. He'll hold out for a long time, there's still a chance. Edwin and Noland, don't get me wrong, I love those brothers, they were both good commanders. But do you think, even if we get them back after all this time, that they will be of any help? Think about it. Trade for a couple guys who will be so badly broken by now that all we can do is keep them safe, wipe the sweat from their brows as they convulse in terror. Even if we get them back now they'll be insane. Or do we trade for Abe, someone who has given everything for the resistance and we get back a full human being? And remember, Abe knows about you and me."

"I'll think about it. You know it's not entirely my choice. Okay, I'll put Abe's name forward, but the council might not agree. In the meantime, I'm going to give you an order that you might enjoy. Go and tell Ben that he might be at risk and arrange some sort of protection."

~

Moccasin Lake stretched north, flat and black until the lake met the black sky and northern lights danced on both. Elsie tugged at Benji's sleeve and they stepped back from the sand beach to where willow grew down to the high-water line. A boat split the ebony lake and headed straight for them. The driver cut the engine as it drew into the shallows, lifted the leg of the motor and let momentum wash the boat onto shore where Elsie and Benji had just stood. The man in the bow jumped out and pulled the boat higher onto the sand, reached into the boat, grabbed a rope and strung it out to the willows intent on tying to something secure.

"What the . . . " he exclaimed when he caught sight of two human shapes behind the willow clump.

"Red." Elsie recognized the voice. It matched the shape of her tall thin cousin.

"Who's that?" Red didn't recognise her voice.

"It's me, Elsie."

"What the . . . "

"What you doing here?" Elsie stepped out of the darker shadows into the mere dark, hugged her bewildered cousin.

Red nervously looked back at his partner getting out of the boat. "It's okay Mike, it's just Elsie lost or something." He turned back to Elsie, held her at arm's length. "What am I doing here? What the hell are you doing here? Come back for the wake or what?"

Mike began unloading plastic twenty-five-litre gas cans from the boat, plopping them into the sand. "Never mind your cousin. Let's get this boat empty."

"Hey, Elsie, kind of busy now. Tell you what, here." He picked up one of the cans and offered it to her. "Here take this, it's pure alcohol. Don't drink it. It's for your car. And I'll come up to the wake later and we can visit, okay."

"Sure, Red." She struggled with the weight of the can. "Where'd you get this?"

"We made it. But it's not for drinking. That shit will blind you if you try. It's just for your car." Red carried a can in each hand. "Go back up to the gym, I'll see you later, okay Elsie? Hey, cuz, it's good to see you again." And he disappeared up the trail toward the shape of a truck parked on the side of a little-used dirt track of a road.

~

"They sure misunderstood Quebec." Leroy the Montreal Canadiens fan re-entered the conversation. "They seemed to think that the French would be on their side for some reason, didn't realize that Quebec wanted independence."

"Yeah, independence from them too. They're sure putting up a fight down there." Roderick looked around to see if the young lady with the big tea pot was in sight. She wasn't.

"It's like the Americans thought that all Quebecers hated Canada." Ben followed Roderick's searching gaze, another cup of muskeg tea would be nice now. His throat was getting dry. "They must have thought Quebec would side with them against the rest of us. They sure got fooled on that one. Did you hear the news today? Sounds like Montreal is a fire storm. Strongest resistance anywhere comes from the French. Who would have thought?"

"Not that hard to predict." Leroy looked for the big tea pot too. "It's like brothers or even sisters. Oh, they might argue between them, even act like they hate each other sometimes, but just try to get in between and you have both of them against you."

The young woman with the big enamel pot did come around again, poured the last of the wild forest-scented tea into Styrofoam cups; it was cooler now and stronger. Ben only wished that he was drinking it out of a tin cup, the way his grandmother used to pass it to him; evenings with Grandpa, stories, and Ben trying not to burn his hands on the hot metal cup. Styrofoam gave the tea a chemical taste. Oh well, it was still good, soothing on his dry throat.

Elsie and Benji came back into the gymnasium. A quiet stillness had begun to settle over the people there and despite Benji's wanting to get to know her more and more, the quiet in the gym prevented him from speaking.

The night deepened. Young mothers took their children home first, then others drifted out. Groups of visitors became quiet as people gradually left. Standing first for a moment by the open casket, touching Elroy's cold, folded hands one last time, they said their final goodbyes, then walking around shaking people's hands, and promising to "See you tomorrow," they found the door and the dark. Roderick followed protocol early, "I'm about done in here, boys," and only Leroy and Ben remained.

Benji came over to the Elder's table not long after Elsie, and Rosie, still carrying Rachel, left. "I guess I'll take you up on the offer of that cot after all."

"Anytime."

"Well, thanks." He wasn't sure of himself, standing half behind Ben, so that Ben had to twist around on the plastic chair to see his face. "Are you staying?"

"I think so, for awhile anyway."

"The door isn't locked. Just help yourself to whatever you need."

And Benji, too, found the door and the dark, but without shaking hands with anyone or going to the casket.

∽

"That's a good looking son you've got." Leroy still wanted to talk, didn't want to be alone just yet. "It's just too bad you missed out on his growing up years." Leroy's voice softened at Ben's pained expression. "It's okay. You have time now. Up to you if you want it."

"I suppose."

The silence of the night drained conversation, took away the energy for talk and both men fell back into the quiet. This was the part of the wake that Ben remembered most, this still, quiet time in the middle of the night when only a few remained to keep the dead company until daylight, his mother only agreeing to go home and get some rest when a much younger Ben had promised, "I'll stay, Mom, you go home before you fall down."

"Don't be falling asleep now. You keep watch."

"I will, Mom. Promise."

"This is the last time you'll have to look after your dad."

"I know, Mom. I know."

∽

Leroy butted his last cigarette into the dregs at the bottom of the Styrofoam cup, adding it to the others. Elroy always hated his smoking. Probably didn't smoke because Leroy did. Well, maybe Leroy could quit now. He stretched his shoulders back, forced old muscles to move, stood, scraped his chair loud in the echo chamber of the school gymnasium and went to stand before the open casket. His brother, his little brother. Now he could say goodbye, now when there were only a handful of people left, Leroy and Elroy one last time and the world would change forever. Leroy would be alone for the first time in ninety-two years.

"Well little brother . . . " He stood straight, looked down into the box at the old face and the long grey white hair fanned out on the pillow, rubbed his hand over his own short-cropped hair. "It looks like it's just me now. You're not missing much. This is a different world than we had. Maybe it's better. Maybe it's as it should be. You and me, we weren't made for this world; this world's gone crazy. Maybe it's better that you're not here to see this." His hands held the edge of the coffin, supported his weight, his heaviness. "Gotcha with this Canadiens thing, didn't I? Got you last." Leroy tried to laugh. It wasn't there. "Your kids were here, your grandkids, and even some great-grandkids, but I guess you know that, eh?" He looked away, around the nearly empty gymnasium, collected thoughts for a second. "Gonna miss you." He looked back. "You know that too. It won't be long, not long little brother. You just wait. Me and you in the happy hunting grounds, and I'll show you how to hunt. Nothing left to hunt around here anymore. You must have shot the last of the big moose to get that set of antlers in your living room. But don't you worry, when I get there I'll show you a really big set of antlers." He touched his brother's scarred, cold, hand, the one with the gold Western Canada championship ring. "When I get there, we'll be on the same team. Promise. I promise." Leroy choked on the lump in his throat, felt the sting of tears threatening to burst. "Promise." He leaned down and kissed his brother's forehead.

~

Elsie wanted to go because Benji was going. Rosie wanted to go because Elsie wanted to take Rachel with her. Give the boy a sense of his ancestry, Ben figured as he manoeuvred the boat a short distance up Witiko Creek from its mouth on Moccasin Lake. The creek ran deep and dark, its water stained with tannins. The sand bar along the south shore was longer than Ben remembered. He let the boat swing in the light current and nosed it in where the trail began, right there where the pines ran down to the water's edge.

The trail ran straight back, up a slight rise and onto the flat, three- or four-acre clearing. Its indentation from years of use ran through the red brown pine needle-covered ground. Some of them lay in clumps, blown from the boss trees of the forest that stood guard around the grey weathered cabin, shaded it from a relentless sun, broke the wind in winter, sometimes gave their life to that wind. Ben was saddened by the sight of a large pine that lay tilted, its roots torn from the earth, brown and grey across the trail that ran under it straight to the door of the cabin. He remembered that tree, remembered his father leaning his big bow saw against it, wiping his forehead with his sleeve. "That's enough for today, *Nikosis*, go for a swim or something. Can't work all the time." And the dutiful son had gladly obeyed in the cool of the creek.

Ben wanted to share his memories with Benji, memories of two old people living quiet and close to the land. He hadn't intended to sound like a professor, but he did. "They lived here all their married lives." Without the feeling, without attachment. "They moved here after their wedding. The story is that someone was killed at the celebration, stabbed. Mom and Dad came here to get away from the drinking. All the time they were here, alcohol was never allowed; might be why they never received many visitors."

Rosie interrupted: "Adolphus and Eleanor Robe. People on the reserve didn't mention them much, kind of forgotten people," as she walked around the windblown pine towards the cabin. She spread out a blanket before unsaddling Rachel from her hip, put the little girl down and lowered herself onto the hand-sewn quilt. The exact place where Mom used to sit on a blanket to do her bead work or birch bark baskets, Ben realised.

"This cabin is in pretty good shape." Benji pushed against the solid log wall.

"It's not that old. I helped your grandfather build it not long before they both passed away. Actually, we built it twice."

"Twice?" Benji turned to his father.

"Yes," Ben was flooded with memories so strong that he lost his words for a second. "Yes, we built it twice. You see, the old cabin, the first cabin was right here where this one stands. It was getting pretty rough and Dad decided to build another one. I wasn't teaching during the summer so I came to help. We built another cabin just over there, and Mom and Dad lived in the old cabin while we built the new one. When we were done we moved Mom and all the furniture into the new cabin. The plan was to use the old cabin as a shed, someplace to keep Dad's traps, and sleigh, and stuff.

"But Mom didn't like the new cabin. It was in the wrong place. It was only twenty feet, but it was in the wrong place. So they lived in a tent and me and Dad tore down the old cabin, tore down the new cabin, and put it back up where the old cabin was."

"I can understand that." Rosie moved to keep Rachel from crawling off the blanket. "You get used to something and it's hard to change."

"The only difference was the place. The new cabin was the exact same size and shape as the old cabin. Even the windows and door were in the same place. She just didn't like where it was, not how it was."

"Place is important."

"I suppose." Ben realized for the first time that it might be, as he watched Rosie in the exact spot where his mother used to sit, sitting exactly the way she sat with her legs tucked back beside her. "At the time though, I thought she was just being old and silly. That was a lot of work for Dad and me. He was almost eighty."

"Then it's a good thing you helped," Rosie placated. "A little work probably didn't hurt."

"Oh, it hurt all right," Ben remembered as he looked back at the heavy log wall.

"Did you come here often?" Benji wanted to know.

"Every summer from when I first went to university until they passed away. I haven't been back here since."

"Every summer?" Rosie questioned. "Never saw you on the reserve."

"Never went there. I'd come out and stay here. Was no reason to go to the reserve."

"So how come you didn't move here instead of building your place next to my mom?"

"This is a hard place to live. No road, no electricity. Not bad in the summer, you can come by boat, or in the winter you can come by snow machine, or dog team the way Dad used to, but it's not good in the spring and fall."

"Why's that?" Benji came back from examining the construction of the cabin, how the logs fit together in the corners.

"Because when the lake freezes you can't use a boat, and you can't walk on it until it's thick enough. In the spring it's the same thing. The ice gets rotten and you have to wait, sometimes it takes two or three weeks. Wasn't bad when I went to school on the reserve — I got a holiday,"

"Couldn't you put a road in?" Benji was thinking construction.

"Too much muskeg, we're kind of on an island here. The lake on one side, but behind here — " Ben waved a wide sweep toward the east — "it's all muskeg. No way to get across. Anyway it would ruin it." He liked this place just the way it was.

Mice dirtied the floor of the cabin, dragged in litter, chewed the mattress and spread out the cotton lining. Squirrels made much more of a mess. They dropped the leftovers of their meals in piles, chewed holes through the walls, widened gaps between the logs. Birds took advantage of the squirrel holes, moved in and built their nests mudded to the pole rafters. One large nest hung from the ridgepole, the log that Ben and his father struggled to put into place. The south-facing windows were stained with years of dust and grime so that the light took on an orange hue where it fell on the floor, adding to the abandoned feel of the cabin.

"They're taking back their land." Elsie spoke philosophically as she followed Ben inside.

"Yeah, Mom would see it that way too. But in her lifetime that floor would shine."

Benji examined a calendar hung from a nail, February 2001. The picture was of a 1962 Oldsmobile coupe, the one that had the unique wrap-around windows, bright green and enamel white.

"Nobody's been here in awhile." He voiced the obvious.

"It's isolated." Ben moved to look over Benji's shoulder, looked for February 10th. The day they found his father, found him sitting under a tree only a half day's walk up the trapline. "He must have got tired," his mother had said, and before the snow melted that spring she got tired too and they buried her beside Dad.

"This would be a great place for a still." Benji sized up the cabin, measured its cubic feet, considered its isolation, the spread of the pines, and the solidity of its structure.

"Over my dead body." Ben was firm.

"Oh, I don't mean for drinking." Benji realized his gaff. "I mean ethanol, for fuel."

"Not even ethanol." Ben remained firm. He felt ghosts stirring, an uncomfortable stir.

"Come on, Ben." Benji wanted to say 'Dad', but wasn't sure how his father felt about that yet. "Think about the money you could save. That truck of yours must suck up a lot of cash in a year. Maybe even burn it in your boat."

"No, I agree with your dad." Elsie too felt the ghosts. "Not here." She saw the homemade curtains, saw through their raggedness, saw the wood cook stove with its stovepipe still going through the ceiling instead of tumbling behind, saw a place where a woman once cooked and baked.

"What's with him?" Rosie asked Elsie. She had caught a look on Ben's face as he came out of the cabin and headed toward the old garden area, a slightly pained look.

"Nothing." Elsie now looked bewildered. She had not seen anything.

"What were you guys talking about in there?"

"Nothing much. Benji was imagining using this place as a site to set up a still, but Ben wouldn't have anything to do with it."

"I guess not." Rosie sat up slightly, looked away from Rachel who lay on her back and kicked and waved and tried to talk through a voice that could only coo and bah. "Alcohol was what killed us. They didn't beat us in war, they used booze to take everything away from us and then used it to keep us down."

"I know, you've always said that. But what's Ben's reason?"

"He learned it the same place that I did. Right here in this cabin. Our trapline and the Robe trapline come together right there at the first point on the lake. I used to come over here to visit with Eleanor, listen to her stories, learn her beadwork patterns; she's the one that hated alcohol the most. I think old Adolphus might not have been so dead set as his wife was. He was easier going. Well not easy going I guess, more quiet in his ways. He didn't talk much, usually just stood there and smiled a lot, at peace kind of."

"How long ago was that?"

"Oh, I was young, before I got married and started having kids. After I met your dad I never did come back here. But I remember all her stories, and I'm pretty sure Ben does too."

"What kind of stories?" Elsie probed. Stories were always good. She stretched out on the quilt and played with Rachel's bare foot, tickled it to see her wriggle and laugh.

"Old time stories, how they used to live. Stories about the Treaty, lots of stories about the Treaty, kind of like she wanted someone to remember that."

Benji now stood just off the blanket where the three females sat or lay, listening, so Rosie helped to fill him in, gave him something he could use without ever looking directly at him.

"Treaty was signed just up at the end of the lake there where the river begins, 1889. She said it was in winter and all the Indians were there when the treaty commissioner and the police came by dog team from the south."

"Eleanor wasn't there." Elsie calculated years to 1889.

"No, she was old even when I knew her, but not that old. She heard the stories from her dad, he was there. You see, Eleanor was the youngest of her family, the baby. Her dad was already an old man when she was born, so she was raised special. She stayed home with her parents until they died." Rosie added a little gossip, just a little, just for spice. "She was almost an old maid by the time she married Adolphus, and he was younger than her, not much just a few years, but still younger." Elsie looked up at Benji, guessed that he might be younger than her, maybe.

"Eleanor used to say that Treaty wasn't what was written on the paper." Rosie fell back to a more formal recitation for this part. "The commissioner promised we could live like before, then they forced us to live on the reserve, pulled us off the land. She didn't like that. She said the reserve was supposed to be just a place where Indians could go if they wanted to go to school or learn to be farmers, but if the Indians wanted to stay in the bush they could." Rosie let Rachel play with her dangling hand, let the little girl swat and pull at her fingers. She looked down at her granddaughter, away from Elsie and Benji, as though she was telling the story to a younger audience.

"Her family came from further north along the Churchill River, moved down here because that area was getting trapped out. You see the Churchill used to be the first fur trade route, they trapped it out first. When there was nothing left, some of them moved into Chipewyan country. Eleanor thought that was why they don't like us Cree very much. But her family came here, not just for the trapping I guess. I sort of got the sense she was telling me they moved here to get away from the missionaries, but she never came right out and said it."

"What was wrong with missionaries?" Benji wanted to know.

"Nothing." Rosie continued Eleanor's conciliatory manner. She wasn't going to say anything bad about anybody. "It's just that Eleanor's family was traditional, kept the old ways. I guess the Christians looked down on that sort of stuff." She remembered why Benji was there and went back to the story she had begun with the purpose of giving him some sense of his lineage.

"Let's see if I remember this right. Her dad was Moise, that was his Christian name, the one he used when he signed at Treaty time. Everyone knew him as Wapos. Wapos had a brother they called Sikos and a sister Piso."

"Rabbit, Weasel and Lynx," Elsie translated for Benji's sake. "And Piso never married. Eleanor said she had six kids but was never seen with a man. She used to live by herself. Had her own dog team, did her own hunting, set fish nets by herself, everything."

"Where did she live?" Elsie couldn't place her.

"Everywhere. When she got tired of one spot she packed up and moved somewhere else, built a new cabin, planted a new garden, wherever her mood took her. The last place she lived was just past where the Treaty was signed, up the river a little. I remember visiting her. She wouldn't speak a word of English, old Cree, a little hard for me to understand sometimes growing up on the reserve like I did. She was at Treaty signing too, had her own stories about it."

"You knew somebody who was at Treaty." Benji spoke slow, unbelieving.

"Yeah, a few. Are you calling me old?"

Benji fumbled. "No, no I didn't mean it that way, the opposite in fact. I always thought the Treaties happened, like a really long time ago, you know. I can't imagine anyone, not even my dad, who might have known someone who was actually there."

"Look around, the land hasn't changed. In real time it was only yesterday that white people came here."

Benji had no means of grasping the enormity of Rosie's statement. It was simply and completely beyond him. He changed the subject. "What about her kids, that Piso woman, what became of them?"

"Some of them are still around, not many though. Philip Charles would be her, let's see . . ." Rosie consulted her inner genealogical chart. "Philip would be her great-grandson."

"Is that the guy who walks everywhere, the one people call Traveller." Elsie tried to connect the name from the chart to a person.

"Yeah, that's him. Just like his great-grandmother, too free a spirit to ever settle down."

~

"What'ja doin'?" Rosie asked as she came up to Ben.

Finally separated herself from that baby, he noticed. "Oh, just looking over the old garden," He pointed with his toe at the long wide leaves growing up through the grass. "Hey, check this out. The horseradish is still here."

"Horseradish." She made a sour face.

"Yeah, Dad really liked it. Mom wasn't much for it. He ate it on almost everything, ground it up and mixed it with a little vinegar."

"To each their own, I guess." The sourness was still on her face. "Looks like the catnip survived." She was over near one of the remaining corner posts, the one that still held a pole rail angled down to where another post had rotted and fallen over. She knelt beside the pale-coloured bush, plucked a single leaf and gently nibbled on it to draw out the mint flavour as though to remove the taste of horseradish.

Ben responded with a slow "Oh yeah." He remembered catnip. Remembered a cup of tea, a blend of catnip and muskeg leaves that drained away any residue of stress a day might leave on a body. "Mom would be happy to know that was still here." He too plucked a leaf to nibble on. The mild mint taste brought back other memories. "Dad used this to bait lynx. Worked like you wouldn't believe."

"I believe it." Rosie closed her eyes for a few seconds while her mouth moved ever so slowly, alone with her spit and her tongue and the roof of her mouth and the sweet mint. "Oh, so nice, so nice." She opened her eyes. "You were lucky to have them as parents."

"Dad, was more the potato gardener. Had a bigger garden down there a ways." He pointed east. "For potatoes, beets, carrots, turnips, that sort of stuff. Mom took care of this one closer to the house. Used to be flowers all along that fence line." He half turned toward where Benji, Elsie, and Rachel were approaching. "I wonder." He remembered something. "I wonder if the raspberries survived."

They had. Large ripe berries weighed down thick thorny branches. "So, why did they grow raspberries?" Elsie asked around a mouthful, crunched tiny seeds with her back teeth. "Instead of picking wild ones? They grow everywhere."

"Why walk." Ben answered as he plopped a single dark, thoroughly ripe berry into his mouth, and another. "Raspberries don't take any looking after."

"I remember years when there weren't any wild berries." Rosie stood waist deep in the bramble, held Rachel high on her hip, held up a berry for the little girl to grasp in her fist and mush into her mouth. "Just makes sense to have a patch you can look after, especially in dry years."

"Self-sufficient." Benji ate a handful at a time, picked until there wasn't any room left in his cupped palm before filling his mouth and himself with tart sweetness.

"No, they didn't go to town for very much." Ben looked around. The rabbit pens looked to still be in relatively good shape, the chicken wire stretched across the doors might need a few staples to keep out weasels, maybe replace a few rotted floorboards. The asphalt-shingled roof had done what it was intended to and protected the low pens from the weather. He remembered rabbit soup, potatoes, onions, thickened with flour, lots of salt and pepper. They could have gone out and snared rabbits instead of hauling in feed every autumn, but why walk. The work of cleaning out the pens rewarded them with manure for the gardens to grow the vegetable leftovers that helped feed the rabbits. A good cycle.

～

Monica felt a tinge of jealousy, not toward Rosie for being out with Ben, not even toward young and pretty Elsie. It was the sight of Ben and Benji each with a hand on opposite sides of the bow of the boat, pulling it up onto the shore, working together. She'd had less than half of an uncomfortable day with her son, and here he was, working beside his dad as though they had known each other all their lives. She had not even acknowledged to Benji that his father was Ben Robe of Moccasin Lake. He must have researched that for himself, not that it would have taken much. How many professors named Ben would have taught political studies . . . ? Internet searching could provide present addresses. The thought bothered her deeper. If Benji could find Ben with the little information he had, so could Homeland Security if Abe gave him up.

"Hey, guys." She hid her anxiety and grabbed the bow of the boat to help. But the boat was as far up the beach as it was going by the time she got there.

~

Hershel Rosche arrived not long after the Second World War on a shiny new diesel train. He liked Prince Albert, a young city, a city that would grow, become something. It had potential. He liked the wide sweeping North Saskatchewan River, liked the architecture of the hotel on Central Avenue, and Indians, the first he had seen since his arrival in Canada, there on River Street, going into a fur buyer's store. Hershel followed them in. He carried a small heavy leather case that he occasionally shifted from hand to hand, but never put down. He walked around the tiny store, pretended he was looking at the scarce merchandise, the six used rifles leaning against the wall, the bins of blue steel spring traps, and the coils of snare wire. He was there to see real Indians. He listened in while the Indian negotiated in his own gentle fashion. Both parties to the negotiation knew that there were other fur buyers and that some of them were only a short block up the street.

Hershel watched the Indian shake out a lynx pelt, hold it out at shoulder height and look down at where it touched the plank floor. Without words, he told the fur buyer. *This is a large lynx, not a medium, it's worth more.*

The buyer stood behind the counter, sifted pelts, not looking at them anymore, just moving them to keep his hands busy. "Tell you what. I like you, Adolphus; you're a good customer. Fifty dollars for the whole pile. What do you say?"

Adolphus didn't answer, he touched the pelts, moved a mink, shiny black over toward his left, sorted through the pile for another, slightly larger mink, and placed it beside the first. He might have been sorting out the pelts by species, but he might have begun to package them up.

"Tell you what." The buyer picked up the first mink. The skinning and stretching skills were obvious. The pelt was perfectly shaped, unblemished, completely dried. "Because it's you, I might go as high as sixty. But don't you be telling anyone now."

Adolphus moved the mink pelt back to the pile.

Hershel was not pretending to look at anything other than the transaction. He was impressed. The Indian knew negotiation, knew how to use time and timing, understood the art of it. He was a man of Hershel's spirit, a reader of humanity.

Three days later Hershel used his skills, sized up the town and its people until he found the man he wanted, someone with refined taste, who wore a good-quality coat, and clean shoes. There were a few around, in the hotel lobby or in the restaurants, who dressed well, who looked like they might have the money Hershel was looking for, but they were too flashy, too new, did not walk with the confidence he wanted: someone comfortable with his wealth, who did not have to show it.

"Excuse me, sir. Might I have a moment of your time? I have something that might interest you." Hershel began the sale. Invited the man to a quiet corner of the Avenue Hotel lobby, the finest hotel in Prince Albert. He sat in a stuffed leather chair with the leather case between his feet, felt its sturdiness between his calves.

"It's Swiss made, very fine quality. Something not appreciated so much over here it seems. I know in Europe it would demand a much larger price, but here I am in Canada, a fine place, someday this country will rival old Europe in fashion, but today very few appreciate quality. I don't expect to get what this is worth. I am prepared to live with that."

Hershel sold his first watch. He built a neat jewellery store just off Central Avenue, where he worked every day from when he opened it in 1951 until he took some time off in 1993, feeling a bit tired. His family buried him two weeks later up the hill. A good quality plain marble headstone marks the grave, nothing fancy, nothing flashy.

The store never did need customers. The heavy leather bag contained the wealth of a family that had presented itself modestly to the world for generations, but always with quiet dignity. Hershel's older brother Marcel had been the exception, liked to show what he had. When the soldiers came to Marcel's, before the paintings were stripped from the walls and an *oberstleutnant* drove away in Marcel's polished black-and-chrome automobile, Hershel fled.

Ben had attended Hershel's funeral. He and his parents, Adolphus and Eleanor, had stood back from the small gathering around the fresh-torn hole in the sod. Shook hands with Hershel's son John, such a simple name, and his sister Eleanor. The younger Eleanor had hugged the older Eleanor before they got in Ben's little car for the quiet ride back north.

Bells tinkled as Ben entered Rosche Jewellery and Collectables. He stood with his hands in his pockets looking into a glass-covered case as John came out of the back. Eleanor was with another customer and did not acknowledge Ben's presence with more than a nod and the faintest of smiles. John held one finger pointing downward by his side, hidden from view as he passed on the other side of the glass case from Ben. Ben did not respond. John pointed two fingers downward and still Ben did not respond. As John passed, Ben extended three fingers on the glass case. John responded, his eyebrows raised slightly, and he went out the door, tinkled bells before he went up the street toward where the banks were clustered on Central Avenue.

Ben continued to look at the selection of watches in the case, one hand in his pocket feeling the small soft metal bars that weighed exactly ten ounces each, until John returned. Without a word, Ben followed him into the back of the store.

"I didn't have that much money here." John reached inside his jacket, inside the breast pocket. "Thirty thousand Ameros raises people's attention." He put an envelope on the worktable, knelt and opened a safe that was out of view under the table.

"Is something wrong?" he asked as he handed over the money and took the three gold bars without looking at them and placed them in the safe, shut the heavy door and turned the brass handle, listening for the double click of the lock before taking his hand away.

"No, not really. Just being careful." Ben put the additional bills into the bank deposit envelope without counting either. "In case something should come up."

～

Ben felt a tinge of guilt as he drove past the building that once housed the Prince Albert Indian and Metis Friendship Centre, as though he had taken the people's money. The envelope in his hip pocket felt thick, uncomfortable to sit on. He took it out, wiggled it around the seat belt for a second before extracting it completely. He went to put it in his shirt pocket. The shirt was damp and sticky, the envelope too bulky. Finally he threw it on the dash of the truck, just as safe there as anywhere.

It wasn't the people's money. It was money that did not exist, erased money. In the first days of the invasion, annexation, everyone scrambled, everyone shifted belongings and assets toward more secure forms. Some people hoarded food, others converted their cash to carryables. The Saskatchewan Indian Gaming Authority wanted Ben on their board of governors, not because Ben knew anything about running casinos, but because he was a respected professor, an Indian with a position of prestige. They didn't want him there, they wanted his image: honest, intelligent, educated, a class addition.

While the planes were bombing the base at Trenton, when the 401 was jammed tighter than that multilane highway between Toronto and Kingston had ever known, Ben took a certified cheque to Sport Gold. He went alone, security guards attract attention, better to be inconspicuous with that amount of money. The exchange was quick, efficient, a heavy oak desk in a large, bare office, two uniformed security guards outside the door, another just inside, his back to the wall. They look thuggish, Ben thought as he entered. The official of the corporation handling the exchange looked too young for the job, close-cropped brown hair, glasses that made his nondescript eyes look larger than they were. His appearance, his choice of clothes, cargo pants with bulky pockets and a golf shirt, did not inspire confidence. Neither did the toothpick wiggling at the corner of his mouth as he spoke.

"So even the casinos think this is going to last. Oh well. Today's price is six hundred an ounce, ten ounce lots."

"Stock price this morning was down to four-sixty-nine." Ben felt an obligation to the board of governors to take care of their investment.

"It went up while you were out front with everyone else. How many lots?"

Ben looked down at the cheque, made a mental calculation. "Forty- two." He handed over the quarter-million-dollar cheque. The toothpick wiggled while the company official made his own mental calculations. "You're short two thousand."

"Yes," Ben faced him confidently, the older man across the desk from the young and anxious. Negotiation is about time. Whoever has the most time will take the hurried. Ben had time. There were still people in the outer room waiting, nervously, rushed, terrorized even.

"All right." He took out the toothpick, and Ben walked away with a cardboard box weighing slightly over twenty-five pounds. He had done well for the board, secured a large portion of their assets against the unforeseeable.

~

"We're done." The voice of Timothy Bird, the chairman of SIGA crackled in Ben's cell phone.

"What do you mean?" Ben looked at the cardboard box on the car seat beside him.

"A virus wiped us out this morning. Everything's erased."

"I have to see the board. I have something to report." Ben did not want to explain over a cell phone, didn't know who might be listening.

"There is no board. Don't you get it? Everything is erased, absolutely everything. All of the casinos are closed, well they're not even closed, abandoned is more like it. When people found out they weren't getting paid, they just walked out. Everybody from the floor sweepers, the dealers, security, management, everybody just walked away. Nobody even had the sense to lock the doors."

"I don't get it." Ben needed reason, rationality that was not there.

"What's to get? They didn't like the idea of casinos so they used a military virus to wipe us out, targeted at SIGA. We no longer exist, you won't find a single byte of information that refers to us. Payroll is gone, Human Resources does not have any records of employees, Security doesn't exist. The board doesn't exist. We have no minutes of meetings, we have no records, no financial statements to review. You don't even exist Ben. The virus must've started with SIGA and spread to all of the directors, every employee's name is wiped out. There is no evidence anywhere that there ever was a board, or a corporation."

"Listen Tim, you have to reconvene the board. It's important. I have in my possession a sizable amount of board assets."

"Whatever you might have is nothing. Keep it. Use it for your retirement, consider it your severance package. And hey, Ben. You take care of yourself, and maybe we'll see you around."

⁓

Dean Fisher stood on his farm, he just stood there, looking north. Six-thousand-four-hundred acres of mixed grain and cattle keeps a man busy, too busy to stop in the middle of the day, but he was doing a lot of that recently, standing there, staring, always north. Not that far, he thought, not that far from South Dakota to Canada. He could almost see it just there beyond the rolling parched yellow horizon. *You have to find some feed for those cattle.* The thought forced itself into his mind. He let it ride there a moment and went back to thinking about Canada; Saskatoon Saskatchewan Canada.

Nothing happened there, nothing was supposed to happen there. Vicky had been so happy that their son Rick had been posted to Saskatchewan and not Quebec City. He would be safe there, quiet, rural, no population to speak of. It wasn't that long ago, in the good days before all this, they had gone to northern Saskatchewan, drove up in the rented RV. Dean remembered Otter Rapids on the Churchill River, little Ricky, he must have only been eleven, twelve maybe — no, he was twelve — just finished sixth grade, the year of the excellent report card. Ricky swam the rapids, seen other kids do it and begged until Dean and Vicky bundled him in an over-large life jacket and stood on the iron bridge with the expanded metal deck and looked down on the rolling blue water, churned into sparkling white foam. They stood holding hands, their hearts racing, while little Ricky floated and bobbed down the rapid, waved up at them as he passed under the bridge. Dean could still see the big smile on his son's wet face. It wasn't that long ago.

Ricky had to grow up, couldn't stay the brave little boy forever. He turned eighteen and they drafted him into their army, not Dean's army and certainly not Vicky's army, that army that belonged to the others, those crazies, those stomping and yelling people, their army. Drafted Dean's son, took him away from the farm. Dean was happy here. His Dodge pickup with the chrome stacks that rumbled when he drove it into Sioux Falls was still in the Quonset for when he came back. He could go to town with a nice girl, take her to a movie, marry her and bring her home to the farm.

Dean kicked his toe into the dry earth, raised powder dust. Missing in action, how can that be? Missing in Saskatchewan; shee-it, they had joked with Rick before he left that where he was going there was no place to hide. "Keep your head down."

"Yeah, right, in a gopher hole, I'd guess."

Three weeks now, Ricky was missing for three weeks; there was hope. If something had happened they would have found him by now. No, as each day came and went, the better his chances, Dean hoped. That was all he had, hope. Hope for the best, hope that Ricky would come home. He kicked the dry dirt again, looked to the west where a promising cloud was beginning to build, maybe it would rain, maybe a thunderstorm would come by with a little moisture, as long as it didn't bring hail.

It was all over by the time Ben arrived in Saskatoon. Idylwyld Drive was open again and traffic flowed down its length over the melted and blackened pavement on the southbound lane. Someone had hauled away both trees, cut them into pieces, left sawdust on the sidewalk and a few small branches too small to bother with. Ester Kingfisher cried often, cried when she thought of those trees, the elms. Mostly she cried when she thought of the elm that had stood in front of her house. Elmer would miss them. Poor Elmer, at least he didn't live to see this.

Roger Ratte's bullet-ridden Toyota Prius sat on its flattened tires on a low trailer in the government insurance inspection garage. The inspector didn't have good news. He could have told Roger when the car was first brought in, but he wanted to hear the story, so he went through the motions of assessing the damage, even wrote figures onto the form clipped to a board. Then he invited Roger into an office, sat across an empty particleboard desk and asked an easy, "So what happened?"

"I was on my way home, Northbound on Idylwyld, about twenty-eighth, twenty-ninth, somewhere in there and holy shit! a tree fell across the street right in front of me." Roger had told the story a few times already, once to his wife over the phone to explain why he wasn't coming home that night, once to the guy at the hotel. He had it down, had practised it again on the way here this morning, each time adding a little more detail, arranging it chronologically.

"There was this old lady, I talked to her after, her name is Ester — she seen everything. I guess she lives right there, all her life she said. Anyway when the tree fell in front of my car there was this guy with his hood up and tied tight around his face so you couldn't see it very well and the old lady, Ester, she was still trying to take the chainsaw away from him. That's the tree on my side of the street. The tree on the other side came down just as I was getting out of my car. So they blocked traffic both north and south. I knew something was wrong then. I knew something was really wrong. The guy with the chainsaw on my side of the street, he gave the chainsaw to Ester, well he sort of threw it at her, or let her take it. I don't know. Then he ran away, towards downtown, right past me; I was on the sidewalk by then. Weird shit, I figured. I went to see if Ester was all right, she was sitting on the grass, it kinda' slopes down to the street there, she was sitting there holding the chainsaw where the guy pushed her down and the saw was still running, and traffic is piling up now if you know what I mean, on both sides of the street, nobody can go anywhere. I sure couldn't have got my car out of there with all the cars behind me and the tree in front of me and the way the land slopes down on each side. I was stuck there. And I knew. I knew something was really wrong. I grabbed Ester, took the saw away from her and tried to get her out of the way of whatever was coming. Tell you the truth, I didn't give a shit about my car at that moment. I was just getting out of the way, and getting Ester out of the way.

Then Homeland Security, they must have been behind me, five, six vehicles of them, all together, you know the way they travel. Well, when the traffic got blocked they must have gone over the meridian there onto the southbound lane where there was no traffic and come up right beside my car on the opposite side of the street where they were blocked by the other tree and the vehicles piled up behind it on that side.

They just opened fire, as soon as they came to a stop, they must have realized it was an ambush and they opened up first, shooting everything. My car got it the worst because it was the closest. They were just, fuck! there were bullets flying everywhere. By this time I got Ester back off the street. There's kinda a cement wall there by her sidewalk up to her house. I held her down in there and laid on top of her. And you know what she's crying about when those bullets are smashing into everything? She's crying about the tree.

Then all I heard was *whoomp* and the first HS vehicle, it's all on fire. Must have been one of those Montreal cocktails we hear about, you know the one with diesel fuel and Styrofoam and oxygen mixed into it like an Aerobar; must have been something like one of those. I didn't see who threw it. I seen one guy on the other side of the street up on the roof of a building come right out to the edge, right out into the bullets. He had some kind of machine gun or something and he was shooting at the first vehicle. Must have been drawing fire so his buddies could get up close enough to throw I figure.

Well they got him. Yeah, fuck man, just like in a bad movie, I watched that guy come off that building, then *whoomp* and that front vehicle, you can't see it anymore, all flames, orange, orange flames, and those HS guys never had a chance, whatever the hell they hit them with, it had some concussion to it. Felt it from where we were on the other side of the street. Then there's more bullets and another *whoomp*, that one must have been the back vehicle, I don't know, I got my head down and there's shooting like you wouldn't believe. Never in your wildest imagination man, you couldn't imagine how many bullets, hundreds, no thousands, thousands of bullets from both sides. Just fuckin' incredible."

Roger stopped, out of breath a little, looking at the inspector, waited for a response. The inspector sat there with the edge of the clipboard on his crossed leg, held it with both hands leaned against the desk, sat there with his mouth slightly open, maybe he breathed through his mouth instead of through his nose that was too small for his face. He sat there for the whole story, didn't flinch even once, not even for the *whoomps*. He waited, possibly for more. But there was no more. Roger wasn't going to talk about carrying Ester into her house, putting her on the old sofa, knocking things off the coffee table, bottles and bottles of medication, of finding a bottle of gin under the pillow when he propped her up and tried to make her comfortable.

"I'm sorry to have to tell you this, but SGI policy does not insure against incidents of war. It's in every policy. War is something you cannot buy insurance against."

Roger put his hands on the edge of the desk, not threatening, not at all; he just needed someplace to put them after waving them around for so long, tracing bullet paths and mushroom clouds. He was tired, shocked and tired.

"Incident of war." His voice was flat.

"Yeah, it's in the policy."

"But the Americans say this isn't a war, it's an annexation, justified in international law as a protective measure."

"Don't matter what spin the politicians put on it; any right thinking court in Canada will determine what happened to your car was an act of war. Fighting an insurgency is an act of war, I'm sure."

"Insurgency." Roger's voice remained flat, questioning.

"Well, yeah, an insurgency is classified as an act of war." The inspector was beginning to feel threatened, remembered his training on psychopathy. *Cold emotionless, kill you as soon as look at you.* Roger was too calm. He should be upset.

Roger remained rational. "An insurgency is when people try to overthrow a legitimate government, right?"

"Uh-huh." The inspector held the clipboard, maybe he could defend himself with it.

"A resistance is when people fight off an invasion, right."

"Uh-huh." Agree with him and maybe he won't do anything.

"So what do we have here, an insurgency or a resistance?"

The inspector shrugged. He didn't know.

Roger stayed still, calm, the car really didn't matter. Insurance, no insurance, fix the flats, buy some glass, maybe even duct tape up the holes, drive it out of here, what the hell, didn't matter. And this guy here with the clipboard, he didn't know shit, not even worth talking to anymore, just a dummy, doing a dummy job, not thinking, not questioning, didn't even know if he was living through a revolution, an uprising, or a resistance. Didn't matter they were all likely incidents of war to him. Did he even know what war was? Probably not.

War is when an old lady cries because a tree was cut down; that's what war is.

~

Monica was not at home. Ben rang the buzzer of apartment 607, waited in the glass case cubical, stood in front of the panel array of names, numbers and buttons and wondered whether he had the right address. He checked the slip of paper again. No this was right. 607- 212 4th Avenue South, Saskatoon. He rang the buzzer again before he went back to his truck to wait, looked skyward as he hurried the few yards between the front doors of the apartment building and the street.

~

Monica sat on the floor with her back against the wall, something about drinking wine and sitting on the floor that seemed right, brought back memories of university, memories that had laughter at their core. This was different, sitting here because they didn't want to be seen through the windows. She leaned as she passed the bottle over to Ed Trembley and he leaned away from the adjacent wall to take it, tilt it, glug it, once, twice, spilt some in his eagerness. He put it down between his outstretched legs, wiped his mouth with his sleeve. "So, was it the full council that decided, or what?"

"Pretty near, there were a few not there, Sakej and Emily are out of town, but most of them agreed. There was definitely quorum, if that's what you're asking."

"No, I don't doubt council. Whatever they said, that's fine with me." His hand on the long neck of the bottle, he lifted it from the floor, held it there. "I'm a soldier, whatever I'm told." He raised it, glugged it again once, and passed it back to Monica.

"Me too, Ed, whatever council says." She sipped at the bottle, looked at the label, a plain white paste-on, a prairie picture and a cherry bush with oversized berries. "I don't believe that people would put their name on a bottle anymore."

"Paul Reiseman makes good wine, always has, why not show that he's proud of it."

"It's not bad." Monica sipped again, lips to bottle, a kiss of a sip.

"Four-year-old chokecherry." Ed leaned his weight into the wall, rested his head against the plasterboard. "Tests out at 18 percent."

"You can tell." Monica's head buzzed, her belly warmed, she kissed the end of the bottle again before passing it back.

"So, you were up north you said. How was that?"

"Not bad, I like it up there, like there's no war going on, trees, lakes, that sort of stuff, and the people, they just keep doing what they always do." She did not want to tell Ed about her son, not that it was a private thing, she could share private things. It was because having an adult son would make her seem old, and Monica did not want to be old, she wanted to be a university student again, sitting on the floor drinking wine from the bottle.

"You went to see Ben Robe. How's he getting along?" Ed needed this visit, needed someone in this barren house besides himself and the prisoners downstairs, needed a fellow human.

"Ben? Ben will be all right I suppose. Took the news a little rough. He's probably never seen himself as part of the resistance, at risk."

"He'll get used to it. Everybody's at risk."

"Yeah, that's true." She reached out, indicating the bottle. "Don't know what he's likely to do. He was pretty quiet." She raised the bottle. "But that's the way Ben is, doesn't ever say too much, so you never know exactly what he's thinking." She drank.

"How much does he know?"

"Next to nothing."

"Then what are we worried about? It's not like Abe. Now if Abe talks, a lot of people are on the line. If they take in Ben, no big deal right."

"Except that Ben could be a power, if we used him right. The man is brilliant. Have you ever heard him speak?"

"Naw." Ed shook his head and a lock of yellow brown hair fell across his forehead.

"He can move you with his words. A natural orator of the old Cree tradition. A magic voice."

"I guess I've never heard an Indian give a speech."

"Did you know . . . " Monica found the space she was looking for, she was a student again. "Commissioner Morris when he came out West . . . "

"Who?" Ed leaned away from the wall; he was either inattentive or having trouble with his hearing.

"Alexander Morris, the treaty commissioner, you know, the Indian Treaties 1874, Treaty Four, Treaty Six up at Fort Carlton and Fort Pitt."

"Okay." Ed was on track.

"Well, he was so impressed by the ability of the Cree to make speeches that he tried to copy them. That's why some people think the words, 'as long as the grass grows, the river flows and the sun shines,' were used. Morris was trying to sound like a great Cree orator. Don't know if he ever pulled it off. But that's where that stuff comes from."

"Doesn't do them much good now, does it?" He was thinking of grass and rivers as he leaned back.

"Maybe not. Ben taught us that the words weren't as important as the spirit of the Treaties. Maybe something there. But that isn't where I was going with this. Now Ben has that gift, that ability to move you with his voice. If we had him in the resistance, or even out of the resistance but speaking for us. He could move mountains for us."

"And so, will he or what?"

"Will he what?"

"Be our speaker, move those political mountains for us."

Monica did not have an answer; she looked through the glass of the wine bottle, held it up to the light, slightly lower than half. Half full or half empty? She drank, more than a sip, a full mouthful, but not a glug.

"I think," she leaned out extending the bottle toward Ed. "I think that if we work it right, Ben might come onside, bring his voice and his knowledge and . . . " she nodded to herself, "and his wisdom. The man has something to offer. A good place for him might be on council."

"Ever think we need more soldiers on council and less old politicians?"

"Council makes the hard decisions. They need both. They need to have thinkers and doers. Council is not afraid to act. Sometimes we get frustrated because they seem to take forever, but when it's crunch time, they act. Like this morning, they heard Betsy's petition, thought about it, discussed among themselves and agreed to put Abe's name on the list of people we would agree to exchange for those two downstairs. I didn't see any delay, or inability to act."

"Like I said before, whatever council tells me to do, that's fine with me. But you try staying in this house for three weeks. I was happy as hell to get out for that bit of action yesterday. It was like a holiday. Fireworks and everything."

"And it was council that planned that out. Every detail of it."

"Well they didn't plan for that crazy woman who was trying to take the chain saw away from me." Ed laughed, a tiny laugh at the thought.

"Yeah." Monica smiled. "You owe the resistance one chainsaw, don't you?"

"They can deduct it from my pay." Ed laughed louder, a real laugh. *Nothing from nothing leaves nothing.* He sang the words to an old song. "Wish we had music."

"Yeah." Monica nodded. Music would go good with the wine. "Why not, I mean this place is supposed to look like a normal house isn't it, not draw attention. A little music is normal you'd think. So long as it isn't loud and blaring and someone calls the cops, right?"

"There's a radio on the alarm clock." Ed pulled his legs under himself, used the wall to help stand up.

"An old rock and roll station. Not that new stuff, and definitely not country." Monica tasted the wine. "Something mindless." she added as Ed walked past.

"It's all mindless."

～

The music filtered through the floor, muffled, undecipherable, but clearly music. Rick Fisher heard it, reached a foot out in the dark and nudged Wally. Wally wasn't doing so good, maybe if he woke up, the music would help. Wally stirred.

"Music." Rick whispered.

"Oh." Wally answered and stayed still.

Rick hoped he was listening.

The music became clear as Ed put the radio on the floor upstairs. It sounded better to Rick and Wally in the basement than what Monica and Ed were hearing. The wood of the floor filtered out the tin sound of the speaker, added bass, added quality.

Rolling Stones. Rick recognized "Street Fighting Man." Leaned his head back against the post and listened. What an absolute blessing music could bring. Rick closed his eyes and let it fill him, lift him. He was in his truck again, blasting down the gravel road from town with Clarice, the windows were down and her hair was flipping around her face and she was tapping on the armrest between them to the music. He wanted to take her hand but he needed both of his on the steering wheel. He was showing off how fast he could drive, and the rush of the truck, and the spray of the gravel, and the pounding of the music and Clarice was laughing, and the sun was shining and he wasn't tied to a post in a dark basement. Ricky went home and the draft notice never came in the mail. Mom and Dad were home, and the grass was green again and the cows were fat and the Rolling Stones were on tour again. He would take Clarice in the truck and they would drive over to Minneapolis and go to the concert, and he would never put on a uniform, or learn to use a gun.

~

The sun was setting straight down 22nd Street West, into Ben's eyes. He flipped down the visor, peered under it, hoped he would be able to see the streetlights in the glare. No telling when Monica might get home, try again in the morning. He turned the truck into the parking area of the Westwind

Motel — out of the sun, out of the glare, he could see again and in a few minutes he would be under the cover of the motel roof, away from the sky that was watching him. A night of television and clean, sterile sheets, something different, wouldn't be so bad. Maybe a T-bone steak in that Montana's restaurant that seemed almost deserted. Maybe they should change the name. But that might seem unpatriotic, or insurgent even.

~

The screwdriver slipped in the notch of the wood screw again. Rosie looked at the rounded end of the Robertson driver, wore out, not of very good quality to begin with, it was all that she had to work with. She reapplied it, put pressure on it and managed another half turn on the screw before it slipped again. Bit by tiny bit, she tightened the hinge on the screen door. Where were the men when things needed fixing?

Lester was out, hadn't been around for a couple days, maybe he found work, doubtful, but maybe. Benji, well could she have asked him even if he and Elsie were there? Probably not. It was too soon in their relationship to begin to consider him a son-in-law.

She stood and tried the door. It swung loosely on the hinge, didn't fit the frame. The hinge lifted as the door shut. The wood frame was rotted, the screw holes worn too large. She opened the door again to look at the frame, three-quarter inch, probably spruce plank, maybe she could find one, somewhere. She could not afford to buy it, damn shame, lumber coming out of the country all over, pulp wood, fibreboard plant over by the highway and nothing in the community to build with.

Even if she had the right board, even if she could get a new one, she didn't have the tools to shape it, a mitre saw would be nice, she didn't even have a chisel to counterset the hinge.

For a moment, just a moment, she missed Lawrence's shop, not the farm, not the prairie, just the shop with the tools hung on a pegboard. Wondered where he was? Drunk somewhere, unable to sober up; definitely not the man she had married, not nearly, maybe not a man at all, not anymore.

Sadness tried to fill her; she pushed it away. *No*, she was not going there; that was where Lawrence was, unable to forget, unable to forgive himself. The sadness tried again, brought an image with it this time. Lawrence on the lower step, Darren in his arms, and Darren's head; warped, not right and the blood on Lawrence's shirt. Dougie standing beside the truck, could not come close, could not face his mother, their mother.

Then the police were there, in her kitchen asking questions, and Lawrence could not stop crying, wiping snot and tears on his sleeve, how it happened, how the handgun was in the glovebox of the truck, for no reason, no damn reason other than Lawrence liked handguns, big handguns, 44 Magnum and a 45 Smith and Wesson upstairs in their bedroom. He was going to be charged with unsafe storage of a firearm. That's it. The police had done their job. Wrote up a charge, left the paper on the table. They had to charge him with something. The death of his oldest son, his pride, was not murder, an accidental shooting and the police fulfilled their duty, took notes, a statement from Dougie and left.

Dougie's statement to the police, was not to the police. He looked at his mother as he spoke. "Darren said, don't play with that. It might be loaded. And I said 'don't be stupid. Dad would never leave a loaded gun in the glovebox', and I pointed it at his head and pulled the trigger just to prove it."

Then Rosie had three children, not four. Lawrence never saw that, he never counted the kids. He never stopped and said "this is what I have left." He didn't know how to bury a relative, mourn for one year, cut your hair and then let the dead go, don't cry for them all the time, that just keeps their spirits around, keeps them from going to the Otherside to be with their relatives over there. Maybe if Lawrence had cut his hair. No don't go there. Don't try to reshape the past. That's what he's still doing. Saying what if, what if, what if, and drinking and crying. It was poor Lawrence. He didn't even have the strength to get mad about it. Poor Lawrence.

Rosie heard that he still gets up early in the morning, five AM but now it's to go out and wander the streets of Prince Albert looking for bottles and cans, until he has enough from the dumpsters and alleys behind the schools and other sure places where people don't bother to recycle, until he has enough to buy his daily ration of rotten grape. Why was it that they made such a big thing about alcohol consumption these days and they still sold that shit in the liquor stores, rot gut wine, cheap, rancid, and twenty percent alcohol?

She put the screwdriver back in the kitchen drawer, the drawer where things collected, things that did not have their own place, shut it with her hip and shut Lawrence and the prairie and the farm and that brief other life, shut them and would not go there, stay there. Wonder how Dougie was doing? Maybe she should give him a call now that Elsie had got the phone reconnected, find out how he's making out with his welding business.

"I'm glad you phoned mom. I was going to give you a call, but we've been busy like you would not believe."

"What's going on?"

"Lined up a contract, a big one. Four units."

"But you only have two."

"I know, that's what's been keeping me busy, tryin' to find two more welders big enough for this job."

"Well that's good, that's good my boy, tell me about this job."

"North Dakota, Mom. North Dakota, can you believe it. Big pipeline, and I mean a big pipeline, this job is good for at least three years."

"So, you're moving." Worry crept into her voice.

"No, no don't worry, Mom, I'd never run off on you." Dougie laughed into the phone. "Marie and the girls are staying here. I'll be gone quite a bit at first, setting things up, but it shouldn't be long and all I'll be doing is supervising." He laughed again "and collecting those big fat pay cheques."

"Good for you, my boy, good for you. I knew you'd do good. You always liked playing with your dad's welder," Rosie caught herself, "and hey, look at you now. So what kind of pipeline is this, gas, oil, or what."

"Water. A great big pipeline all the way from Lake Winnipeg to Texas and the best part is that I don't need pressure tickets. Not like a gas pipeline, where they're super fussy. No this is high volume pipe, big diameter. And I mean big Mom, you can drive a truck down the inside of this pipe. Those must be some thirsty Texans."

~

Lester shovelled grain from the back of the pickup into the fermenting pot. This was something he understood, a bit bigger scale, but not that much different than jailhouse brew — yeast, sugar, and something to rot. Farmers were happy to get rid of poor quality grain, stuff that wasn't worth putting on a train and, besides, brewers paid in cash.

Lester stopped, leaned on the shovel for a moment before rolling back the blue tarpaulin to reveal more musty grain. He tired easy. Out of shape, that's all. Just out of shape. Maybe he could find a set of weights and work out, get back that muscle he used to have, muscle that rippled under a tight tee-shirt and warned others not to mess with Lester Bigeye.

He looked around as he rested, both hands on the end of the handle. This used to be somebody's garage, a place for repairing heavy equipment, loaders, dozers, graders. A heavy plank workbench ran all down one side. There were still bits and pieces of engine, or maybe transmission, Lester wasn't sure which, scattered about. The concrete floor still showed black from spilled oil and grease and years of big rubber tires or clank of steel track.

This was a good job he had. It paid not bad, pretty good in fact. The only requirement was the ability to keep his mouth shut, not rat out. He had years and years of experience at that, was well qualified.

The roll-up door creaked a warning and Lester put the shovel back to the grain. The door lifted on its rusted track until it was waist high, the spot where it always stuck, needed a good jerk to get it past and moving again. Red ducked underneath, scraped his back against the battered rubber weather guard on the bottom of the door and let it fall behind him.

"Hey, there."

"Hey, yourself." Lester stopped shovelling again.

"Hotter'n a bitch outside, least you got some shade in here." Red lifted the brim of his canvas hat — green with a gold star on the front, the Castro hat, the kind of hat that the new revolutionaries, and anyone else who wanted to say something to the world wore — and wiped his forehead.

"Not so bad." Lester was feeling good today and that was different than most days.

"Smoke?" Red had the package out, flipping back the cardboard lid.

"Sure." Lester moved to the side of the truck, dragged the shovel and leaned out toward Red reaching. "Marlboros!" he recognized the package.

"Yeah, it's all I got. Hard to get Canadian smokes, even on the Rez."

"It'll do." Lester reached again, this time for the lighter. He sat on the edge of the truck box, liked this position, a little higher than Red, who stood with his elbows rested on the truck, not that Lester had any concerns about Red. Red was a decent enough of a guy, Lester just liked being in positions of advantage. "So, what's up?"

"Nothing much. Just stopping by to see how you're making out."

"Wish I was making out."

"You're too ugly for that man." Red grinned up at Lester.

Lester took a deep pull on the cigarette, let Red's little jab go past, wait for his turn to jab him back. "How many gallons did we get from that last batch?"

"Five full barrels. We'll make about three grand on that."

"That's a lot of work for three peesly grand. You know," Lester paused for emphasis, "if we ran this like a business, we might make some decent coin."

Red was alert. The business word he'd heard before. "We're doin' all right. Might not be getting stinking rich, but we're doin' okay. This is more a community service kind of thing anyway."

"I know some people, could really set this operation up right. Supply, distribution, protection."

"I know those people too, and no thanks. Listen Lester you forget about that. We don't want to attract attention here.

We're small scale and it works. We make a little coin and people can afford to drive their kids to town for happy meals."

"Up to you." Lester straightened his back, gave himself a little more height over Red. "But if you ever want, just let me know and I'll put you in touch with NS management."

"Not today, Lester my man, not today."

~

"So why do they call this Skunk Point?"

"Don't know, it's always been called that."

"Maybe should have called it Rocky Point." Benji was having trouble walking on the smooth, wet stones along the shore. Elsie was doing better, up a little higher where the stones were drier, away from the breaking waves.

"There it is. That's the spot I remember." She pointed ahead to a grassy rise that sloped out toward the water. She let go of Benji's hand, a bit reluctantly, but the choice was walk or hold hands and the rocky ground made doing both difficult.

"Beautiful. Just beautiful." Benji stood on the highest part of the knoll and looked out across the water, at the hills on the opposite shore, distant blue, the roll of the waves way out and closer to shore where they occasionally broke white and foamy. Southward the lakeshore curved in a long sand beach, rushes grew lush, deep dark green and filled the bay. Poplar and large white spruce crowded down to the edge of the sand, and no people, nobody other than him and Elsie on the whole of the lake.

She snuggled against his side, her arm around his waist. She felt his solidity against her thigh, the strength of his back as she ran her hand under his flapping shirt. He might be a half-inch shorter than her, she thought, as she leaned her head against his shoulder. It didn't matter, it was only a half-inch, and he made it up in other ways.

"You know, this is a waste. An absolute waste, all this beautiful land and nobody using it."

"We are."

"But we're the only ones."

"Do you need people to watch?" she snuggled closer.

"No, no." He turned and kissed her forehead, the spot closest. "But just think." He turned to look out again, to wave with his free hand at the expanse. "This could be a resort, easily a resort, people swimming, jet boating, water skiing. Just think of it."

Elsie thought of it. Didn't like what she saw. "I like it the way it is." She understood that Benji came from a city, probably the only time he ever saw nature was at a crowded cottage subdivision north of Toronto on a long weekend. But that's okay. Give him time, he'd learn. And Elsie would be there to help him learn about natural things, about wind and water and trees and how people fit in, how to be an Indian, how to appreciate what is, instead of what could be. Benji was half Indian. His father gave him that. He had good blood, he would have a good spirit, she would find it for him.

"So, did your dad say why he was going south?" She changed the subject.

"Not really. Just said he has something to take care of, said I could use the boat, make myself at home in the cabin, whatever."

"Was he going to see your mom?"

"Maybe. I don't know. He never said."

"That was strange, your mom showing up like that. Like she knew you were here. Mother's instinct."

"I suppose. I don't know what her and Ben were talking about. Whatever it was it got him moving. I've never seen a man pace like that. Walked back and forth in that cabin for hours. I fell asleep and he was still pacing. Next morning he says, "Help yourself to whatever you need, and if you go out don't lock the door. I don't have a key.""

Elsie sat down on the grass, pulled Benji by the hand to join her. "Do you and your dad talk much?"

"Not really, no deep conversations, if that's what you mean. But it's okay, it seems like we communicate in different ways. We do things together, I like that. I like it that we don't just talk, we get out and do stuff."

Elsie nodded. He was getting it. He was learning. You don't have to talk all the time, deeper communication happens in different ways. Benji was learning to become an Indian. The tall grass swallowed her as she laid back content with the wind off the lake and a blue sky and waving slender green blades beside her face.

"What's your favourite song?" Benji laid down beside her.

"Oh, that's easy. Bob Dylan's 'Ange'."

"That's that old guy."

"I like the lyrics. 'Under a sky of orange, God help our Ange. It's not the end of the World, but you can see it from here. Courage Ange Courage'. What's yours?"

"Me, I like 'Universal Soldier' by the Last Temptations."

"I like them too." She felt around for his hand. "The granddaughters of the original Temptations. Did you know that that song was written by an Indian?" She found his hand. "Buffy St. Marie wrote that."

"Who?"

"Buffy St. Marie, from Fort Qu'Appelle, Saskatchewan. That's her song."

The wind rustled the leaves of the poplar behind them, bent the grass over their faces. Tiny white clouds, bright against the deep blue sky, shape shifted, challenged imagination, became beings and entities of drift and change, always change.

⌒

"Dark roast," Ben answered the very young woman behind the counter.

"Need room for cream?" She let the black pour into the glass cup.

"No, I don't use that." Ben liked bitter coffee. Here at the Roastery brought back memories of when he first lived in Saskatoon, mind, the Roastery then was still only on Broadway Avenue. Now it dominated the city, pushed Starbucks to the fringe and as people discovered the merits of fresh roasting, the Broadway Roastery chain could be found in all the western cities as far west as the Rockies. It never made the jump to the coast. Out there, they were still drinking Seattle slough water.

He found a table by the window facing the street. Twenty-second had changed over the years; now it rivalled Broadway for interesting little shops. First Peoples Publishing across the street looked to be already open, or maybe it was just someone coming to work early before the heat of the day ruined inspiration. A little after six and the sun was beginning to climb the highrises down town, spreading tall square shadow fingers, and blinding drivers heading into the heart of the city.

Ben flipped the pages of the *StarPhoenix*, found nothing interesting, or nothing that he could believe, nothing he could trust. If this were his only source of information, he would think that Canada was better off under the new regime. Programs were working, employment was stable, healthcare functioned. The new president of the university denied that enrollment was dropping. The mayor was in negotiations to have the entire city declared an urban First Nation. With a First Peoples population of seventy-two percent, and two thirds of council from First Nations, it was obvious that Saskatoon should have reserve status. He reiterated that non-First Nation peoples within the city would be accommodated. Private property could exist alongside community property.

Ben looked up. Monica was watching him through the glass. Chance, coincidence, destiny, didn't matter. He came here to see her and there she was.

"What brings you here?" Monica liked a little milk in her morning coffee, not cream, not thick, she liked the thin taste of coffee, the water part of the blend between flavour and liquid.

"You."

"Me?" She felt his eyes, held her cup to her mouth longer, hid behind it, tasted it again and held it with both hands, elbows splayed on the table in front of her. She looked to be in a pose of worship. Blessed is a morning cup of coffee.

"I want to know about That Jack." Ben folded the paper, put it aside.

"Do you have a platform?"

"I never went with that technology."

"Too bad, you still using a laptop and a cellphone and a video and a GPS."

"No GPS."

"Still using paper maps I suppose. Maybe that's better, nobody can track you with a map. I left my platform at home — come by and I'll introduce you to That Jack." She slid her chair a fraction of an inch back, needed a little more distance between her and Ben, now that he was leaning forward. She could smell herself, maybe he could too, smelled Ed's sweat, his sperm, her sweat; she could even smell the spit of his mouth on her breasts. She should have gone home for a shower before coffee. "If you've never met That Jack, you're in for a surprise." She fastened the top button of her blouse.

⌒

Rosie could not stop thinking about that big pipeline full of water, sacred water in a steel pipe, trapped, condemned to chlorine. How was it that those people never learned anything about water? Well, they didn't know anything about life either. How could they know that water and life are connected — if they didn't know that life was sacred, they would never figure out that so was water. Maybe someday, after they ruined all the water they might realize that there is no life, nothing without water. Oh, well, it was up to them to learn.

Same as Dougie. He'd have to learn too, in his own way. Someday he would realize that money was not important, that his wife and his daughters were. Going away to work, well that's what men do. When they're young they're supposed to go out into the world, travel around, explore, face the world and its challenges, burn off some of that craziness that young men get sometimes; but then, they're supposed to come home and take care of their families and the community. This thing that had been going on now since the mining companies began hiring our young men, taking them away and sending them home with pockets full of money, wasn't the way it should be. But how can you tell a young man that he has to think about his life when that's what he's doing? Thinking about his life and how he'll support his family, how they'll have all the things, all the cars, and computers, and toys. That's what it was all about wasn't it — the toys? The little boys never grew up, never went through that phase. Nobody went out on the hill to fast and suffer and look for their vision anymore, they just stayed little boys and never got over wanting more toys.

Rachel crawled off the blanket spread on the floor. Not on her hands and knees yet. She still mostly dragged and pulled herself along, her legs kicked to little affect. Rosie let her go, didn't pick her up and put her back on the blanket, let her find her own way; she had to figure it out for herself, wouldn't be long and she would be crawling for real, a month at the most, then in another month, maybe two and she would be pulling herself up and trying to walk. Rosie had never helped her babies learn to walk, never held their hands, helped them balance and encouraged them to move their feet. It happened too fast as it was, she didn't want them to walk too soon, before they had their own balance.

This was Elsie's first baby. She would learn, same way that Rosie learned, from heartache and joy, if she was around to see it. Maybe Elsie would be like some of those mothers who left their kids, either didn't want them, or got caught in something they thought was more important. "It's okay, *Eskwesis*, little woman, you'll always have your *kokum*. Come back here now, you can't go downstairs yet. Wait, soon enough you'll be running out the door." Rosie picked up her granddaughter, carried her down the short flight of stairs to the front door and out into the wind of the afternoon. "Is this where you wanted to go, my girl? See, it's all wind and dust out here." Rachel gripped Rosie's shirt in strong tiny hands, buried her face in the folds of cotton for a second, caught her breath stolen by the wind and then twisted to look around again at a world where giant trees waved and bent.

~

"That Jack used to work for CSIS. He was assigned the American files, to watch the neo-conservatives and the militias that were forming in some of the western states and starting to come into Canada." Monica's wet, freshly shampooed hair clung to her face as she prepared breakfast. It was more for Ben than for her. Her stomach wasn't up to food yet, young wine had that affect. "He predicted that the Americans were going to invade long before it happened and nobody would listen. So he dropped out. By the time the bastards got here, That Jack was just another guy with a computer." The toaster popped two slices. The butter dish was empty. She looked in the fridge for margarine, found a tiny yellow tub with a little in the bottom, enough. "He still had all his connections. They think he's one of theirs. Some of the stuff he gets is just incredible. Must be in tight with Homeland Security." She spread margarine thinly on the toast. She was talking as fast as she worked. "How he gets stuff is pretty impressive, but his real genius is how he gets it out there."

"And how does he get it out there?" Ben looked out the apartment window, nice place, you could see the river from here.

"Do you ever read your Spam?"

"No, I've got good filters to keep that out. I'm not interested in discount Viagra, or ultrahigh definition monitors and I definitely won't buy internet pharmaceuticals. I get enough advertising during my day now that CBC radio has had its public funding cut."

"Spam isn't all advertising. It's not just people trying to sell you stuff. A lot of what you're getting is computer-generated nonsense. Try reading it sometime."

"So why do people send it?"

"'Cause they can." She carried a plate, two eggs, sunnyside up, micro-waved bacon and hashbrowns, toast cut corner to corner, something traditional. It was good to keep tradition. Tradition was more important than ever now.

"You're not eating?" Ben saw only one plate.

"Girl has to watch her figure." Monica placed the plate in front of Ben, leaned across in front of him, exposed her nakedness under the thin bathrobe, throat to pale breast. Nice figure to watch, Ben thought, as he respectfully averted his eyes, looked down from the flesh inches away from his face to the food on the plate. The pair of eggs, white and soft, hinted of breasts.

"The reason That Jack can get away with it is because most people are like you. They don't read their Spam." Monica brought out her platform, unfolded the screen, slid the lens cover closed on the camera and spread the keyboard. A computer generated face, not dissimilar from Ben's, appeared on the screen and immediately began to speak. "Good morning Monica my dear. I hope you had a pleasant sleep. The news overnight has been relatively quiet. Homeland Security reports that they have captured two insurgents in Val Dore, Quebec without casualty." The face smiled, showed perfect teeth. "Of special interest, the Sami Parliament has announced that it expects to use more of its share of North Sea gas profits to support Indigenous Peoples in the Americas to negotiate modern Treaties, and hopes that the United Nations will respect those Treaties as international instruments."

"Would you open my email please." Monica's voice was flat.

"Whatever you want, my dear." The face winked.

"Let's see." Monica ran her finger down the screen to a blue icon. The screen shifted to lines of text. "Here," she pointed to a heading that read *Jack Richards*. "Anytime an email comes from someone named Jack or has Jack, or Jacqueline, or Jackie in the sender box it's worth looking at." She touched the screen twice and the text shifted again. Ben read down from the top: *Universality does not require expertise nor amendments. When the first spacemen arrived on the earth, they were not met by mammalian beings. Justice needs just people to proliferate.*

"No need to read all of it. It's mostly nonsense and jibberish anyway." Monica interrupted Ben's reading with her hand running down the screen. "All we're looking for is the word *that*. Here we are." She pointed to a line of text: *when you sing about that two men from Val Dore were taken last night and a third was summarily shot.* "When you read That Jack, the truth is between the word 'that' and the next period."

"So, the report we just heard wasn't correct. There was a casualty."

"Not completely. Homeland Security didn't have any casualties. Truth is tricky stuff, it depends on who is doing the reporting."

Ben forked some of the egg onto the oily toast. "Isn't the web being constantly monitored? I've been under the impression that it was impossible to use it for subversive purposes."

"It is monitored. Always has been. But their search engines can't read everything all the time. The web is too big for any one computer, that's the beauty of it. So they use key words. You'll never find That Jack using words like insurgent, or even Homeland Security or democracy and definitely not resistance. And he hides it in Spam. Nobody reads Spam, apparently not even Homeland Security." Monica grinned, pleased with herself to share in That Jack's brilliance.

"So, what does That Jack have to say about Abe Friesen?" Ben needed to know.

"Yesterday." Monica ran her finger across the screen again. "Here." She removed her hand so that Ben could read. He quickly found the word *that* and read: *foes of the people that will not speak, Abe Friesen, John Doe and Jane Doe, live in pain.*

"And what does that mean." Ben wasn't hungry. He put down the last strip of bacon that he had been nibbling on. "He's being tortured. Right."

"That's what it looks like. But have faith. He hasn't talked."

"Not yet."

"Maybe never. It's not true that everyone talks. Sometimes they overdo it and the prisoner can't talk."

"You mean they kill them."

"That's blunt, but you're right. Sometimes they end up killing a prisoner before he or she talks."

"I can't even let myself imagine that for Abe. Even if it means they don't find out about me. I can't wish for Abe's death." Ben stood, grinding the chair against the ceramic tile floor of Monica's dining nook. Sunshine through the big bay window, refraction of light off the spread of trees along the river, bright cheery tapestry, and a Che poster all dimmed, suddenly became sullen.

"Listen, Ben." Monica put a hand on his shoulder. He faced away from her toward the river. "There's still a chance, there's always a chance." She could not tell him about the negotiations, about prisoner exchanges. But she could assure. "I know for a fact that there is still a chance that Abe is going to get out of this."

Ben turned at her touch. "I never wanted to be a part of this. This isn't my fight."

"It's everybody's fight, Ben." Monica stood back, faced him "This is the way the world is and we all do what we have to do."

She suddenly felt naked in his stare, as though he was looking right through her robe, right through her.

Ben wanted to tell her he had been fighting all his life, but could see that it wouldn't do any good, she would not understand, would try to argue her point, prove that she was right. He looked at her, at the length of her, at all of the parts that showed through the gap of her robe, at the height of thigh, and slant from throat to navel, at a familiar face, at the drape of her hair, at the single heavy gold hoop in her left ear. Monica thrived on being a revolutionary. It gave her purpose. He could not take that away from her. She was doing what she believed in. This was Monica's reality and it was too far away from Ben's understanding to even begin a conversation.

"Do you know where I can buy a gun?" The words surprised him as though someone else, something else, something deeper spoke. He wondered if it was his fear.

~

A squadron of fighter jets smashed the air, just above the tree tops. They didn't see the planes coming across the lake. At seven hundred miles-per-hour, they had only been visible for half a minute and Benji and Elsie were too busy with each other to be watching. Thunder, thought Elsie. Thor's hammer, thought Benji when he had time to recover, to stand naked in the wind.

"What the hell was it?"

"Jets." Elsie had caught the flash of metal against the sky a half second before the sound slammed into them. She stood stooped beside him in the wind, pulling jeans up muscular thighs. "We should head back." She was now thinking about her daughter. She also noted with a little concern that the wind was pushing the water into large waves.

"Ever drive a boat?" Ben had asked.

"Yeah, on Lake Ontario." Benji had answered his father. He did not say, "once, a boat with a steering wheel, while my friend untangled fishing lines."

They had trouble getting Ben's boat away from the rocky shore with the waves pounding in. Elsie stood in the water and held the bow while he lowered the leg and started the motor. Now out in the roll of the lake, Benji was more than a little unsure; he was on the border of panic as the boat pounded against the waves, nosed high in the air, and splashed down into the next draw only to begin to nose up again. He gripped the tiller, concentrated on his heading, southwest across the wide part of the lake toward the reserve, not that very far, just there under that part of the sky that was deeper black than the rest: ten kilometres maybe, ten impossible kilometres. There may be shelter from the wind along the west shore, he thought, shifted his concentrated stare toward the hills for a second, but even that was six or seven kilometres away. He looked back to where the reserve should be, at the next wave, larger than the rest. The bow of the boat rose, obliterated his view until all he could see was aluminum and wood-covered seats and Elsie sitting dead centre facing him, holding on to the seat under her with both hands, her hair blowing forward, hiding her face.

The rain hit, hard, stinging his face, forcing him to turn away, take his eyes from the horizon that his heart pounded for, ached for. He wanted to cry, cry like a little boy who could not have what he wanted and all he wanted was to get this boat safely to shore. He looked down out of the driving rain. His feet were in water. It sloshed half way up his calf. He was going to drown out here because of his own stupidity and worse he was going to drown Elsie. He looked up, at her face. She either was not afraid or was not showing it. She sat hunched away from the sting of rain on her back, looked up as he looked at her. Their eyes met.

She read his fear, saw the shock-etched face with the mouth pulled hard into a straight line. She looked around, beyond the roil, the mash of waves, capped in white foam. She was pointing with her right arm extended straight out, her mouth moved and the wind tore her words away. Benji looked to where she was pointing. He didn't understand. She made big full arm-pointing gestures; he heard the word cabin and turned the boat out of the wind.

Running with the wind was suddenly smoother, easier. The backs of the waves were not as steep as their face. The rain lost its sting, was not in his face, he could see. There was the shoreline, the point of land he remembered. Just to the left of that was where the creek led back to the shelter of the old cabin.

Elsie spoke into the wind again. Benji did not hear. She was not speaking to him. She was talking to her mother, words into the wind.

~

Rachel began to cry, little whimpers of discomfort. Rosie picked her up, held her to herself, felt the baby's face buried in the soft between her throat and her shoulder. "It's okay, my girl. It's okay. Your mommy is okay." She crooned and swayed, gently rocking Rachel as she walked back to the kitchen. Nothing to do with a day like today but stay inside and bake a pie. A nice plump apple pie, lots of cinnamon.

~

Elsie stood naked again in front of the stove that crackled and snapped. Dry pine wood does that, she remembered, turning to warm her backside. The cabin smelled slightly of the smoke that leaked from the pipes they had fashioned together. Their clothes steamed on the string lines stretched above the snap and crackle. Elsie laughed, not at anything, lifted her long wet hair from her shoulders with both hands and let it fall. Benji turned at the sound, his hands still outstretched over the heat of the stove. His laugh joined with hers, not at anything, nothing more than relief. Naked, wet, and shivering needed to be laughed at.

~

Strong winds never blow for very long and the sun always shines again another day.

"You and Elsie are getting along well." Ben wanted to talk.

"Yeah, pretty good." Benji appreciated the question, appreciated his father showing interest in him. He turned from the computer after he tapped the keyboard, once, then again, waited for the shutdown page to appear where the video had flashed before folding down the screen to better see his father. Nothing there but cinematic flitter anyway. His father didn't own a television, obsolete things now that internet provided complete entertainment, complete communication, despite those out there dedicated to crashing it.

Ben's cabin appeared spartan to Benji. It was not filled with the collection of a lifetime, not at all like his adopted parents' house, where clutter ruled, and people moved carefully around the assorted and arranged. Here was open, from log wall to log wall, a larger version of the cabin he and Elsie had spent half of one day, a sleepless night, and most of the next day in.

"She's quite the woman. A bit of a flake if you know what I mean, otherwise . . . " Benji searched for the words. Words that would tell his father that he was falling, crazy in love. But how does a man say something like that, especially to another man. "Otherwise she's perfect."

"I've known her mother since I was a kid. Good family, Rosie is good people, so were her parents and Elsie comes from there. But what makes you think she's a 'flake'?"

"Oh nothing, really. We were just out at the cabin and I asked her if she was concerned that her mother might be worrying about us and she says no, she sent her mother a message on the wind that we were all right."

"And that's being a flake?"

"No, it's just that she insists that she can communicate with her mother without words. It's a little weird, but it's nothing, really."

"What makes you think she can't?" Ben faced his son squarely across the table.

"Not you too. Is this some kind of Indian thing or what?"

"I don't think you have to be Indian to have a sense of how your children are doing." Ben paused, wondered how much to tell Benji. "It's not like vision quest or sweat lodge ceremony, not even the sacred pipe. It's more personal than that. Intuition."

"Intuition I can understand, but she insists that she sent her mother a message."

"Well, intuition is part of understanding. You can't know anything completely if you only apply logic." Ben felt the professor within him stir. He suppressed it. "Intuition can be developed, learned. Maybe Rosie and Elsie have learned how to use it, how to use the connection between family."

The word family hit Benji, stopped him from his quick answer. Family he did not know about, was not sure enough to insist upon his otherwise clear perspective. He sat still, looked down at the folded platform on the table. There was a communication device, understandable: microchips, circuits, wireless connections, solid, real. He looked back up at Ben, checked flannel shirt, red and blue squares, something out of history, at the wind-tanned face beginning to be gouged by the lines of age, at the eyes that looked beyond him, not at him, not challenging.

"We understand family, maybe a little differently than you've been taught." Ben was not the professor now, he was his own father and grandfather speaking. "Our ancestors are always behind us, a line of them going back; we're connected to them. The things they did in their lives affect us, just like the things we do in our lives affect our children and grandchildren. If our grandparents did something good, helped someone, that help might come back to us. That's why in this life we should try to do good, so that good brings a blessing to our children." Ben wanted to talk, felt the need to pass this on, understood his own father, and the warmth of the wood stove and the cabin and the quiet of a winter evening while he sat and listened to these same words. He now appreciated his father's need to speak. Time was short, was always short. "You should remember seven generations behind you, and think seven generations ahead of you. Those are your connections. Imagine a string running through you, out your back to your ancestors and out your front to your great grandchildren that are not here yet. When you can imagine that, you are getting somewhere. Then you should try to imagine how you are related to everything else, how you are related to the trees, to the animals, the fish and the birds. Those are our relatives too." Ben held back, did not talk about the other relatives his father told him about. Those could wait. Benji had enough to think about for now.

Benji was thinking. "What about my adopted parents?" he asked.

Ben sat back. The connection between him and his son felt strong. "We knew about adoptions, we used to adopt each other as brothers, people would adopt the children of their friend. That child then would have a second set of parents and when that child needed they could go to them. It didn't get in the way of the child and its biological parents. You could adopt anybody, get new grandparents, or a new sister. It even went so far that nations would adopt nations. That's what the Treaties were to us. We adopted the white people and as relatives they got the right to be here, on our land, we shared with them." Benji was looking up, listening. Ben looked into the young face, at the eyes that were open to understanding. "Your adopted parents are part of the string of ancestors behind you. That string I was talking about. It doesn't have to be only biological. Anybody who loved you in their life, will be there in the Otherworld, looking out for you, will help you when you need help." Ben stopped. This was going too far for Benji to grasp just yet. He needed to experience it before he got it.

Benji did not get what his father was talking about. He thought that the man across from him was trying to explain Cree mythology, trying to explain some ancient superstition. He was not sure which world he was in, which his dead adopted parents might be in and which world Ben might occupy. He was careful enough not to say anything that might be insulting. He had learned not to speak quickly from Elsie, her back straight. "Be careful what you say about things you don't understand." Her voice stern, clear, her head high, her eyes meeting his directly, equally.

"I'll have to think about that," Benji murmured.

It was the perfect answer to Ben. He sat back from the table satisfied. His son was developing understanding. Maybe if he thought about it long enough he might learn how to use his connection between the worlds. He might reach the point where he would settle comfortably into his own life, into his own skin.

⁓

Lester waited. This was easy for him. Sitting around the gas station, listening in on conversations; weather, mostly weather:

"Too damn hot, never seen it this hot."

"What a storm yesterday."

"Heard about the forest fire way down in Regina, I guess the little park downtown burned up, hell-of-a-thing."

Local stuff; going to town, someone needs a ride:

"Chief is at the band office today for a change, better catch him while he's there, before he has to run off again, meeting with officials."

"Is it true the southern Indians are moving up here? What we going to do when that happens? There isn't enough moose and elk for us as it is."

"Heard they're changing the hunting laws."

A man in a suburban truck pulled to the pumps. "Fill," he commanded the young woman attendant.

"You got it." She tightened the leather glove that was slipping off her free hand, teeth to the cuff, the taste of gasoline now in her mouth.

He looked around at this environment: dark green trees of some kind, no one had ever told him the difference between white and black spruce, of pine and poplar and birch. Trees were things along residential streets in the old parts of the city, important to some people, especially important to dogs. Here they were everywhere, the clear areas were the exception, here trees ruled, pushed to the edge of the gravel road, surrounded the back of the gas station — a rectangle cleared into the thick of them for a house across the road from the gas pumps — a pole fence bleached in the sun, marker for a square of faded grass in front of the house that looked like every other reserve house on every other reserve, government issue.

He stumbled, one foot dropping into a pothole between the pumps and the gas station — only savages would live like this, without pavement. He walked carefully, hoped that the dust he raised would not cloud his leather shoes, fine Italian leather, not moosehide. He was not a savage, not a bush Indian, not naïve. He was business.

He recognized Lester sitting on a bench in the shade in front of the gas station, convenience store, grocery, post office, snack bar, coffee shop, lottery distributor. Lester stepped from shade into the August sun. "Richard." He held out his hand.

"Lester." Richard's tone matched the formality of his strong handshake. "So, do you own this place yet?" He indicated with his chin the graffiti-splashed metal-sided building.

"Not yet. I've got something else going on. Something I need NS to help with."

"We're not charity, Lester. What can you do for Native Syndicate? Not, what can we do for you, remember."

Lester nodded, looked down, then quickly back up. Never be humbled. Never feel shame. "It's a good project for NS. But, you look it over. You decide. If it fits in with our other work, maybe we have something. If it doesn't then it doesn't. But between you and me, Richard, I think we have something here."

"I'll have a look." Richard slid a slim wallet from his hip pocket. It was made with smooth nearly shiny material, light and strong. Slim because it did not have any cards or identification, no photos of loved ones, nobody's business card or folded piece of paper with a phone number. It contained one commodity — cash, Amero hundred-unit bills. He gave five to the attendant for the fill. Lester was impressed.

When Lester was in the Suburban, listening to the very good stereo sound of powwow blended with hip hop, absorbing the chill of the air conditioner, reclining in the comfort of leather, Richard reached under his seat for a bundle wrapped in red cloth. "Here, something for you from head office."

Lester unwrapped the cloth around the stainless steel semi-automatic, hefted the weight of the piece, felt the solidity of the grip fit to his hand, pointed it, found its balance, let it rest there, easy, so easy. He checked the magazine, fifteen rounds, pulled back the action, there was another in the chamber. Ready to go, ready to go anywhere with class.

"Nine millimetre Browning." Richard looked back to the gravel and potholes. "Fast as you can pull the trigger."

"Nice." Lester held it to the light, away from the tint of the side windows to see the shine of steel in sun.

"I'll have a look at what you phoned about. But that is not why I'm here." Richard poured bottled water into a glass with his right hand, offered the glass to Lester. Lester declined. The pistol in his hand filled him. His thirst was quenched.

Richard eased back into the seat, drove left-handed; drank water from a glass, not the bottle, not like a wino. He didn't like it here, on the reserve, on dusty rough roads. He didn't like the houses — spaced, each in its square cleared of trees;

these houses were cheap. You could tell just by driving by, nothing solid about them, cheap siding, cheap roofs.

No sidewalks anywhere, no pavement; there was nothing here that Richard wanted, and Richard did not want to be here; did not want to be reminded that this was where he came from — not Moccasin Lake, but from a reserve, a reserve just as dusty and poor and cheap. He was better than this now. He had class. He drove a Suburban, a GMC, with a full-size gasoline engine, not a hybrid — fully loaded, nothing chintzy, nothing routine, nothing working class, or worse — reserve class.

Lester was spinning the pistol on his finger, finding the balance of it; spin it, grab the grip, point, aim.

The music through the clear speakers chanted a song of resistance, banned lyrics; a song of rights, freedom, and homeland, a version or perversion of "Oh Canada", depending upon your perspective. Richard heard the words and dismissed them, this resistance stuff wasn't real fighting. Real fighting was north-central Regina nearly a decade ago. Now that was war. The enemy didn't wear a uniform, you shot at blue bandanas or red bandanas or white and they shot at you for the colour of your clothes. Then killing was all revenge and honour and control, and you never slept.

Native Syndicate rose, became great, faded, and rose again. Now Richard had command and NS had purpose, it had place; and the respect they had fought for all those years in crumbling apartment blocks and slumlord rented collapsing houses was finally theirs. Native Syndicate was the battle arm of the resistance. It put more soldiers onto the streets than anyone. And, whether the resistance liked it or not, NS reaped the profits.

Everyone wanted to get high and hide. The war on the insurgents replaced the war on drugs. While the police chased the bombers and watched the marchers, cocaine flowed freely, morphine was almost as easy to supply as cigarettes, and the OxyContin Blues was becoming the most popular song on the streets. Richard and Native Syndicate were the link between the powder and the profit; and the police were busy elsewhere.

The best part, the very best part; no rats. No one was phoning Homeland Security because there was a crack house in the neighbourhood. And the RCMP, well most people saw them as just an adjunct to HS.

"So, what do you want me to do with this?" Lester toyed with the Browning.

"It's business — not mine — I'm just bringing a message, an assignment for you."

Lester rested the pistol on his lap, kept his hand on it, listened. "Yeah?"

"Someone for you to watch for us. It probably won't go anywhere. Far as I'm concerned it's someone pulling strings, getting favours, wants someone out here looked after."

"You want me to babysit."

"You have a problem with that?"

"No, no problem. You tell me what you want done. It'll get done." Lester tipped the pistol sideways, movie gangster style, and pointed it straight ahead.

~

It's too early, Monica thought, at the sight of a single faded orange leaf on the maple that a city worker had planted, gouged a hole and plopped into the boulevard in front of the new apartment block twenty-seven years ago. It's way too early for the leaves to change. But then she thought, well maybe because spring came so early they are just tired of it all, tired of the constant heat. Summer can become tiring, dust, daylight that comes way too early and wakes you, the buzz of flies, and that dry wind that keeps blowing up from the Arizona desert. Some days she thought she could smell cactus mixed with the grit. Maybe winter would be good this year, some snow, just a little, just enough to settle the dust and make the city look clean again.

Ben loved autumn, used to come back to the university after summer tanned a full shade darker, brought the wilderness with him into the classroom, brought energy and light. He used trees as metaphor to explain to the seminar class how an ecological society might function, how balsam and birch lived together, put thoughts in her head about how she might live. But Ben's utopian society only existed there, in her head, maybe in his; it was not here, on the concrete where grass grew through the cracks beneath her boots, here where the boulevard ended and the busy 23rd Street — a couple more blocks and they would be at the bus depot.

～

Rick hurt, this was a sick he had never experienced before. It was more than the sick that might be expected from six weeks of confinement in a basement without light, more than the sick that might be expected from the beatings, the kicks, the punches to the temple. Why did he always hit me there? What was the damage he hoped to inflict with punches to the side of the head? Brain damage? No, the brain was functioning perfectly well. He knew where he was, knew that the explosive taped to the small of his back was armed, knew the woman behind him held an old-fashioned garage door opener in the pocket of her floppy jacket, knew that if she pressed 'open', the explosive would certainly smash his spine if it did not kill him. Rick's brain was fine. It was the rest of his body that was having problems, serious problems.

"Do not get on the bus until I say so." Monica's voice behind him was indifferent; at first Rick confused it with kindness. Six weeks of anger can do that; make you believe that indifference is kindness. Sunshine and light can give you hope, keep you walking when your body wants to lay down, there on that bit of grass, or even here, right here on the concrete, just lay down for a moment. Rick kept walking, putting one foot in front of the other, promised himself it would be okay once he was on the bus. Buses have reclining seats.

At the station, Rick tried to stand away from the other people waiting to board. If this was all just a set-up, if she pushed the button anyway, he did not want to be standing close to someone who had nothing to do with this. He looked at her, standing in the shade, watching people getting off the bus two lanes over. She nodded and he pushed himself the three steps to the door of the bus, handed the driver the white stiff paper ticket, used the handrail to climb the narrow stair, turned left past where the driver would sit, waited for his eyes to adjust to the dim light, and made his way to the very back of the bus where the man was signalling him. He would have preferred to sit anywhere closer.

"Here, lift your shirt." He felt the rip of tape removed. "Anywhere else?"

"No. That's it."

"Okay then, just sit tight and we go for a short ride." The man sat back, turned away from Rick, toward the window where the light was better and disconnected the detonator from the explosive. "Everything is going to be okay now."

Rick knew it wasn't. Knew that the man with the dirty blonde hair and hawk nose had poisoned him. That was why he stopped the punches and kicks, stood there and grinned while Rick ate cold canned beans that tasted of grit. No, it was not going to be okay.

~

"Everything is going to be okay now, Abe." Monica put her arm around his waist and helped him to walk to the depot.

"No it isn't. Monica. I told them everything."

"It's okay, Abe." She squeezed him tighter, reassured. "We'll handle it. Let's just get you out of here. You're safe now." Quickly through the station, past the ticket counter, out the street doors, into the taxi. "No, the other one." She guided him to the third cab in the line, the one that Ed was driving.

"Where to?" Ed joked.

"You know fuckin' well where to." Monica was not in the mood for jokes as she slammed the door behind her. "Are you wired?" She had her hands under Abe's shirt, feeling.

"No, nothing. They put me on the bus at Dundurn and told me not to get off."

"Nobody rode with you?"

"Not that I know of. Monica, I talked. I told them everything."

"It's all right, we'll handle it. You just take it easy."

Abe wanted to talk, needed to talk. "I don't know what I said, I just started babbling. They gave me an injection, fire in my veins, I don't remember. I couldn't concentrate, confused. That needle, whatever it was, and I couldn't stop talking, babbling was more like it. It was like I was somewhere else listening to myself. It was like I was trying to put the fire out with words, trying to make the pain stop, anything to make the pain stop."

"Bastards." Monica sat back, let the taxi carry her, let herself go with it, wherever it was going. The resistance would continue and she was along for the ride, all the way. The taxi turned hard right, leaned her against Abe, shoulder to shoulder. She put her arm around him. "It's all right, Abe. Like I said, we'll handle it."

Ed sped the taxi through the old warehouse area, the area that had once been converted to nightclubs, offices and restaurants, but was now deserted again. The once bright paint, the purples and oranges that had attracted people at the turn of the century now faded, peeling and empty.

Abe sat up straighter, his strength returning; he did not need sympathy, did not need Monica's arm around him. He relied upon his own strength.

"What did you tell them about me?" Monica needed to know.

"I don't think I did." Abe turned slightly to look at her. "I rambled a lot. They wanted to know about the gathering on the farm, who was there, who said what, and the person that I kept talking about the most was that guy you brought, Ben Robe. Of everyone who spoke at the gathering, it was Ben Robe that stuck in my head, and it was Ben Robe that I gave to them. I don't know if it was the drugs or what, but I remembered everything he said. In my babbling I gave them his speech word for word. I've got to find him and tell him."

"I'll take care of that." Monica looked out the window, looked north.

The rifle kicked into Ben's shoulder. Not the slam of a hunting rifle, more a push than a hit. He lowered it, looked at it again. It was shaped like a rifle, barrel, forestock, trigger, scope. But it was as different as it was similar. Ben was more familiar with walnut and blue steel. This was flat black and plastic, electronic rather than mechanical action.

"It fires three rounds for each pull on the trigger," Monica had bragged when she showed him his purchase. "Laserscope tuned to four-hundred metres, put the red dot where you want, squeeze the trigger, and one dead bastard."

Ben looked back at his target, a plastic bottle hung by a string from a tree branch two-hundred metres distant. He did not need to check, he knew it had three holes in it, saw it jump when he squeezed the trigger. Easy enough, but could he shoot a human? Could he put the red dot on a man? Take a life?

"In self-defence," he answered, but the words were not his, they were his father's: *"When a man takes a life, that man takes that other man's life as his own. If you murder a man you take that man's sins. That man they electrocuted there."* The old man had pointed at the newspaper a young Ben was holding. *"They took all his sins onto themselves when they killed him. The wrong that man did, they have to pay for it now — him, he goes to the happy hunting ground."*

"The one that pulled the switch has to pay?"

"Not just him, all of them. All of them that decided to kill this man, they take his sins. You watch, they keep doing this, they keep electrocuting and hanging people, all of them are going to pay. It's going to come back on their people."

"They've been doing this for a long time."

"And look at the suffering it brought them. They still have murderers and rapists, lots of them. Just watch. It'll keep getting worse."

Ben put the rifle away. It did not hold any answers.

~

Rosie knelt, moved aside a branch to check the underside of the faded blueberry bush. There weren't any berries there either. Nothing. She felt tired, wore out, more from disappointment than from exertion. In a good blueberry-picking year she could stay out all day, walk with a pail for miles, happily filling it and spend her evening cleaning the berries, picking out the occasional unripe green one and the very rare unwanted leaf, packaging them up, and stocking her freezer. Blueberries were Rosie's staple. She depended upon them for the pies she baked over the winter, her famous pies that she could sell when she needed a little extra during the last days of the month when things were running low.

She had heard of years like this. Her mother had told her about the year they had a big snowstorm in June that killed all the young berries. But even that year her mother had found berries. The snow had come while her mother and father were travelling. They had stopped overnight, made a camp, the next morning when they started out they found the snow had come all around them but not the place they had camped. Her mother had gone back to that spot and sure enough there were berries there, not much, but enough.

Rosie wondered if she would be the first in her family's history to ever get skunked. She picked up her pail and started walking, looking for that one spot where the sun had not burned away the berries, where there might be some, enough. Maybe in the shade of poplars. Maybe there were saskatoon berries on the island at the north end of the lake. Maybe Ben would take her there in his boat. Maybe Elsie and Benji would come and they could take Rachel. There was a nice beach there, a little cove of sand and driftwood. They could have a picnic. It would be good to be on the lake, on the cool of the water.

~

The hitchhiker looked like the Indians that showed up on movie sets, with a pair of long black braids tied with leather, darker skin; he could have been Indian, wore denim, and boots. Even the name he gave, Billy Thunder, sounded Indian. But the accent that accompanied the name was not Indian, not Cree, not Saulteaux. Ben suppressed a laugh at the thought, maybe he was Dene. He thought of asking, making a joke, but Billy Thunder or whoever he really was would likely not appreciate the humour, would not understand that the Cree and the Dene were once enemies and still teased and made jokes about each other.

The more Ben thought about it, the more honoured he felt that an Arab man would disguise himself as an Indian. It meant that there were a people more reviled than his people. Someone had said that the Arab in America was in as much jeopardy as the Jew was in Nazi Germany. Ben didn't know if that was true. It might be. The average German did not find out exactly what was going on in the concentration camps until the war was over. Maybe, you never know. That was the thing of it, you never know.

He had found Billy standing at the junction. He looked undecided, like he was not sure whether he was going down the gravel road to the reserve, or up the paved highway to the north. So Ben stopped and asked. "Where you going Bud?"

"To my reserve," Billy answered quickly. He walked across the road toward the driver's side door until he was close enough to get a good look at Ben. "*Tanisi.*" Billy said the Cree word that meant How are you? the way that it was written, instead of the way it was commonly spoken; without dropping the unneeded middle "i". That was when Ben first wanted to laugh but kept his face deliberately stoic, very Indian. "Jump in, I'll give you a ride."

"You live here at Moccasin Lake?"

"Yes, I was just in town to buy some paint for my fence. Here let me get it out of your way." Ben moved the four-litre pail from the front passenger seat to the back.

~

"You are not under arrest, Mr. Robe. There are no charges pending. We merely wish to discuss some matters with you."

"I have nothing to say until you remove this hood."

"The hood is for your own safety, Mr. Robe. When you were found you had a person in your company who gave the name Billy Thunder. What can you tell us about this person?"

"Remove the hood."

"Only innocent people do not have to wear a hood, Mr. Robe. We found an M-37 assault rifle in your dwelling. You are not an innocent person."

"Remove the hood." Ben's voice was as flat as the voice asking the questions.

"Mr. Robe, you attended a clandestine meeting on the farm of Abe Friesen earlier this summer. Do you recall this event?"

"Remove the hood."

"Mr. Robe." The voice beyond the hood might have been a principal speaking to a schoolboy. "Do you understand where you are? Do you know the seriousness of the allegations against you?"

Ben did not answer. He rested against his arms handcuffed behind him, shifted them into the lower part of his back. He knew the answers to the questions, knew where he was. He was in a prison, not far from Moccasin Lake; Prince Albert maybe, more probably Saskatoon at the old correctional centre out in the industrial section. His calculation of time under the hood was limited by his inability to see the sun, but he knew he had not travelled far in the back of the Hummer, bound underneath a tarpaulin, rattled down the gravel highway, then smooth pavement when the throb of diesel engine became a whine of turbo, to here. Here was a correctional centre from the stop and go of their movement when they dragged him in. Stop and wait, held up by his arms, his hands handcuffed behind him, his feet tied together so he could not walk. Stop, wait, listen to the sound of steel doors clang shut behind them, listen to the grind of steel doors open in front of them. Then dragged, one person at each shoulder, arms looped through his, his feet dragged on concrete, carried too low to get his feet under himself to stand, ankles bound together so that he could not walk in any event, and when he tried to stand, while they waited for doors to grind or clang, his feet were kicked out from underneath him. Dragged to here. Here was a table and Ben lay on his back, on his arms, on his numb hands behind him, and the hood kept out the light.

~

"It was your responsibility."

"I gave the prisoners to Ed Tremblay. He captured them. I trusted him." Monica defended herself.

"It was still your responsibility." Councilwoman Betsy Chance sat across the long table from Monica, looked directly at her. Monica stood straight at the narrow end of the table, not quite at military attention, but in a formal pose, stood for this dressing down from the full council. "Council appointed you to look after the prisoners."

Councilman Moosehunter leaned forward slightly to see around the person to his right, so that he could see Monica. "It's not that we really give a damn about whether the prisoner was poisoned, you realize. We're dedicated to killing as many Americans as we can, same as you. The problem lies in two separate factors. First, we traded a prisoner for two of ours, one of those was at your urging. Council went with your recommendation." The person beside him leaned back so that Councilman Moosehunter did not have to lean so far forward. "By poisoning the prisoner you jeopardized all future exchanges. This is very delicate. The process of a prisoner exchange requires a great deal of good faith and it exposes our negotiators to incredible risk. Councilwoman Chance negotiated that transfer for us. Her credibility is now tarnished."

Monica glanced at her friend Betsy who sat shoulders back and stared directly at her.

"The second factor," Councilman Moosehunter continued, "maybe the more critical factor, is that the prisoner was poisoned with yellowcake. The Americans now know for certain that we have it. We've been able to keep them guessing so far. Do we have the material or not? Now they know. Maybe it's a good thing, maybe it was time to let them know that we have it. But, that was for council to decide, not you."

"I was not aware of Ed Tremblay's actions. He acted without my instructions."

"It was still your responsibility." Councilwoman Chance repeated.

"I am not denying my responsibility." Monica stood a little straighter, a little more formal. "I am merely advising council of the facts. I take full responsibility for my actions and ask the indulgence of council once more. Please tell me what council needs done to repair the damage."

Council sat back in unison. Each of the seven looking down the table at Monica. Chairman Booth sipped water from a plastic bottle before he spoke, straightened his glasses to see the length of the table. "We are going to ask you to do something that you might find goes against your sense of loyalty. You will have to decide where your loyalty lies, with this council or with Ed Tremblay."

"I assure council that my loyalty lies here." Monica indicated the table.

"One thing more." Councilwoman Chance turned slightly as she spoke. "Your friend Ben Robe has been taken in. We appointed someone to watch out for him, but our man was obstructed by a neighbour woman."

"Rosie?" Monica guessed.

"Whoever she was, she grabbed our man's gun away from him as he came out of her house. The arrest did not take long. Your friend Robe apparently went willingly, did not resist."

"That is just for your information. You are not to do, or try to do anything more about it." Councilman Moosehunter did not lean forward to speak this time. He did not even bother to look at Monica.

"Should I have the barrel of yellowcake moved from the house?"

"Where to?" Councilwoman Chance spoke in a sarcastic tone.

Monica shrugged, lost for a second. She had never received a dressing down before, did not know how to react. She was determined to stand up, say 'yes sir', 'no sir', 'three bags full sir', 'never complain, never explain', 'take your lumps', 'maintain honour', all those military axioms. Yet she was shaken by Betsy's behaviour. Betsy her friend was a different person from Councilwoman Chance. Councilwoman Chance obviously was not her friend.

"That barrel is in the best place we could find." Chairman Booth spoke quietly, explaining to a five-year-old patiently. "There aren't many houses left with cold war bomb shelters made of a foot of reinforced concrete. That barrel is giving off radiation, radiation that can be detected by satellites. Radiation that can only be stopped by an inch of lead or heavy concrete. As Councilwoman Chance asked you, where do you think we could move it to?"

Monica shrugged again.

"So you realize, Miss, what needs to be done is not to move the yellowcake, but to remove the risk."

"You mean Ed."

"We mean Ed." Councilman Booth stood abruptly; his chair scraped back loudly. "You will cooperate with Councilwoman Chance in ameliorating the problem." The meeting was over.

~

His body was shutting down. Rick did not need Doctor Finlayson's report that his kidneys and liver were failing. He did not need to look at the intravenous tubing stretched to the hum and bubbling machines, did not need to crane his neck to see the digital readouts. He knew, felt the slowing of his life, felt it fade, drip away. The time would come soon when he closed his eyes and would never open them again. He forced them open now, to look around the hospital room, at his mother sitting in the armchair by the window where there was good light. She was keeping her hands busy with her knitting, found comfort in doing, in making. His father would be pacing — the room was too small for him, he needed the hallways, and the little green area outside where patients and visitors sat at plastic picnic tables, ate a sandwich or drank a coffee and smoked cigarettes.

Vicky looked away from her knitting for a second, at her son in the bed, the back raised. He was looking at her. She smiled at him, put down her needles and yarn on the floor beside her.

"You okay, Ricky?" She asked leaning over him.

"As okay as it could be, Mom. Where's dad?"

"He's around somewhere. Do you need something."

"I need lots of things. But nothing you can bring." Rick lifted his hand, the right one, the one without the tube, reached feebly with it. Vicky took it, held it, squeezed it, took it in both of hers, patted it, leaned over and kissed the back of it, smiled down on her son, put as much happiness and kindness as she could find into the smile, but her eyes showed her pain.

"Your dad needs to be on his feet at times like this."

"I know, Mom."

"He never was a man to sit down. He's trying to stand up the best he can."

"I know, I'm trying to stand up too."

"You don't worry about anything, Ricky, you just rest and get better."

Ricky looked directly into his mother's pained eyes. Breathed in slowly. "I'm not going to get better." He was standing up the best he knew how, he was not hiding behind a lie, he was standing straight, honest, like his father. "U238, the doctor said. There's no magic cure. I'm not coming out of this one. I'm not coming home." A tear began at the inner corner of Vicky's left eye, welled out and ran the length of her nose, around the end and hung beside her nostril, bubbled there while she sniffled.

"Don't cry, Mom. Please, that makes it hard."

She took one of her hands away from his to wipe away the tear and snot, breathed in deeply looking for strength in the air, wiped her face with her palm.

"I don't want to die, Mom."

Vicky's tears poured, dripped down her face into her mouth, she tasted salt.

"It's not fair. I should be on the farm." Ricky gasped air between words, sucked it in, whistled it past the plastic tube in his nose. "It wasn't our war. You and me and Dad and Clarice, we never started it, never wanted anything to do with it. You know what we did wrong, Mom?" He waited for her to answer. She didn't, couldn't, her mouth was full of tears.

"We didn't do anything to stop it." Ricky answered for her. "We never stood up to the crazies. Never put them in their place. They came and said that God wanted us to do this and we would not talk against God and we went to war; that's what we did wrong."

Vicky knelt beside the bed, her legs would not hold her up anymore and she could not let go of Ricky's hand. She laid her wet cheek against that young hand, rested her upper body on the starch white bed and poured tears onto the hand.

"Mom," Ricky tugged at his hand to get her attention. "Mom." She looked up. Raised herself on her elbows, found the strength she did not believe she had. Raised herself until she could see his face, his serious young face. "I need you to know something, Mom. It's important." Vicky nodded and wet dripped from her chin with each nod. " I never killed anyone. I never shot anyone. I want you to know that."

"Uh-huh," she dripped more tears.

Rick relaxed back into the pillows, looked toward the tiled ceiling. "I never killed nobody." He sucked in air, hospital air, air that smelled of disinfectant and linen. "I never killed nobody."

~

"You'll have to stay and look after your dad's place." Rosie was standing in Ben's big garden. It was full now, beets were ready, potatoes were beyond bloom and needed another hilling up, the squash were not doing so well, too dry; squash need lots of water.

Benji leaned on the hoe, looked toward the house, at the red truck parked beside it. "I guess, eh?"

"Someone has to." Elsie was thinking of moving the last of her few belongings over from her mother's place. She had only come home for a visit, to see how her mother was doing, had stayed the entire summer. She had no wish to return to the little apartment in Red Deer. There was nothing there that she wanted. It was Bert's apartment, his family would take care of it. Elsie didn't want to go back there, that little life ended with the message that Bert had been killed, ended before it started. It was a false chapter in her life, a promising beginning, not more than a couple of weekends with a soldier home on leave, a pregnancy and emails and phone calls and she promised she would stay at his apartment, look after his stuff, wait for him to come home. She kept her promise, stayed and waited. He did not keep his promise. They sent his coffin to his family in Edmonton. It was a very short chapter that ended in loneliness despite the company of her daughter.

"How long do you think they will keep him?" Benji was not asking anyone in particular. He felt a tinge of guilt at not being there the day his father was arrested; he'd been occupied with Elsie.

"Who knows." Rosie felt the dryness of the soil as she dug for the root of a dandelion. Sandy soil grows good root crops but it doesn't hold moisture. It would be nice to mix in some clay. There was that blue clay up the little creek where her father once killed a caribou, but it was a fair distance even if they used Ben's boat, and how would they carry it?

"Your dad is going to be okay." Elsie picked up Rachel, fingered the dirt out of her mouth, wiped the grit from her face and put her back down on the centre of the old patch quilt.

"I've got that same feeling, like there is nothing to worry about. It's strange. I'm not at all worried about him. Even when I try to imagine the things they could be doing to him." Benji continued to lean on the hoe, felt the heat of the sun on his back through the thin shirt.

"Trust that feeling." Rosie sat on her legs, straightened her back, stretched it out.

"You think it's intuition?"

"You can call it that if you want. You and your dad are connected, learn to trust the connection." Rosie wiped the loose soil from her hands against her dress. "I feel it too."

"But you and him aren't related are you, Mom?"

Rosie turned to look toward her daughter. "No, Ben doesn't have many close relatives left. Most families back then had lots of children, Adolphus and Eleanor only had Ben. They used to gossip about her that she was using Indian medicine for birth control."

"Was she?" Elsie wanted a bit of gossip, even if it was ancient.

"What kind of medicine?" Benji wanted to know what it was made from.

"I don't know if she was or not." Rosie deliberately answered Elsie instead of Benji. Some medicines were dangerous if you let people who didn't know anything use them. The medicine Rosie knew about caused abortions and sometimes sterilization, not something to be given out randomly. The world did not need that medicine anymore, there were enough birth controls and procedures. She looked down at the pile of plants she had pulled from around the row of carrots, weeds some people might call them.

Benji went back to thinking about Ben, put the hoe to the earth again, chopped the little green that grew up between the rows of onions. Yeah, his father was all right. He would take care of things here until he got home. It wouldn't be so bad. He had the house to live in, a good solid truck to use, a boat to go out on the lake whenever he wanted. He was learning about boats, listened to people who knew about crossing big water, how to take the waves on the beam instead of dead on. He had the monthly allowance his adopted parents willed him, a trust until he was thirty.

Benji had not thought about them in a long time, those two people who should have known they were too old to take in a child. Something was different now when they came into his mind. They did not stir the anger. He imagined what they might have said if he had brought Elsie home, Elsie with a baby, an Indian woman and a papoose into the home of a retired diplomat. How would they have introduced their daughter-in-law-to-be to their circle, an all-white circle of elites? Benji could not hold the thought of their possible discomfort. Instead he wondered whether they would like her. Probably, they probably would have liked her, taken her in and made a fuss over her and Rachel, poured tea for her in the middle of the afternoon and offered cookies and little cakes. And

Rachel, well they would have been proud to be grandparents and they would have made good grandparents. He could see them spoiling the little girl with frilly dresses and fancy hats and teaching her to speak English like the Queen. He could hear Joyce calling her princess, and James with her on his lap in the big recliner chair reading her a fairy tale book. Here in the garden, with his hands sore from the wood of the handle of the hoe, the sun on his back and the smell of water from the lake on the little wind, he wasn't angry at them anymore. In a way he missed them, wished they could see him now.

"What was Lester up to the other day?" Elsie asked her mother.

"I don't know what he had in mind. Came out of the house with a gun just when they were putting Ben in that truck. He came running past me. I just reached out and grabbed it out of his hand." Rosie laughed. "He ran another three or four steps before he realized he didn't have it anymore — Rachel is eating dirt again."

Elsie picked her daughter up, brushed the soil from her face and held her wiggly and flailing on her hip. "Don't eat too much of that, my girl."

"Yeah, Ben needs all the soil he has." Rosie pushed herself to her feet. "We really have to do something about this garden. Maybe haul in some peat from the muskeg or something."

Benji leaned on the hoe again. He was beginning to like this long-handled thing. "So, why did you take the gun away from him?"

"What was he going to do? Him with one little gun and all them with machine guns and who knows what else, all he was going to do was get himself killed. I didn't want him to get Ben in more trouble than he was."

"But maybe he could have surprised them, got Dad free."

"Then what?"

"Then Dad would be free."

"No, then they would have sent more men and more guns and more trucks and Lester would have to get a bigger gun, and your dad would have to hide out in the bush for the rest of his life."

"RCMP never chased anyone who went out in the bush." Elsie hoisted Rachel a little. It seemed that gardening was done for now. She picked up the quilt with her free hand.

"No, that's true, they never did. But these aren't the RCMP. Maybe these Americans would go into the bush to look for someone. But even when the RCMP were after someone, they never stayed out there very long. Longest I remember was John James and he only hid out four months. Gets lonely out there." Rosie dumped her weeds onto the compost pile she was starting by the gate and headed toward the house, Elsie and Rachel followed. Benji looked around. No, there was nothing left to put the hoe to. He leaned it against the rail, closed the gate, looked back again at the garden, the freshly painted pole fence that did not keep anything out, at the rows of vegetables and the potato patch that took the whole northeast corner. There was a lot of food in that garden, he thought, as he followed the women. A person could survive off that for a while if they had to.

~

The voice beyond the black hood asked. "Are you a Christian, Mr. Robe?"

"Remove the hood."

"Now, Mr. Robe, we have been through this before. The hood is for your protection. It's a reminder to you that you live in darkness and only when you have accepted Jesus into your life will you see the light."

"So you're going to torture me in the name of Jesus."

"No, Mr. Robe. Nobody's going to torture you. I have a checklist here in my hand and do you know what? There's a little box on it that says Imminent Threat. That box is not checked off. No, Mr. Robe, if that box had a little x in it, you wouldn't be here, you would be somewhere else answering questions for someone else. This is just an interview we're having here, not an interrogation. You have nothing to worry about, all we are going to do is talk. Now, again, Mr. Robe, do you believe in Christ."

"If you remove the hood, I'll tell you about how he was a medicine man."

"A medicine man. Really, Mr. Robe, you don't follow the heathen way of thinking do you?" The voice waited for an answer. Ben waited for him to remove the hood, knew that it was too soon, that it would take much more before he saw the face of the voice, knew also that the voice would give in, knew that he had won the moment he was asked if he was a Christian. In the silence, Ben could hear the sound of metal against concrete, of people moving, talking. This place was never quiet. It echoed every move, every footstep, every human motion bounced and rebounded as though resisting its confinement.

Ben began to dig in his memory, those things he studied, the memory of hours under a coal oil lantern in a cabin just back from the shore of Moccasin Lake. He found the image first, felt the warmth of a woodstove, then he began to retrieve the contents of his study. "In the beginning was the word," it said. Words that are like the sounds that echoed around him, wanting to be free, words, who would be the master of the words? Ben or the voice, or would the words be masters of them?

"Mr. Robe, you were found in the company of a charlatan, an Arab man who was pretending to be an American Indian — do you have a plausible explanation for this?" The voice spoke first and Ben relaxed. He was in a contest of wills and he was winning.

"Remove the hood." Ben's voice was flat, fixed.

"You have not earned the right to see. You cannot see until you find the truth. Tell me what you intended to do with an M-37 assault rifle."

Ben listened to the sounds that echoed through the concrete and cinder block — waited, found his own inner silent place and waited.

"You attended a meeting earlier this summer, Mr. Robe, a very important meeting on a farm not far from here. Can we talk about the presentation you gave? I understand that you impressed a lot of people with your little speech."

"I spoke without a hood."

"Now, Mr. Robe, that is not getting us anywhere. I'll remove the hood when you earn the right to see, until then you and your soul are in the dark."

Ben only heard "I'll remove the hood." Time did not matter. Time was on Ben's side, his friend. His father had given him the gift of time, how to use it, bend it, stretch it, a lifetime of time.

~

Monica checked her watch. Cute, she thought when she bought it, a Swatch, nice bright shiny plastic band, something fun to wear, even fashionable. But, that was a long time ago. Now the hard plastic band wore into her wrist and she wished she had worn a different watch, maybe the one with the cloth bracelet, much more practical for what she planned for today. The planning had been easy. Ed was easy. "Want to go stubble skiing tomorrow? Something different for a change."

"Yeah." Ed let the thought sink in. "Yeah, sure. Haven't done that in a while."

"Abe's farm?"

"No, I want wheat, Canola is too damn hard on the body."

"South quarter was wheat. Heard they took the crop off already."

"South quarter of Abe's farm it is then. That's the one with the rolling hills by the river, right?"

"That's the one."

"Yeah, let's do it." Ed's face had lit up, stupidly she thought now.

Even with the traffic it only took twenty minutes to get to the wheat field. She checked the passenger side mirror. He was still on his feet, leaning hard against the ten-metre towrope tied to the truck, his heavy work boots ploughing up the soil as he skidded an arc. He turned his body against the rope, dug his boots into the earth and crossed back behind the truck again out of Monica's view. She checked the speedometer, forty killometres-per-hour, right where he wanted to be, fast enough to be able to really skim along, slow enough that if he fell it wouldn't hurt too bad. It would hurt, but not that bad.

She noted the knuckles of her left hand — they were white. She was gripping the steering wheel too hard; switched hands, drove with the right as she clenched and unclenched the left for the circulation.

Was she scared?

Maybe she was being set up.

Would Betsy give her away, offer her?

Possibly.

Would council?

She wasn't sure. Council was not pleased with her.

Maybe.

Maybe her fate was tied to Ed's. One at either end of a long rope.

She pushed down on the accelerator, moved the needle up gradually, forty-five, forty-eight. Now Ed was skimming nicely, almost elegantly, as he slashed back and forth behind the truck. She put the truck into a long slow turn. Ed leaned away, dug in the edges of his boots and arced out across the wheat stubble, skidded and gouged the dry earth

She began a turn in the other direction and lost sight of him as he crossed back behind the truck. She checked her watch again before she began to accelerate toward the poplar bluff along the west edge of the field. "Stay on your feet, bastard." She spoke to the mirror as the truck rounded the north end of the poplar. She turned sharply, way too sharp for Ed to make the corner and sent him tumbling across the stubble. He held on to the towrope and rolled through the wheat straw and chaff. He stopped tumbling, found his knees first, then his feet. "Crazy fuckin' woman!" he yelled, wiping the grit from his eyes and mouth. Those were his last words. Two black uniformed Homeland Security officers began firing in unison at the man promised and delivered at exactly 2:00 PM on Thursday, September 18th. Two other men dressed in civilian clothing stood behind the officers, witnesses of the delivery and execution.

Monica drove away without looking back, without looking into the mirrors to see what happened. Her assigned task was complete. She had only to phone Betsy and make the report and that would be two words — "It's done." When she reached the approach to the grid road that would take her first to the highway, then back to the city, she got out, unhooked the rope from the trailer hitch behind the truck and dropped it there, left it lying stretched out in the stubble.

Late that evening, That Jack sent out a revised Spam to a select list of recipients. Included in the garble were the words: "that Edward Riley Tremblay did not survive this day, he will be missed by those who loved him."

~

A hush of wind rose and fell in the big white spruce. It deepened the silence of the boreal where Benji stood and listened to the nothing, the absolute nothing now that his boots no longer clomped the trail. He listened for something, anything, and only heard the sound of his own breathing, his own heartbeat. That's the problem he thought. That's what's wrong. Nobody is making any noise. Ben's beloved forest didn't care that he was arrested, a political prisoner. "Where was the outrage? Where was the indignity of humanity?" Humanity sat comfortable in its own silence, speaking of its own discomfort, not caring about the plight of one man. This quiet, empty land needed someone to scream, to shout and stomp and rage. He would have raised his own rant at the trees, shouted the needed words into the wood and branches, but the forest was stronger than Benji, smothered him in green stillness, siphoned away his hurt and anger and left him muted, with only thought swirling, coming back to the need for someone, anyone to speak out.

He turned on his heel, gouged a hollow in the earth trail, left a mark at his turning point and could not help but listen to the sound of his own feet, heavy on the trail as he plodded back toward the community beside the big lake.

"Thomas, Thomas Larson." Benji spoke resolutely into the phone. "This is Ben Ferguson. James and Joyce's son, James Ferguson remember, from the Foreign Service. You worked with him . . . I'm glad you remember.

"How am I doing?

"Not too bad, not bad at all,

"No I'm not in Toronto anymore.

"Listen, Thomas, I need a favour from you. Are you still with Amnesty International?

"Good, that's good.

"Yeah, I know Tom. I should have stayed in touch. My parents put a lot of faith in you.

"Year-and-a-half ago. Yeah?

"Yeah, she was quite the lady.

"But, Thomas, there's this thing happening here I think Amnesty might want to get on."

⁓

It's better that he is home, even if . . .

Vicky looked over at her son flailing slowly in the hospital bed. Fighting it, she thought, fighting to stay home. Rickie eased a bit, sighed around the hoses, rested. She fell back to her first thought that it was better that he was home even if it was just to die, to slowly die. She didn't have to worry anymore. Since Ricky came home she had not once turned on the news. Not like when he was gone, every morning, first, before she even brushed her teeth or combed her hair, she tuned in, listened for news from Canada, and hoped she never heard it. She lived by the news, trapped by it, unable to break away, in case she missed it, in case they announced something from Saskatchewan and she was away, rushing through the shopping in town, worrying that she would be late home for the six o'clock, staying up, forcing herself to stay awake for the eleven o'clock, and hating it, hating the horrors broadcast, sanitized horror, bombs and guns and Montreal cocktails, torn bodies and black smouldering twisted metal. She wouldn't have to watch that ever again. She could go back to the farm when this was done.

The machine beside the bed beeped loud, steady. Vicky put her knitting aside, and was almost to the bed when the nurse arrived. She must have been standing outside the door. Vicky noticed that she checked the machine first, before Rickie. He was shuddering, his teeth clenched on the plastic tube, his eyes open, staring hard at the dream catcher hung above him, its web to catch the bad dreams, something from the gift shop, the little folded card said the Indians used this, maybe it would help Rickie to rest. Maybe this was just a bad dream caught and struggling. Rickie's shuddering subsided, eased to twitches, his jaw relaxed its clench, he drew in a long rattled breath, and let it go — let go.

The beep became a steady howl, a wail. The nurse slapped a switch and it quit, left Vicky in sudden silence standing beside the bed holding Rickie's hand. What did he see in the dream catcher web? What final image struggled in the strings?

She heard Clarice's sobs behind her, her daughter-in-law-to-be, or never be; felt the grip of her hand clenched to the back of her shirt. Clarice was using Vicky to stand up, pulled at her, would pull her down as her knees weakened. Vicky found the strength to stand against the added weight, gently closed her son's eyes, brushed with the palm of her hand, shut the sight, hoped that it was a good dream that came and carried him away.

It wasn't a full military funeral. There was an honour guard, regal dressed, spit shine shoes, brass buttons, a dozen men to march their son across the close-mowed grass, green still despite the lateness of the season, greener than the surrounding fields. They must have watered it often, Vicky thought, as she followed the honour guard toward the open hole. She looked up, Dean's attention was on the fields, she held tighter to his hand. He'd escaped already. That was not a bad thing. She wished she could join him there. It was lonely here when Dean went away into his mind She put her other arm around Clarice's thin waist, more for the company than to give comfort. The girl was cold, shivering, wobbly on her high heels. She pulled her close, to hold her up and to lean on.

Vicky stood like this through the ceremony of going to the earth, holding her husband's hand to keep him from wandering too far away, holding on to Clarice to hold her, to hold herself up.

Then it was over. The flag and the box and the earth, the march, the drill and they were coming one by one in the closing ceremony of shaking hands with the family members.

"My condolences."

"I'm so sorry, Mrs. Fisher. Your son was a good man."

And they took the hand she needed to hold Clarice with, pumped it twice.

"He served his country."

Just a nod, "Ma'am." Pump the hand and shift over to pump Dean's hand and then wander over to where they grouped, uniformed, taking off their brimmed hats, wiping their brows, shuffling. Vicky watched, wondering what they might be talking about. Not her son she knew, maybe there was still time to gather at a pub later, she suspected.

"Ma'am." The officer in front of her did not let go of her hand after the two pumps. Held it as gently as he could. "Ma'am, I'm sorry that for security reasons the media was not allowed to be here for this."

"That's quite all right." She didn't have the energy left to explain. "We're private people." That was all she had for words. It would take too much effort to tell him her fear that Ricky would become part of the daily diet of horror, an episode, a string of words across the bottom of a screen and somewhere someone would rejoice that it was not their son.

"But I do have some good news, Ma'am. Something to take comfort in."

Vicky looked up at this man who stood in a military stance, feet apart, head high, chest out, so much a part of him that it was his relaxed pose. "The man who poisoned your son was taken care of. He was executed three days ago. I'll have to ask you not to speak to the media about this. The information is very classified. I'm only sharing it with you for your own comfort. Please understand."

Vicky nodded. She understood, but there was no comfort in it. There was no comfort at all in it. She looked over at Dean, but he was gone, maybe he was already back at the farm. "Thank you, officer." She wanted to go home, just go back to the prairie house and look after Dean.

~

Too many years of not doing, of swinging a mop, not with any effort to it, just sloshing the painted concrete floor, too many years of waiting, maintaining, left Lester without the stamina for a full day of physical work. He rested, found reasons to stop, to straighten out the logs piled in the back of the truck rather than join Red and the others hauling them on their shoulders out of the bush. Red was in a good mood, joking, teasing all day, lifted peoples' spirits with his banter. Late autumn, now that the leaves were off the undergrowth, now that the mosquitoes and flies were not so thick, was the best time to cut firewood. Red said it was almost tradition for him. Put up a big pile of wood and then go shoot a moose. Then you could spend the winter with your feet up in front of the fire and eat ribs and brisket.

Lester wasn't so sure it would work out that way, wondered if he would make the winter, wondered if he could find the money for the meds. This work was not bad. Paid a bit, but they sure wanted a lot for a little bottle of green pills. Red could turn this into a real money-maker if he wanted, but Red didn't have any ambition. He only wanted enough for the moment, and enough for Red wasn't enough for Lester.

Short time on the inside, when the sentence is running down, stand away from trouble, stand aside, watch the fights; but keep your record pure, be patient and pure, abide the rules. But short time on the outside felt the opposite. Lester wanted these last months, these possible last months to be worth something, anything. If it wasn't for Rosie he could have had a moment of glory, walked into the face of authority with a nine millimetre and carved a path of fame for himself. Damn Rosie. Then Lester laughed at the memory of it. How he was walking past her, not thinking of her, she was just old ,fat Rosie. But old fat Rosie snatched the gun right out of his hand and he took two more steps before he realized his hand was empty. Then she put it in her pants and how was he going to take it back.

"What's so funny?" Red flipped the log from his shoulder onto the already large pile in the back of the truck.

"Oh, nothing"

"You were sure grinning about something." Red gave the end of the log a flip to roll it over, fill a gap.

"Looks like we might get some snow." Lester looked toward the grey sky.

"Maybe. It's cold enough." Red thought about the possibility, considered the weight of the clouds. They were heavy enough for snow. "We'll get what we have cut off the ground just in case it does snow and bury them, then we can call it a day. I'm feeling a little crappy anyway. Damn cold, just can't seem to shake this one." He sniffled. It wasn't enough and he wiped his nose with the sleeve of his canvas jacket, coarse against the tenderness of his nostrils. "What have we got today? Is this the third or fourth load?" Red was the type of guy who in his enjoyment of working, especially working outside, could lose track of such things.

"Fourth load." Lester wasn't.

"That's not bad." He struck a flame to the end of a cigarette. Lester swung his legs over the side of the truck box and sat on the rail. Looked like they were taking a break. Red wasn't quite ready to stop yet. He took a few drags from the cigarette, handed it to Lester. "Here, finish it." And went back to hauling the last of the logs out of the bush.

⁓

"It's snowing." Elsie watched the first flakes; small, drifting, lazy white specks. "Wonder if it will last." She followed a flake to the ground to see if it melted right away. It didn't. The ground was frozen enough to hold. First of winter. Something new. She was about to turn away from the window when the truck stopped next door at her mother's house, a load of wood sagging its springs. She waited until it came to a spot where she could see through the trees. It was her cousin Red bringing

Lester home. A good thing to know that Red still cut wood. She'd wondered where they might get their winter supply. Ben had a chainsaw and a truck. Benji could do the work. She could help. She would be happy to help, to be outside, physical work, fresh air. But, there was just the thing about Benji and a chainsaw. Grew up in the city. Would he cut his leg off? Or worse.

She turned away from the window, instinctively looked around for Rachel. The little girl had been quiet for too long. It meant she was up to something, and she was. Standing on a chair, trying to reach Elsie's now cold cup of tea.

"Come down from there, my girl. Come on over here and see. Look out the window, see that? That's snow. That white stuff. That's snow, my girl." They stood together and watched it fall. There were more flakes now, and not lazy. The wind picked up and slanted them, gave them purpose and destination. The sight chilled Elsie. She added another block of wood to the steel fireplace. Not that it needed it. Forced it in and shut the glass-screened door. "You stay away from this stove Rachel. It's hot. Don't touch. Hot."

She wished she could build something around the stove. Something to keep Rachel away. But this wasn't her house. It was Ben's. And someday Ben was going to come home. What would he say when he found her here, living with Benji. Shacked up, like they used to say. What would she say? "We were looking after your place for you. Taking care of things." If he ever came home.

She wished she and Benji had their own place, a small warm cabin, built of logs, like the one up the lake where Ben was raised. That would be nice. She could live without electricity, without all the distractions that came with it. But, could Benji? Or was he still too dependent, too modern to ever give up the comforts and ease. Not that there was anything wrong with comfort. She felt the heat of the crackling stove. But some comforts are better than others. Some don't cost your soul so much.

~

"You have mail."

"Mail?" Ben didn't get it.

"Well, not for you, but about you."

The daily interview, at 2:00 PM. The guards came to the cellblock, beckoned Ben to come with them down the concrete hallway to administration, into the office complex where the floor was tiled and the offices had glass in the windows, where coffee and doughnuts scented the air. Someone here liked Tim Hortons. Brought in a half-dozen sugared old-fashioned every afternoon and spread the smell of cinnamon into the otherwise still, dead air.

The interview would last an hour, the same questions, the same answers. "Why an M-37?"

"Because my eyesight is fading."

"That's not the average hunting rifle you have there."

"It works for me."

Ben sat in the chair, kept his feet flat on the floor, never stretched out his legs, never relaxed. The voice had a name now, John Penner, and a face. The hood was negotiated away. "I'll trust you, if you trust me. It's about answers." Ben knew it wasn't about answers. It was about questions. The questions John Penner wanted answered weren't about guns or meetings or the hitchhiker. The daily interview always started with those questions, repetitions, rote to the point of becoming custom. The answers were slight variations of more of the same.

Ben watched the time, the big office clock on the wall in the next office, there where the window let in the light from outside. John Penner came to believe that Ben was looking in that direction because of the light, outside, freedom, believed that it tormented Ben. He liked it that he sat between Ben and that freedom and that Ben had to go through him to get to where he knew Ben wanted to be. He sat in the seat of power, his legs stretched out under the desk.

Always take your time, my boy. Don't rush things. Those old people, when they negotiated the Treaty, they took their time. It was the government people that were in a hurry. Us Indians, we sat and talked about things, all kind of things before they got here. We were ready. We knew what we were going to say. We sat on the ground, on our Mother, got our strength from there. They sat on chairs. It was always the treaty commissioner who tried to hurry things up. Remember that my boy. When it's important. Don't rush. Time is your friend.

Ben had one hour with John Penner. He had the rest of the day to listen to the words of his father. One hour in an office, and then he would sit by the fire in a log cabin, hot tea in his hands, a willing receptor of the wisdom of generations and their stories. Even here, even in this concrete and glass, in this office, he heard his father, heard the slow speech, the short sentences, each filled with importance, never an empty phrase, a wasted word.

"It seems like you have some friends, Mr. Robe."

"I'm sure I have one or two."

"Oh, there's more than two. We're starting to get a little pile of letters, people are writing, saying you're a political prisoner. Are you a political prisoner, Ben?"

"I am a prisoner."

"That's not what I asked. Are you political?"

"Wasn't it George Orwell who once wrote that everything is political?"

"So you admit that you are part of a political movement?"

"I've told you over and over again, John, I am not part of any organized resistance. I speak only for myself."

"Maybe not organized, as you say, but you are resistant."

"I accept that you are here and that you are not going away, that we have to learn how we will live together."

"Good answer, Ben. But between you and me, we know you would prefer that I went home to Richmond. I'd like to go home to Richmond too. Especially now with winter coming on. But, we have things to take care of here first. Satan walks these lands, spreading lies, spreading his hatred of the holy." Ben watched as Penner's hands began to wave the air. The beginning of the rant, the calling down of the wrath of God, the demand for repentance that began with admission of sin. Soon he would be begging Ben to save himself, save his soul from eternal damnation, admit his wrongs so that he could experience the salvation of the lord.

Ben tuned him out. Would not follow him into the circular depths of his rant. Instead he wondered why Penner had told him about the letters. People on the outside were putting on a little pressure. He imagined the content; held without charge, principles of fundamental justice, the rights of humans.

But why tell him?

To give him hope?

Maybe. Probably. Give him hope so that there was something to take away. The problem was that Ben had no hope, had taught himself to not hope. Hope exists for people who never learned to live entirely in the moment. Ben stayed in the here and now.

"Repentance is the path to salvation."

Ben didn't need salvation, or the promise of salvation. His Mother, the Earth, was still somewhere beneath the concrete. His Grandfathers were in the air around him. He didn't need promises of somewhere better. He was home.

"'I am the way, the truth and the light. No man comes unto the Father but by me'." John Penner stared straight into Ben's eyes. "Jesus said that. Know what he meant?"

Ben kept silent.

"He was telling us that the Muslims and Buddhists and Indian spiritualists and Atheists, and all of them are deceived by Satan. There is only one way, Ben. You have to follow the truth and the life."

Ben refused to respond, kept his face calm. He realized in that minute, even though he had thought about it before, the power of a few words. He counted them in his head: *I am the way, the truth and the light. No man comes unto the father but by me* . . . Eighteen words. How many millions have died for so few words? The phrase was the epitome of intolerance. There it was, clean, simple, deadly, perfect. It didn't say go and kill everyone who prays differently than you. Ben couldn't resist. He asked, "What did he mean, he was the truth, the light and the way?"

"That's not important, Ben. The important part is that no man comes unto the father but by Jesus. If you understand that part, then you are on the path of righteousness."

But Ben couldn't stop thinking that he knew a little about the truth, that *the light* was synonymous with *understanding* and that he definitely had a *way* to pray that was humble and honest.

"Do you think Benji could set a net?" Rosie was talking to Elsie, but her eyes were on Rachel. The little girl toddled, holding on to the edge of the cot, her feet unsteady. Going, always going. The little girl had two speeds, flat out and stop: she was either asleep or moving, a handful.

"He could." Elsie forced confidence into her voice. She had never seen Benji set a net, didn't know for certain that he could. "Are you hungry for fish again?"

"Oh, not for me. I could use a big feed of pike, maybe make a fish pie. No, I was thinking about Duchess and her puppies. Whitefish run this time of year, we might want to put up a bunch of fish to feed them over freeze up. Might be a long time until we can set nets through the ice."

"I don't know if Benji can set a net through the ice. His dad showed him how to set a net in open water. But, I don't think he ever saw fishing through the ice."

"That's okay, we can show him." Rosie moved to stand behind Rachel, let the little girl fall against her legs.

"Now, how in the world did you know she was going to fall right then?" Elsie stayed seated at the table, her tea cooling in the cup, no need to move, her mother had things under control.

"Four kids, no help from anyone." Rosie offered an answer that didn't satisfy Elsie, didn't at all explain how. Elsie let it go, one of those things about her mother that she might never understand.

~

Benji pulled the boat up on the beach. Setting the net had not been too difficult, he tangled it a couple of times, it hadn't been a smooth set. But now it was in the water and tomorrow there should be fish in it. He stood for a moment before unloading the gear, a moment to take in his surroundings. It was one of those perfect fall days, crisp; a light wind out of the west that rippled the lake for no apparent reason other than to give the sun something to reflect off of. A large flock of snow geese swirled off the northern horizon, formed patterns, waves that broke and reformed chaotically. Nearby a gull screamed its demand for food, or just yelled for the joy of its own voice in the wind and sun.

Benji noticed a bit of ice on the deck of the boat, it didn't mean much to him, other than the day was colder than it looked. He packed the gear into the back of the truck. No need to put the boat onto the trailer. He would be back out onto the lake tomorrow. He was thinking about a hot cup of coffee with Elsie and Rachel when he put the truck into gear. The rear wheels spun in the sand, the truck bounced up and down. He pushed a button on the consul and the bouncing stopped. Four-wheel drive was such a nice option.

〜

A large black and grey pup jumped at the hanging fish, out of reach. It stood and bent its neck back, blue grey eyes begging. "That fish is for you, but you can't eat it all today." Rosie's soft voice shooed the puppy as she hung another string of fish, a slender, peeled pole pushed through holes cut in their tails, shoulder-high on the drying rack. "These are for winter, little guy — you go eat with your brothers. Benji brought you lots of tasty fish."

She knelt and petted the pup, felt it along its broad chest already muscled, ruffled the fur along its back and its narrower hips. "You're going to be a good size dog in a few months. Before winter is over you'll be big enough to pull." The pup wriggled with the petting, turned and licked her hand. "I'll make you a harness the way my mother used to. A nice one with lots of padding so it doesn't rub. Yes sir, little guy, you are going to become a good-size dog."

"Having trouble, my girl?" Rosie returned to the gutting table under the pines where Elsie struggled with a knife.

"Just this part gives me a hard time. How do you get the little bones out."

"Here, I'll show you again, just run your knife along here." Rosie started a cut down the inside of the pike fillet. "Well, here is your problem, your knife is dull." She ran the edge of the knife against a honing steel hung with a string from a branch. A half dozen quick strokes and she handed the knife back to Elsie. "Try it now."

"Benji did good. I didn't think we'd get this much out of one net." Elsie's knife found the line, made the shallow cut the way her mother showed her, felt the click of it against the line of tiny bones, another cut above the first line and a sliver of flesh fell away. Elsie held up a perfectly boneless fillet.

"Pretty good," Rosie agreed as she prepared the next string of fish. She watched Elsie without being intrusive, let the girl learn, even though Elsie was leaving way too much fish on the bones. She had to do it to learn it. Rosie prepared the fish that would go to the dogs and let her daughter prepare the fish for the frying pan.

∼

The wind died overnight. The water calmed, Benji slept content in the silence.

∼

"Rosie said we had enough yesterday. I should have listened. But man we were catching good, I just wanted one more lift, just one more." Benji tugged against the boat frozen into the lake.

"That's the way it goes." Red agreed. He was happy to answer cousin Elsie's phone call, *I need a favour, cuz.* He looked out across the frozen bay. "Where's your net set?"

"Off Willow Point."

"That part still looks open, lucky thing. It's hell chopping out a frozen net."

"If the boat isn't buggered up."

"It's not the boat you have to worry about. A little chopping and we'll have that out. You left the motor down. If there was any water in that gear housing, it'll bust sure as shit."

~

Elsie helped Benji to hang the net. "You've had quite the day."

"You can say that again. If it wasn't for Red we'd be in real trouble. He not only helped to get our boat up onto shore. He chopped ice for about fifty metres so that he could get his boat out to open water to go rescue this net."

"Red's a good guy."

"I like his attitude. Know what he said about the motor? 'Well good thing it happened today, now you have until spring to get the parts.'"

"So, how bad is the motor?"

"Broke the housing around the gears and the water pump is shot. I should have known better. It's not like Dad doesn't have enough going on right now without me wrecking his stuff."

"Don't worry about it, it's just stuff." Elsie hung the last of her side of the net on the peg, turned, and wrapped her arms around Benji from behind.

He turned back for the kiss on the cheek he knew was coming. "Dad might not think of it as just stuff."

"Like Red said, you have till spring to fix it." Elsie hugged him tighter.

~

"'I am Alpha and Omega, the beginning and the end, saith the Lord, which is, and which was, and which is to come, the Almighty'." John Penner nearly screamed.

Ben thought about this simple linear construct of time. It wasn't at all relevant to his experience; he let the thought go, let it drift out into the cyclical universe that Ben chose to exist in.

Penner was in the middle of his daily rant, and Ben knew from experience not to push his buttons. Penner's vomit of words excluded rationality, excluded Ben, excluded even Penner himself. The words poured, spewed, angry and raw. This wasn't a preacher bent on conversion. This wasn't a teacher explaining. This was hate wrapped in gospel, hate warped by gospel. Hate that surfaced and subsided quickly. Penner stopped. Briefly the interview room fell silent. He looked directly at Ben and asked. "Do you believe in Democracy?"

Ben hesitated, looked for the trick in the question and decided it would be safe to answer "Yes."

"That is absolute foolishness. Democracy is the work of Satan. Satan puts ideas into men's heads to lead them away from the Kingdom of Jesus. There is only one rightful government. That is the government of God. Jesus came here to create his kingdom on Earth. It is his kingdom that we should be working to create. Not our, or your kingdom, Ben." Penner's voice changed. It became a pleading. "Do you honestly believe we could create a kingdom on Earth that would be superior to

Jesus' kingdom? Do you believe that man is better than God?"
He didn't give Ben an opportunity to answer. "Of course not.
Now you are asking, what would this look like, this kingdom
of Jesus on Earth? Well, let me tell you. It would be Christian
Totalitarianism. Mao had it right, even Hitler knew what he
was doing. God chose those men. He chose them to get the
world ready for the day when he puts his kingdom back on
Earth."

For the remainder of the interview Ben sat and listened to
the words of hate, the words that were part prayer, part calls
for help, part confession (though this had to be read in) and
part demand for the damnation of everything not Godly.

~

The chainsaw screamed in Benji's hand; he concentrated on
Red's instructions. "Cut out a wedge on the side you want the
tree to fall toward. Then when you make the back cut, don't
cut all the way through, leave a little wood, that's what you
use to steer with." The standing dead pine was a nice size. A
good tree to learn with. Red stood back and watched Benji fall
his very first tree. Eighty feet, at least eighty feet. Red looked
toward the heavy crown where dwarf mistletoe cancered
the ancient tree, rapid growth, branches twisted into thick
brooms. The disease clustered in stands of pine, leaving dead
wood for insects, and the birds that feed off them and easy
fire wood for people like Red who still enjoyed simpler though
harder ways of living.

Red didn't notice the change in colour of the sawdust, from
white to orange brown sprayed out onto the thin covering of
snow. He was looking toward the crown, feeling pride in Benji,
a good sized tree for his first. Fall a tree like that and a person
couldn't help but to feel proud of himself. Neither of them

knew about the ants. Big carpenter ants that ate away the tree's core, left a honeycomb labyrinth at the centre. The little wood that Benji was to use to steer the tree with had no strength. The big pine leaned, twisted on the cut at its base and slowly began to fall. Red saw it first. The tree was coming toward them. He grabbed Benji's shoulder, pulled and stepped aside. They stood still and watched the tree pick up speed. Benji screamed a silent "*No!*" when he realized where the tree was going. "*No!*" his heart sank "*Please No!*" The top of the tree hit the cab of Ben's truck where the passenger door met the roof, smashed glass and warped metal, the weight of two hundred years growth and the inertia of coming to earth drove the tree until the roof of the truck touched the seat. The steel frame under the cab bent, then held, snow caught in the branches and released in the fall flittered down for a few more seconds, then everything was still and quiet.

⌒

"You were trying to do something good. You were getting wood to keep me and Rachel warm for the winter." Elsie hugged Benji tighter. "Don't be too hard on yourself. Your dad will understand, you were trying to do something good."

⌒

"Happy birthday, Lester." Rosie hoped to lift his spirits.

"How'd you know it was my birthday." Lester lifted his head and a bit of one shoulder from the couch.

"I remembered when you were born. Your mom came over to our house to ask for a ride to town. December first. I think she came to her big sister's house, half expecting my mom to midwife for her. But in the end we took her to the hospital instead."

"You got a good memory, Rosie." Lester let his head rest back on the softness of the overlarge couch, let the foam and fibre swallow him.

"I remember when she brought you home too. She pretty much lived with us that winter."

Rosie's memories drew Lester backward through time. "Where was my dad?" he wondered, looking upwards at the tile of the ceiling.

"Work. Cutting pulp. Something, I'm not sure. Only home on weekends. During the week, your mom stayed with us." She remembered the baby and the fussing. It was her first experience up close with a baby, a young girl trying to be a part of this woman thing that was happening between her mother and her aunt. She was playing with dolls with her aunt again, and the doll was wriggly baby Lester. "Anyway, that was a long time ago." Rosie suddenly felt uncomfortable, talking about her aunt with the man who murdered her. She came back to the present. Lester on the couch with a bad cold. A cake in the oven. Not one of the big cakes she used to make for her children, she was a little short on ingredients, just a little something because it was his birthday and he was sick. Cake and a little kindness can be good medicine.

~

Winter, again, another cycle of the great wheel. We count winters because they are the most memorable. Ben wondered if he would spend this entire winter indoors. What would be his memories? This cell, concrete and steel, not so different from the winters in the university; thinking, re-gathering, ordering thoughts, finding the order that organizes chaos. The cell was not so different from his university office; windowless, cinder block cold, only his body confined, now by guards, then by exam schedules, his mind free as ever to fly, to find the truth in itself, or out there in the snow and wind, flying above the boreal of his home, or walking the ancient trails. Ben walked often with his father, listened again to his stories, spent hours in front of a warm fire again and reheard the wisdom. The thick of winter, silent, smothered in hip deep snow, when the magpie circled the cabin looking for scraps, the storyteller, just through the window: *"The people moved around lots back then, whenever you wanted, pack your tent, harness your dogs or make a new birchbark canoe. I knew whenever my dad made a new canoe, as soon as it was finished we'd move again. It was like a new canoe was a good reason to move."*

Ben had been reading history; stories about Indians who moved to be closer to the missions, the priests, the documentation of conversions, and asked his father. *"The truth, my son, is that some people did move to the missions. But a lot more moved away. That's why we're here. Your grandfather moved away from the Churchill River because there were getting to be too many Christians up there. He came here. Strange though, I met a young man a while ago. He was from that Churchill River area. Out travelling, the way young men are supposed to, came back to see the land of his grandfather, the Thunder Hills. Seems, that old man moved away from here for the same reason, to get away from the Christians. You know, you hear how we used to banish people. Even Chief and Council nowadays want to banish people. Got a drug dealer they don't know what to do with and they tell the court to banish that person, kick him off the reserve. That's not how it used to be up here. Maybe in the South they did that. But up here, there was lots of room. People could move. What happened most often if a person was acting up, didn't get along with everyone else, well, the people would move, leave that person behind. That's a good way to do things. Banish somebody and you make hard feelings, and things were hard enough before. Make a hard decision like that and you make a hard thing harder. But now we can't do that anymore, the land is all taken up. Did you know they cut lines around the reserve to mark the boundary? As if the reserve wasn't too small as it was, the government paid to cut lines, wide ones all the way around, I think just to rub it in. 'You Indians stay there' and what are the people going to do when someone acts up, what choice do they have? They have to move to the city."*

Ben left his father, reached down and touched his toes, both hands, slowly, stretched out the back muscles, felt the tightness in his lower back resist the stretch, pushed through the resistance; and again, straightened and bent, this time a little slower as he bent through the range of muscle tightness. He bent his knees, squatted and rose, listened to the leg muscles speak to him through his bones. Then, he began his push-up routine, not worried about the count. There was nothing important about one hundred, that was a number, a favourite number of the younger men, a hundred push-ups at a set, repeated several times a day. Ben was thankful for them, their dedication inspired him, reminded him, mind, body and spirit all need attention. He repeated the motions, push slowly up, feel the muscle, experience the ache as tight becomes loose: push slowly up, the burn of the rise felt different than the pain of the slow, controlled down. Repeat, listen to the body, push against the pain beyond the pain of yesterday, beyond where he stopped last time, forced another, one more push-up and then down, then relaxed, lay for a moment on the hard concrete floor of the cell, remembered that Mother Earth, the great grandmother was there under the cement and stone. He laid in her arms for those last few moments before lights out and felt her comfort.

~

"Did you laugh?"

"I couldn't, you had to see his face. I wanted to. It was hard not to. His first tree." Red shook his head, "His very first tree. It looked like he was going to cry."

"I would've laughed anyway."

"I know you would, my dear." Red brushed his wife's hair away from his face, it tickled his nose. He slid his arm under her pillow so as not to pull her long loose hair, intent on drawing her close. He missed in the dark, put his arm inside of the pillowcase, fumbled until he realized why he was unable to hug her, pulled his arm out and tried again. Lorraine snuggled against her rail-thin husband, ran her free hand down his back, felt the cool of his skin. She rolled away onto her back, looked up toward the ceiling. The night was young, lots of time yet for talk.

"You should have laughed at him. I know he's mostly white and doesn't get it yet. But he has to learn sometime. Know what I mean?"

Red ran his hand over Lorraine's stomach, made another circle, then stopped, let his palm absorb the warmth. "If you'd seen his face."

"I know, you said that already. But," she put her hand on top of his before he could begin circling again. "But, if you laughed at him, laughed right away, maybe he wouldn't've taken it so seriously."

"I didn't want to see him cry." Red defended himself.

"I know you didn't. You were trying to be kind." She pressed his palm against her belly. "That's the way you are. All

I'm saying is that it might have been kinder in the long run to have laughed at him right away, instead of letting him feel bad, know what I mean?"

"Yeah, I guess."

"Know what?" she held his hand from moving, kept it from making the circles again. "You should take him hunting."

"Aow." It sounded like a sigh.

"No seriously." She kept him from drawing his hand away. "Think about it."

"I am." It wasn't a good thought.

"Somebody has to teach him."

"I know, but why me? That's a lot of teaching." Red remembered the way Benji clomped when he walked.

"Somebody taught you."

"That's different. I didn't grow up in a city."

"Not his fault, take him with you. It won't be so bad." She moved his hand in a little circle, enjoyed the feel of the rough of the callus and the cool of his palm.

"You don't know what you're asking."

"It won't be so bad." She rolled over onto her side again, drew Red close. "It won't be so bad." She whispered into his ear, felt his palm climb her spine.

～

"Collaborators?"

"Yeah, collaborators."

"No, Betsy." Monica did not like where this was going. All she wanted was a nice dark roast coffee, a little demerara sugar, very little, just enough to counter the bite of the coffee, and conversation with a friend. Then Betsy had to start talking like this. They should have been talking about anything else, the weather even. Snow was swirling out the window of the

Roastery. They used to come here and sit for hours Saturday mornings and discuss political ideas, or listen to the chatter at other tables. "That won't get us anywhere." Monica wanted the conversation to go in another direction, or stop. "If we start hitting our own, they'll turn against us."

"If we don't hit them, and hit them hard, the people will follow who they think are the strongest. Strength Monica. We have to show that we're strong. Otherwise we become insignificant. They have to learn there's a cost to doing business with the enemy."

"But they're our own people. Remember Ben, he always said that the people were ultimately in control. Even in a tyranny, the people decided at some level to live with it, made the choice, whether consciously or not, to accept where they were. Without the people we will never succeed. Start hitting collaborators and we lose. That's the path to our own end."

"Your rationalizations start out correctly enough, the people are the key to final success. But we are losing them, every day, more and more, they're lining up for the easy money. We don't have the money, we can't compete. We teach our children not to take candy from a stranger, and when they dig in the cookie jar too often we slap their hands."

"You're not talking about slapping some kid's hand here. Agribition, that's been around for probably a century."

"And they've always collaborated with the Americans. What do you think Agribition is about? It's about selling beef to the devil."

"Oh, it's more than that. Farmers from the whole country come to show off their stuff, not just to the Americans. Lots of people from Europe come to it."

"Used to come, Europeans used to come. Not anymore. Now it's about supplying the bastards with T-bones, giving the fat of the land to the new master."

"Maybe, but I can't stop thinking that if we hit them, the people will turn against us and we need them." Monica looked to the snow, watched it swirl. They sat at a corner table, each with their backs to respective walls. The tables near to them were empty. Maybe it was the snow that kept people away. Maybe it was something else. Monica did not want to talk about this. The thought of security might have been a good reason to bring it to a stop, but they had talked here before, made plans, successful plans. Homeland Security could not listen to everything, all the time. The Roastery was as safe a place to talk as anywhere else, maybe safer. It had a proven track record. She tried another approach. "Has council thought this through?"

"As far as you need to know, I am council."

"I'm not doubting." Monica ran a thumbnail under a fingernail, nervously, realized what she was doing and stopped. She reached for her coffee, not because she wanted it, just to give her hand something to do, something that did not show Betsy that she was in anyway nervous, or distrustful. This was a first, this feeling, this sense, a sense of doubt, and doubt was dangerous. It led to fear. If Betsy was acting alone on this, Monica could not go directly to council, could not go around her, ask her superiors. That would be insubordination and the insubordinate, undisciplined did not survive long. She remembered Ed Tremblay.

"On a final note, I have some good news for you."

"What might that be?" Monica was thankful for the topic shift.

"We found Ben."

"Where?" Monica leaned forward with the word, closer to hear, pulled by the promise.

"He's here."

Monica waited for the rest of the good news, wordless.

"He's here, in Saskatoon." Betsy fed a little more.

Monica waited.

"At the correctional centre."

"Not Dakota Max." Monica sat back.

"No, he's here."

"Then he should get a hearing and be allowed a lawyer, everything else." Monica spun possibilities.

"Not necessarily." Betsy enjoyed feeding Monica little morsels of words.

Monica waited for more. It didn't come. They sat in silence a moment. Monica looked out the window at the gliding snow, let her mind go out into the city to look for Ben.

Betsy looked at Monica, weighed her, weighed her strength, didn't find any weakness and fed her the remainder. "Ben never went to Dakota Max. He's been here all along under psychological review."

"But what does that mean?" Monica came back into the Roastery, looked into Betsy's face, a long, hard face with new lines around the mouth adding to the old lines that were becoming deeper.

"Don't know. Usually politicals get sent south and the correctional centre is used for criminals. Don't know what they're up to. Maybe psychology is the new word for torture. Maybe they don't have enough on him. Maybe Dakota Max is full. Who knows."

"Maybe we can get him out."

"A jail break."

"Why not?"

"Because, my girl, Ben is small potatoes. He doesn't know anything. Council will never authorize it, and even if they did, then what? Ben goes into hiding. He goes to the bush. We have hundreds out there now, just here, under local authority. Imagine there must be thousands across Canada hiding out there. Great thing about Canada, we still have lots of bush. In the summer it's not bad, kind of a picnic, an outdoor adventure. But now with winter, everyday we have people showing up, hungry, frozen, begging council for a place to stay, a blanket, a bed. Hell, we even have people turning themselves in because they think jail is better. At least it's warm."

"Not Ben. Ben can survive out there."

"So much faith. In a way it's good to see. It's good to see faith in something. But, I think you're putting it in the wrong place. Ben is an old man, he doesn't know anything, he can't do anything. He is just not a priority. Not for council and probably not for Homeland Security. Give them a little more time and they'll figure it out for themselves. Then you're beloved Ben can go back into retirement, fade away into the bush."

"Maybe." Monica looked out the window again, the snow was getting heavier. "Maybe, but I still think that he knows a way out of this."

～

Elsie stood with her back to Benji, felt the smooth round of the log on her palm. She leaned against the wall, not for support, it was her stance: she touched the wall beside the window for the sensation of its solidness, its security, as she looked out at the snow on the pines, building on the ground, becoming deep. "Mom's alone over there." She spoke more to herself than anyone.

Only Benji heard her. "Where's Lester?"

"Medevac yesterday. Mom helped him walk to the clinic. They took one look at him and put him on an ambulance to Prince Albert." She turned to look at him, "It doesn't look good. Pneumonia."

"Pneumonia's not a big deal. A couple of days rest, some antibiotics and he'll be back."

"It's not a big deal unless you have AIDS."

"Lester has AIDS?" Benji put the book down.

"Thought you knew."

"No. I thought he was just being lazy. Red needs him to work and he keeps staying home. I thought he just had a cold." Benji spun thoughts, rapid thoughts, a blur of experiences with Lester. Had he ever had an open wound when Lester was around? Had he ever drunk out of the same cup, shared a bottle of water? His thoughts slowed to a stop without finding anything, realized the senselessness of his fear. "Is he going to be all right?"

"Don't know." Elsie turned to slide a chair away from the table; she wanted to sit and watch the snow fall. She never got the chance. The chair scraped against the floor. The sound woke Rachel. She had been asleep for over an hour. Wore herself out, little legs that have just learned how to walk tire easily. The little girl fell asleep on her blanket spread on the floor, across a cushion she had pulled from the couch. Elsie had found her and put her on the bed. The floor was too cold a place for little ones to sleep.

A north wind hammered down the length of Moccasin Lake, flew full force into the tiny community at the south end, brought with it any loose snow and piled it in the willows along the shore. It shaped drifts, then reshaped them, created its own abstract art forms: lines and swirls, depths and hollows — piled snow in one place for no other reason than it chose to, and in others exposed the naked black ice.

Cut by the pines around Ben's cabin, the wind lost some of its force before hitting the solid logs. It tried to find any loose chinks, a place where insulation was thin. Thwarted, it passed, without looking back where it would have seen Elsie standing in the window, her daughter held on her hip with one hand; the other against the wall, drawing strength in the middle of the storm. She was looking south toward her mother's house.

"I love you." Benji put his arm around her waist; stood beside her, pulled her close so they stood hip-to-hip, thigh-to-thigh, rib cages pressed together.

"I love you back." Elsie turned from the window to kiss his cheek, a gentle brush of lips against bristle.

Benji sought what Elsie was watching. All he saw was snow, swirls of it, skittering across the spaces between the trees, piling into, onto itself. He soon tired of it, could not capture whatever it was that had captured her, could not comprehend that she appreciated the power of the storm, the power of those forces that shape and form everything.

Red's truck ploughed through the drift that was forming across the driveway, cut two parallel tracks up to the house. Elsie and Benji watched as he walked, head bent away from the wind to the door.

"Want to go hunting?" he asked as soon as he was inside.

"Today?" Benji wasn't sure.

"Best time. Good wind."

Benji looked back toward the window, at the swirls on the other side of the glass.

Elsie figured this out, saw what was happening. If Red wanted to go hunting today, there was a reason, probably a good reason.

"You should go," she urged. "Get us some moose meat."

"Why today?" Benji wanted to know.

"He can't smell us coming. Best hunting weather. We can walk right up to him if we do it right. Come on, I'll show you." Red was excited, in a rush, his words as fast as his thoughts.

~

"You guys all need names." Rosie scraped leftovers from a plate onto the ground. Six half-grown dogs scrambled, nosing each other aside to get at the bones and scraps. "Here Duchess, saved a piece for you." She tossed a bit of meat aside for the mother, then stood and watched the action. If Ben was here, you guys would be in harness by now, earning your keep." She thought about what she had just said. The words had come before the thought. If Ben were really here, then he would need harness and a sleigh. She could make harness. That was easy. She needed snaps, rings, nylon strapping, something for padding so the harness did not cut into shoulders. Six dogs, she counted, imagined freight harness, not bad, only a dozen snaps and rings, it was do-able. The sleigh, that was a different matter. Her dad used to make his own, bent birch runners, a frame tied together with rawhide or sinew. It needed to be sturdy and flexible. Someone has to remember how to make a sleigh. She couldn't think of anyone alive anymore who would know how. She remembered all of the steps. Her dad had built his inside the house; boiling water to bend the hand-hewn boards, a drawknife leaving piles of shavings on the floor. It wasn't that she had watched him build sleighs; it was that he had done it in front of her so many times that she absorbed it.

She thought it all through again. She could make harness. That was easy, a little sewing. Could she make a sleigh? The hard part would be getting the right tree. Now was a good time to cut it, winter when the sap was all drained away, the boards would be half dry to start with. Red. Yeah, Red, he could get her the wood, probably cut it into boards too. Rawhide and sinew — someone needed to kill a moose. Rosie was beginning to feel chilled. She went back into the house, now with a purpose, not to watch television.

She gave her house a thorough cleaning, not that it needed it. She needed the movement. Lester's duffle bag behind the couch was half open, the leg of a pair of jeans hung out. She stuffed it in and zipped the bag. Everything he owned was in there. Not much. She lifted it, checked its weight, was about to put it back where it had been since early summer and realized, "Lester isn't coming home."

She stood a moment, holding the bag, half bent over. She straightened. No, he wasn't coming home. She put the bag in a closet, made room for it on the shelf, then reconsidered the sudden thought. It came to her as soon as she had touched his bag, his things. Lester was not coming back. No, that wasn't it. She had thought, Lester is not coming home. This had been his home, Lester's home. Now it wasn't anymore. But he wasn't going to die homeless. She took the bag down from the closet shelf and gently put it back behind the couch.

～

"Hurry it up, you old fuck. Against the wall."

Ben did not hurry any more than he had before. This was routine. Against the wall, hands spread on the cinder block. That's all he has, Ben thought. All he has is that I am older than him.

Even the shove between the shoulder blades was routine now. The hands patting, feeling through the coveralls, striking; chest, belly, thighs, ankles, looking for a shank, contraband, drugs. An excuse to hit, even with an open hand, is still an excuse to hit, to demean, punish, force a hand into the crotch, grab, exercise power.

Ben turned his head, looked over his right shoulder. She stood aside, watching the male guard, the one without hair and a belly that pushed against the black shirt, with the hands that hit when he searched. Her face tried to hide what she felt; a brown face, frozen, flat, cold. It was trying to say, "I am doing my job." But it wasn't. It mumbled something else, something quiet. How did she feel? Ben wondered. Collaborator. Her hands were on her belt, the right one near the holster with the pepper spray. "I am doing my job." Her feet were spread, ready, her back straight, her neck straight, her eyes straight, the crease that ran down the front of her legs, straight, stiff, starched. Everything said "I am doing my job" except the eyes. The black, intelligent eyes said something else, they said "I am doing my job, but I don't like it. I don't like to see old people pushed around. I especially don't like to see old natives, Elders treated without respect."

There was no real strength in the hands that hit. These were the hands of a man who never had to work, never used an axe or a shovel; maybe at one time they lifted weights in a gym, but today the memory of the steel bar was distant. Ben noted the feel of the hands the same as he noted the belly. It was not a belly that bulged. The male guard did not know that it was noticeable. He thought it was hidden under the black shirt, covered. Mostly it was, but the shirt touched the roundness just above the wide belt. Ben imagined a puppy with worms, its weakness exposed by a round hard belly.

She walked at Ben's left, he walked on the right with his hand constantly on Ben's shoulder, steering, commanding. A buzzer sounded a long second before the steel door slid noisily to the right, clanged when it was fully open. The hand shoved, pushed Ben through the door that he was ready to walk through on his own. The strength of the push did not come from the arm. It came from the man's waist. Ben noted, stored the memory. The guard with the belly used his weight to compensate for his lack of muscle, a dangerous practice; weight needs balance, unbalanced weight can be toppled. She had balance. Ben watched her feet, watched her walk beside him, watched how she stepped, set her feet down toe first, then rest on the heel. She also had strength, more than muscle. She had the strength to stand still and watch a bully push an old man around; even though it went against everything she had ever learned.

She opened the door to John Penner's office. Ben walked through. The male guard did not push, did not put his hand between Ben's shoulder blades. Ben noted that the bully in him was too much of a coward to act in front of a superior. The door shut behind him with a thump. Wood makes a different sound than steel. The office was slightly different. Ben looked around. The desk, bare, was in the same spot, as was the chair he would sit in. The difference was on the wall. A single framed diploma now hung on the panelling. University of California, Berkeley, Bachelor's degree in psychology. Penner saw Ben read it.

"Yes, Ben. I went into the den of Satan and took that away as a trophy. I matched wits with the liberals and in the end they were forced to concede that God might exist."

"Berkeley is a noteworthy school."

"Berkeley is the home of Satan. He walks those halls and his minions bow and grovel. It is the ultimate denial of the holy."

"So why did you go there?"

"Like I said. I went into his den and walked out with a trophy."

"Psychology."

"A degree in the art of denial. Know your enemies, Ben, always know your enemies more than you know your friends. Don't put any trust in that piece of paper, my friend. I assure you I am not who it says I am. The only reason it is up there is because someone in this organization has succumbed to the liberals' propaganda that we are not qualified, and now we have been reminded in a memo to nail our credentials to the wall."

John Penner has a superior, Ben thought, as he took the familiar chair.

"Something you asked the other day got me thinking." John leaned his elbows on the desk and stared into Ben's face, looking, always watching for the opening, waiting for Ben's face to betray him. It didn't. Ben waited.

"You asked me how many trees are in the Bible."

"So, How many are there?"

"Quite a few. Of course the ones that jump immediately to mind are the Tree of Knowledge and the Tree of Life in Genesis, that, and of course we refer to Jesus being hung from a tree, but I was amazed at the number of references to fruit trees, fig trees, the tree that is pleasant to the sight, people sitting under trees, cedar trees, the tree that Moses threw into the water of Marah so that the people could drink." John leaned harder into the back of his chair, felt the metal dig into his shoulder blades, enjoyed the discomfort. This was not going to be comfortable. He flipped over a single sheet of paper, turned it scribble side up on the desk and read: "Psalms 96:12. Let the field be joyful, *and* all that *is* therein: then shall all the trees of the wood rejoice. Isaiah 14:8. Yea, the fir trees rejoice at thee, *and* the cedars of Lebanon, *saying*, Since thou art laid down, no feller is come up against us."

Ben noted that John did not use his memory.

John continued. "Isaiah 55:12. And all the trees of the field shall clap *their* hands. Chronicles 16:33. Then shall the trees of the wood sing out at the presence of the Lord."

He turned the sheet of paper over and continued, "The burning bush of course was a tree. So, I see what it was you were getting at Ben."

"And what was that?"

"Don't be a smart ass. I get it. You asked me how many trees are in the Bible to get me to think about God and nature. Nature, that's your thing." John leaned forward, elbows on the desk. "Like I said, I get it; references about trees rejoicing, trees singing. Yeah, trees are in the Bible in a big way, and yeah, trees are an important part of the story, a part of the story that scholars tend to miss. You showed me that there are things about the Book of God that you know more than I do." John sat up straight. "You win that round, I concede. You have a unique understanding. You know something that I didn't."

Ben didn't like where this was going. John was working himself up for something. This thing about trees was not about bettering him, it was to give him something to think about, to consider in his interpretation of his ultimate authority. John had accused him of worshiping trees;

Ben had just wanted John to know that John's God also had an affinity for the forest nations.

The door opened and the two guards re-entered the office, the guard with the belly came in first, she followed.

"Handcuff this bastard." John stood, kicked back the metal chair, it scraped against the floor.

She held him by the right shoulder, he held the left, it was his weight that pushed Ben face down on the desk, his left cheek pressed into the fibreboard finish. He could see her, felt one of her hands on his elbow, the other on his shoulder. She gripped his shirt, a solid grip, different than the hand on his other shoulder. That hand was flat against his back and pressed down, hard.

The opening of the drawer vibrated through the desk. Ben felt it in his cheek and the slam of its closing. John held a screw in front of Ben's face, about an inch long between thumb and forefinger. "See this, asshole, wonderful technology, self-tapping. That means that I don't have to drill a hole first. This little beauty will bore itself into solid metal. Screw with me and I'll screw with you."

Ben fought down the fear. Breathed, drew in a chest full against the pressure on his back. The screw pulled hair with the first twists, tore them out by the roots. It ripped through the skin without effort and began to bite into the bone of Ben's skull. Pain has colour. This was brilliant white with orange and yellow flashes, bright to the point of blinding. Pain has heat. The fire began above Ben's right ear and spread around his head, flamed through to the desk and danced down his spine. Pain has sound. Ben heard the bloodrush, heard the roar, heard the scream of it in his ears. It wasn't his scream. He was too busy breathing. Bringing in air to put out the fire.

John Penner wasn't thinking about God as he torqued the screwdriver. This had nothing to do with grace, the right way to pray, the wrong way to pray, which direction to send the prayer. This was about John. Simple. This had nothing to do with Sodom and Gomorrah, though John could tell you every sin ever alleged to have occurred there. This had nothing to do with Canada, or God Bless the United States of America. This wasn't political, secular. This was simply *Don't fuck with John Penner*. This came from the idea that Ben was screwing with John's head, and now John was screwing with his.

He didn't taste the bile in his mouth, or feel the throb of his own headache. That would come later, when Ben was carried back to the cell block and John sat alone at the desk, gasping, gagging. Then he would absorb the bitter acid at the back of his mouth, across his tongue, coat his teeth; teeth clenched until his jaw ached and pain throbbed in his temple. When he unclenched his jaw and the tension in his arms, so strong that he shook, drained away with the sweat from his chest and his throat, then John would realize what it was that he had done, even though he had planned it, every detail of it, from putting the screwdriver and screws in the desk, to arranging for the guards to return exactly two minutes after they shut the door; now the full realization hit him, hit him hard that Ben did not scream, or beg. When the guards stood him up, it wasn't fear in his eyes, it was pity. Ben stood against the pain, breathed hard against it, and felt sorry for little John Penner.

Ben walked between the two guards, held his head up and breathed, drew in air, deep, held it, pressurized his lungs, released the air for room to draw in another deep breath. The pain tried to pull his head down. He held it up to keep his air passage open for the cooling air against the fire in his skull.

He felt a tug at his right shoulder. She was pulling at him, turning him toward the hallway in her direction.

"No, this way." The guard with the belly pulled at Ben's left shoulder.

"The infirmary is this way." Strength in her voice.

"We weren't told to take him there."

"We weren't told not to."

The guard with the belly was confused, off balance, even though he stood flat footed. She turned Ben. He breathed and followed. The guard with the belly caught up, took Ben by the left shoulder again, but now he wasn't leading, he was following.

John Penner opened the computer, looked into the camera that read his retina, identified him, and gave him access. His shaking subsided as he entered information onto the form.

The subject complies with all requirements. His attitude toward authority is within the normal range. Release recommended.

He read the form over again. It felt right. It felt like redemption. He pressed his right forefinger to the little scanner at the bottom corner of the keyboard and his signature appeared in the form's authorized box.

~

Rosie woke with a steady pain in her head. Menopause was a long time ago, she thought, as she walked softer than usual around the house, getting dressed, getting breakfast. Those headaches throbbed. This pain was unwavering, burning inside her skull. Maybe she should go back to sleep. Try again in a few hours. But the sky in the east was brightening. In less than an hour it would be daylight. Rosie waited with a cup of tea and a biscuit that ran over with strawberry jam, pampering against the pain.

It was going to be cold out there. She looked out the window at the pines still black against the birth of morning. Cold, and the snow was getting deep. Maybe she should have picked medicine last summer while it was nice, brought it into the house and stored it in a jar, handy. Maybe start a medicine chest of her own, pick a little of each that she knew for certain, put them away and keep them. Put labels on the jars, this one for headaches, this one for sore throats. Then she would have to keep her house clean. Clean of people who had angry thoughts, and people who used alcohol or drugs. She would have to keep herself clean. She couldn't indulge in fantasy or foreboding. She couldn't rant against the stupidity that entered her house through the television news. Medicine needed to be kept in a clean place. If it wasn't, if it became contaminated, it picked up the anger, frustration, stupidity and could put that into the person who took it.

No, this was the better way. Rosie walked through the snow, Duchess at her heels. The fungus she was looking for grew down by the lake, in the willows. It was easier to find now that the leaves were gone, easier to see. She didn't find the one she remembered from last summer. She found another one, a smaller one, enough for what she needed. As she thanked it before picking it, she thought, this is the right way to keep medicine. This is where it belongs. In the big medicine chest, and the labels were in her memory. She remembered Ben's mother, old Eleanor, telling her of a time before. *"Everywhere we looked, there was our food, there was our medicine."* Everything was where it was supposed to be. Everything was as it should be. Some days are hard. Those days you just have to get through. Some days are better. Some days are really good, and Ben would be coming home soon.

～

That falling dream again, falling through darkness as thick as black water, smothered scream, heart racing, pounding louder than the scream that didn't make it past her teeth. An afternoon nap should not end this way. It was supposed to be an indulgence, a refresher, a break from the stress of work. She checked the time on the clock radio, twelve minutes, that's all; she had only been down for twelve minutes, not enough, not nearly enough. She thought about putting her head back down on the too small cushion but it wasn't on the couch anymore. It was on the floor. She thought about picking it up, knew it was useless, knew she would just lie there, too afraid to fall asleep again.

Monica hated the smell of this; gasoline fumes burned her eyes, there was nothing about this that smelled right. The tiny hollow glass wand connected to a rubber hose hissed as she stirred oxygen blended with hydrogen into the goo, and slime of Styrofoam dissolved into gasoline, putting the bubbles back in. This was the dangerous part. Flow anything past anything and there was a risk that static electricity would build up. Enough static and it would want to go somewhere, jump from one surface to another, spark, a single tiny flash to ignite the fumes and oxygen and Monica would not have to worry about getting the mixture fully fluffed. She would never worry about anything ever again.

She hated all of this, this windowless concrete cave, that bare electric bulb, this rough wooden workbench. She hated the steel door and its complicated latch and lock. She hated the tank where electrical current ran through water, breaking down the bonds between hydrogen and oxygen. *Hydrogen is lighter than oxygen, it rises up here and comes out the red hose. Oxygen is heavier. It comes out here, this blue hose.* She hated the sound of Ed Trembley's voice in her head, but listened to him again. *"It's simple. Just common everyday stuff, water and electricity. They can't prohibit those, or gasoline, or Styrofoam."* But mostly she hated the black steel barrel in the corner there, with the bolt-down lid and the bright yellow trefoil symbol painted on its side.

Maybe she was hating this because out there, on the other side of the steel door, was where Ed Trembley had shackled the American soldiers, where he fed the contents of the barrel to Rick Fisher, where Wally the other soldier died, and Ed left the body chained to the water pipe until it began to smell.

A feeling crept into the bomb shelter, mixed with the fumes of gasoline, mixed with the escaped hydrogen and oxygen. It wrapped itself around Monica and her hate armour, worked itself through the hate shield and touched her. Loneliness drained the hatred, drained the strength that kept her standing. Her knees weakened and she would have sat down, there on the cement floor. All that kept her standing was the fact that if she sat down without grounding out the glass wand, a spark would end all feeling.

Monica sat on the couch, the little cushion still on the floor. She held the bottle of cranberry juice in both hands, because neither hand by itself was strong enough on its own. She held herself up with the little strength she had left. She wanted one thing in that moment, she wanted another human being to touch her, touch her anywhere. What good were legs, if you had nowhere to walk to and hands never stroked them. What good was a flat belly if no one ever kissed it, or a throat, or arms, or even hands. When was the last time someone touched her hand? Just touched it, a finger. When was the last time someone shook her hand, just in greeting, just in politeness even? She remembered the last time she made love. That was easy. That was here on this couch. Was that the last time a human had touched her? Was long dead, forgotten Ed the last human to touch her?

Her body dragged her mind back from the past. She experienced the couch against her back and beneath, experienced the fabric of her clothing, the tightness of an elastic waistband, the bite of her bra strap. She felt the ache in her flesh to be touched, not even caressed, just touched, anywhere.

A man's callused hand, cupped, thumb against forefinger, held her. He didn't drop her. She jumped. Monica found the beginning of the falling dream. She sat motionless on the couch, absolutely still and pushed with her mind against the darkness, sought in the black for more of the image, looked for a face beyond the hand. Nothing. Her mind found only emptiness. She came back to the couch. Breathed again, broke the meditation, became aware of her body, now without the burning desire to be touched, now that she was aware that it was her who jumped from human touch, her choice to leap into the void.

Her sadness rose in her throat and began to choke her, a burn ignited beneath her eyes, and the moisture started to flow high in her nostrils. The door slammed behind her as she continued to button her parka, marched down the unshoveled walk toward the street. She would not cry, would not be weak. Cold air filled her, purified her. She drew it in deep, gasped it, pushed it out and drew in more. It opened her throat and eased the sting, promised to freeze any tears that dared to appear. Monica found gloves in her pocket and pulled them on, continued to breathe deeply and walk. Walk an empty street. She stepped off the snow-covered sidewalk, to march down the hard pack of rare traffic.

She wasn't going anywhere. She was just going.

~

Freedom Friday marchers, silent, voiceless, only the crunch of boots on snow, walked four abreast down Idylwyld Drive. Jason's marched in unison with his wife on his left. The woman on his right was more often out of step than she was in. It didn't matter. She was a body, another body in the march. That's what it was about for Jason, the number of bodies that showed up every Friday at four. His personal count was ninety-seven consecutive Fridays, even last Christmas that just happened to fall on the chosen fifth day. For Jason every Friday was a Good Friday. His wife Elise, her arms swinging beside him had a personal count of over a hundred.

The marchers did not speak. This was not a chanting, screaming demonstration. He liked it this way. It was more dignified, solemn. Words are useless when they are shouted, or screamed, or mindlessly chanted, sound for the sake of sound. He liked this form of protest, this serious, almost religious form, a moving vow of silence, in unison. He took a quick half-step so that he was marching with the woman. She was in step with the man beyond her, an older man, almost old, with a slight but noticeable limp. The marchers tried to step in unison, but were often unable. With time and repetition, the veterans learned how to accommodate the novice, to shift step, and fall in. Mostly it worked.

Homeland Security watched the marchers, one at every intersection from 33rd all the way down the hill to 22nd, cold, stamping their feet to keep warm, shifting their weapons slung over their shoulders. The men and women and the occasional child, stomped past the black uniforms, looked straight ahead, heads high, determined, serene.

Monica stopped when she saw the soldier. He was not the human she was looking for. Then she saw the marchers coming down the street behind him. Fools, she thought. They could march forever and nothing would change. Change needed action. A couple hundred people every Friday didn't even make the local paper, an exercise in futility at worst, at best just exercise. But, they were human. She walked forward, past the black parka, stood at the curb, watched for a place where she might step into formation, watched the faces of the marchers coming down from her left. A mix of ages, an occasional teenager, but most of them were older, some were even old.

The first ranks were all full. Monica hoped she would not have to fall in at the end. She did not want to be last, a tagalong. She wanted to belong, in the middle somewhere, shoulder to shoulder with someone. If not, then she would carry on alone she decided. Why participate in a fool's parade?

"*Ben*" she almost shouted at the old man in the green canvas coat. He turned at his name. A smile twisted his face. "Monica, come on." He swung a weak right arm out as if to draw her in. Monica skipped along as she tried to get into step with the marchers beside him. "What are you doing here?"

"Later." Ben continued to march, kept protocol.

The woman at his left touched his elbow, indicated with a twist and nod of her head that she would give her spot to Monica, and graciously stepped out of rank behind him.

Four more blocks, just four more, Monica's head swam with questions as she marched along beside Ben. She wanted to lean over and brush shoulders with him, but she was afraid to bump him. He looked as though he was using all his strength just to keep walking, stumbling, as though he was dragging his left leg. The limp was slight but noticeable. A stroke, she concluded. Ben has had a stroke.

The march ended in a jumble of people, smiles, chatter after the silence.

"Jason." He held his hand out first to Monica, then to Ben.

"Monica."

"Ben."

They responded and shook his hand in turn.

"My wife, Elise."

Another round of handshakes. Monica removed her glove for the pleasure of it.

"We're going to Tim Hortons. Why don't you join us? On me." Jason indicated down the street.

"Sure," Ben wanted something hot.

Monica wanted to be wherever Ben was. "Before we go anywhere, you are going to tell me how the hell you got here."

"I walked."

"You walked?" Monica held Ben's arm, walked beside him, pressed against him. "Where from?" She looked into his face. It was different, twisted sort of.

"From the Correctional Centre out at the north end." Ben was having trouble walking with Monica hanging onto him. "I'm not sure what happened. This morning she gave me this coat, walked me to the gate and stood at attention while I walked out. She never said anything. Just pushed some papers into my hand. I haven't even read them yet."

"Who's she?"

"A guard. Just one of the many."

"So how did you come to be marching with us?" Jason was listening, walking behind Ben and Monica, holding Elise's hand.

"You were going the same direction I was." Ben looked over his shoulder. "I just joined in."

The coffee at Tim Hortons was okay. Ben would have preferred Roastery coffee for his first taste of freedom, fresh roasted, fresh ground. But, Timmy's wasn't bad he had to admit. Not bad at all.

The lineup at the counter grew as Freedom Friday Marchers sought to warm themselves with a hot cup. Several who walked past their table stopped to pat Jason on the shoulder, on the back, or just to lay a hand on his head, a ceremony of touching.

"You're well known," Monica noticed.

Elise explained with a proud smile at her husband. "He started the march."

"You don't worry about HS?" Monica looked at Ben. " Leaders are known to disappear."

"They haven't bothered us." Jason's elbows were on the table, his cup held in both hands. "It seems that if the media are watching, HS behaves. Lance from CTV is there every week. Even though it rarely makes it on air, just the camera keeps us safe."

"But then I guess you're not doing much. I mean you stop traffic for a bit. But everyone has learned not to take Idylwyld Friday afternoon."

"We're doing a lot." Elise defended against Monica's dismissive comment. "Look at how many people are out every week. That in itself is something."

"But, you're not going to chase the Americans out with a few hundred marchers."

"We're not marching to chase the Americans out. Freedom Friday is about an end to all war. It's about imagining peace. That's why we don't yell and chant. We come together and walk together and imagine peace. It's also a prayer, a silent prayer. And it's working. Every week there are a few more people. One or two more that can imagine a world without war."

"Prayer!" Monica was indignant. "Religion is a weapon. Look at what happened historically in Afghanistan. When the Soviets invaded it, the Americans joined with the Muslims in Pakistan to fight godless communism. They printed thousands of Korans, created religious fervour, and it came back to bite the Christians in the ass on September 11th. Look at what's going on now. It's the Christian Right that feeds the government that attacked us."

～

The wind stopped.

Red stopped.

Benji kept walking.

"Hey!"

Benji turned at the word, loud in the new quiet broken only by the crunch of snow around his boots.

"What?"

"I don't know."

Moose tracks, fresh, led away through the stark black tamarack, trees highlighted here and there with phosphorous-coloured hanging moss.

Benji turned, faced Red, shifted the strap on the rifle higher on his shoulder, the borrowed rifle, the rifle Benji desperately wanted to fire to kill the promised moose. Red looked at the sky, a boiling grey black low sky, a sky that should be accompanied by wind.

"I was thinking about maybe circling ahead if we found an open spot for you to wait. Let him get a sniff of me so that he turns back."

Benji looked around, looked for the open spot. It wasn't anywhere near. Here was all thick, stunted muskeg tamarack standing in bough-deep snow. Only the moose tracks and their own tracks broke the whiteness.

"There's no wind." Red explained.

"Hey, that's right." Benji looked around again.

There had been wind all morning, strong wind that rattled the snow loose from the trees, wind that buried the moose tracks. Red, the hunter, needed wind to hide in, to show him how fresh the tracks were, to silence the clomp of Benji's boots. Wind was his friend. He looked at the sky again.

"We better get out of here, over there to that stand of spruce." Red pointed north.

"What about the moose." Benji looked at the tracks that led west.

"Later." Red started running.

They were not quite into the spruce when the first hailstones hit, driven hard by the new stronger wind that wasn't Red's friend anymore. This was an angry wind that tried to find the two men huddled under the heavy spreading boughs of the towering white spruce.

"This ain't supposed to fuckin' happen. It's January." Red's curses didn't slow the hammering ice. He crouched close to the tree's trunk, circled around to the lee side and sat down with his back to the rough bark. Benji followed, sat beside him, fumbled with the rifle and strap that tangled him. Golf-ball-sized hail beat fiercely against the branches above them, blocked out the world in a violent curtain of white beyond the edges of the bouncing boughs, roared its anger and punished the earth as it tore down smaller branches and broke the weaker trees.

"It's not supposed to hail in January," Red repeated.

Benji wasn't sure, depended upon Red, to track the moose, to say if tracks were fresh or old, to know which direction was home, which was safe, which would lead to the end of the hunt. Benji didn't want to hunt anymore. He stared at the wall of driven ice, listened to the rough rattle of it. He looked to Red. Red wasn't afraid. He was angry. Benji let go of the fear that had been tightening around him, accepted what was happening as nature.

"Did you do anything to piss Rosie off?" Red stopped, waited for Benji to catch up, a few steps behind in the tracks Red ploughed through the snow. The snow wasn't fluffy anymore. It was hammer-packed by the hail that lay in a solid layer on top and made walking difficult.

"What's that?" Benji caught up, shifted the rifle strap.

"Did you piss Rosie off?"

"No, not that I know of. Why?"

"You don't know?"

"Know what?"

"Your mother-in-law is a witch."

"A witch?" Benji pulled off his hat, wiped sweat with his mitt, shrugged under the rifle strap that slid on his nylon parka and settled in the same spot on his shoulder.

"Maybe she sent that storm against us."

"You're serious?" Benji searched Red's face for a hint of a joke.

"If she was pissed off at you, she could do that."

"No, me and Rosie get along good." Benji was serious too.

"There!" Red pointed over Benji's shoulder.

"Where?" Benji turned around. The moose looked more confused than Benji. It stumble-shuffled toward them.

Red waited. He wanted Benji to experience the kill, but Benji was taking way to long, fumbling with the rifle, tangled in the strap. The moose wasn't going to keep coming. It was going to see them, or smell them, and run. Red pulled the butt of his rifle into his shoulder, sighted centre, glanced over at Benji who had his rifle down looking at the mechanism, trying to find what was wrong, why the rifle hadn't fired when he pulled the trigger. Red looked back down the barrel of his rifle. The moose had its head up, stopped, straight on. The rifle kicked into his shoulder, cracked incredibly loud. The moose shifted back onto its haunches a little, then fell forward, its front legs buckling.

"I guess you didn't piss Rosie off after all." Red found the jugular with a knife, let the animal bleed out for a few minutes before they began to skin it. "Unless it was her who put the safety on when you were trying to shoot." Red smiled, he wasn't in the least serious.

~

Theresa poured dry cereal into a brightly coloured ceramic bowl, measured this bowl against the box, allowed for the next bowl and two more bowls tomorrow. Her daughters, Dorothy and Rose, eight and ten, sat sleepy-eyed at the table, quiet. There was enough cereal for tomorrow, but the milk was not going to make it. She made a note to herself to pick up a carton on the way home from work. She didn't want to. Monday was her day off and she would do a complete shopping then.

She checked the clock on the microwave. "You girls have twelve minutes to eat and get ready."

Day shift on Saturday wasn't fair to the girls. It was their weekend. They should be able to sleep in. During the week she left them to get themselves ready for school, a five-block walk, lunches left on the counter and she would be home by four. But weekends meant they had to go to the sitter's and be out of the apartment by seven-thirty.

Her thoughts turned to the old man as she buckled the wide leather belt that held her pepper spray, handcuffs and baton. It matched the black uniform. She wondered where he was today, remembered how he turned and looked into her eyes before he limped through the gate. Looked right into her soul. She wondered if he liked what he saw there.

She tied her hair back, tucked it down, where it could not be grabbed. Safety first.

"Come on, girls, time to go." Ben Robe was not her problem today. He was out. She had to go back in there.

～

"Aren't you afraid of criminals, Mommy?" little Rose asked, she squirmed under the seat belt that at her present size tended to run across her face.

"No, my girl, there aren't many criminals in jail, mostly it's people with addictions."

"Junkies?" asked Dorothy.

"Where did you hear about junkies?"

"School, of course." Rose answered for her little sister.

"All kinds of addictions, not just junkies. I'm . . . " Theresa hesitated. "I'm more a counsellor than a guard," she lied.

"But are there junkies there?" Dorothy asked with the shoulder strap under her chin.

"Not many." Theresa really didn't know. "Mostly it's people who have troubles in their lives, one kind or another who get in trouble and can't find a way out."

"But is it dangerous?"

"No," Theresa lied again. "Most of them are addicted to tobacco." She told the truth. Enough tobacco for a cigarette sold for more inside than either marijuana or coke.

Theresa kissed the end of her finger and pressed it to Rose's nose before her daughter could get out of the car and run to the sitter's.

"Love you back, Mom." Rose found her pack with the books and crayons for Dorothy, and a snack.

"Hey, you girls want to go visit your grandma next weekend? I have four days off. Why don't you take Friday off from school and we'll go up north?"

"You are not going to work overtime." Dorothy's words remained in Theresa's head as she drove her Land Cruiser, the Land Cruiser that almost belonged to her; two more payments. She liked this truck, all-wheel drive, heavy, reliable, Toyota technology. She liked the way it handled in the corners, its four hybrid engines, one for each wheel, computerized to apply the perfect amount of torque.

She accelerated hard at the change of the light. The truck responded with a smooth, quiet rush of power. She was reminded for a minute of the reason she had purchased it, her excitement about the cross between the rotary gas engine and an electric engine, how one fit inside the other, how she had phoned her brother Dougie to tell him about it, and his excitement.

"So they must've built the armature into the rotary part of the gas engine. That means the stators must act as seals." He figured it out in his head. "It would make one hell of a welder."

"I don't know how it works, I just know it's really easy on gas."

"A rotary engine has unlimited RPM. There's no top end." Dougie's mind was working with this, imagining it from a thousand kilometres away.

"It goes as fast as I want." Theresa didn't need details.

"No, think about it. What you have there are three things all together. First you have a rotary gas engine, an electric generator, and an electric motor all in one unit. It's brilliant."

Theresa liked it that her big brother approved. It was a good truck to take to Moccasin Lake.

Red dropped the front quarter of the moose onto the table, slid it off his shoulder, red meat and bone. He straightened once the weight was off, stretched his tired shoulder. "This is the last of it."

Benji looked for space on the table for the set of ribs he held away from his body, not wanting to bloody the front of his parka, his arms tired.

Red made space on the counter and helped Benji to lay it out. "There's some good eating there." He noted the layer of fat that covered the outside of the ribs.

Lorraine put a knife to the flesh, separated gristle and bone.

"Lots of people are going to eat good for a while." Rosie moved the men away from the meat with her hip and shoulder, simply took up the space they occupied until they stepped back. They had no business here. This was her place, her business.

"You men must be tired, that's a lot of meat to pack." Rosie was reminding them that they should go sit down now, relax, drink tea, tell stories. They should be keeping an eye on the children running around, gently teasing, scolding the more mischievous ones. There should be children here. Rosie looked away from the meat, around the room — the only child was Rachel. Three women and two men, enough people to get the work done, but there should be more, more women laughing, more men bragging, more children getting in the way, learning.

"It wasn't as bad as I thought it would be." Benji got Elsie's attention by touching her elbow. "Red made a sleigh out of the hide. We just wrapped all the meat in there, tied it with a rope and pulled — amazing how easy it dragged."

"Trick to that," Red was happy to explain, to teach, "is pull in the right direction. All the hairs lay one way. You have to pull it forward." Red felt good, tired, sore and complete. He brought home meat, he fed his friends. It was said that when Red shot his first moose he was holding his diaper up with one hand. That wasn't quite true. He shot his first moose when he was eleven. Uncle John and Simeon had shot a moose across the bay from the village, a cow moose, they were saying that the calf was still out there. Red and three of his buddies went looking with a .22. Red saw the calf first, put a bullet between its ribs, came home a man, with that same complete, strong feeling he was feeling today.

~

Dean wasn't thinking about his wife, Vicky, he had not thought about her in a long time. His thoughts rolled back to the Canadians who killed his son Ricky. He tried thinking about other things, tried thinking about the farm, the equipment that needed repairs before spring seeding, about the cattle. When she was there, or when he was there on the farm, they talked, said "hello," "good morning," "I love you." Then he went back to the world of thoughts; in this world revenge dominated. The Canadians took his son, a cheap, dirty trick. Dean would not stoop that low. He imagined he would kill a Canadian honourably. Walk up to him, face him like a man, put the gun in his face, look into his eyes.

He did not tell Vicky about the handgun. He was not keeping a secret, he didn't care if she knew or not. They just never talked about things like that. She refused to leave the farm, gave Dean lists to take to town, odd spices and particular flour, specific ingredients for the constant baking, creating, cooking. He ate well when he was home, pastries to try, something new and different every supper. Strange breakfasts beyond eggs Benedict that included fruit and smoked salmon.

Dean stayed in his mind, even when he was all the way over to Minneapolis, in the big mall, wandering from store to store with Vicky's lists. Then he found the handgun, an American-built handgun in the Mall of America, a forty-four calibre, an American calibre, not a foreign nine-millimetre, something heavy, something steel, and solid, a gun that fit a man's hand.

A small box of ammunition, nothing extravagant, little cardboard box, not much bigger than a deck of playing cards really, fit into a shirt pocket easily. Now all he needed was a Canadian.

~

For no reason at all Dougie suddenly thought of his mother. He stopped and looked around. Did these people ever stop shopping? The mall was busy, filling the nine-million square feet of the largest mall on earth. He tried to imagine her here. He couldn't. Rosie simply would not stroll among the shoppers, drink coffee from a paper cup, dangle a handbag fashionably, lean over the rail and examine the plastic model of the planned phase III. He stopped trying.

Work on the big water pipeline was going well. His four crews looked after themselves pretty much, giving him time for a leisurely trip over to Minneapolis to spend a little time and more than a little money. There was lots of work in North Dakota, but not a lot else. Dougie was enjoying his time in the Mall. Looking around, eating, drinking, he even went to the amusement park and rode the big roller coaster alone. It would have been better if his wife and daughters were with him. Easter. He imagined, Easter he would bring them down when school was out, if she could get time off work. Maybe they should ask his mother to come with them. Give her a break from the cold of Moccasin Lake. But Rosie still refused to come. He let it go.

～

"I have something to do before we leave." Monica thought of the house, the equipment, the open door to the bomb shelter. "Why don't you wait here until I get back."

"Sure, no problem." Ben relaxed into the kitchen chair.

"I won't be long." She wrapped a scarf.

"No problem."

"It's this house. I have to take care of a house and . . . "

"No need to explain."

But she did need to explain. "It belongs to the resistance. I could take you, you could wait in the car, but even that is against the rules. If anybody saw you there I would be in trouble."

"I understand, No problem." It didn't matter to Ben how long it took to get back to Moccasin Lake. Time was his friend, it was no longer his master. There was another cup of coffee in the machine, the sun was beginning to show through the window lighting up the trees outside, spreading its copper colour across branches, across snow. He was silently saying 'thank-you for another day' while Monica went out the door.

～

"Theresa phoned." Elsie wrapped meat in brown waxed paper.

"So did Dougie." Rosie cut meat as fast as Elsie wrapped it, her knife finding its way easily around bone.

"What did Dougie have to say?"

"Not much, he's in Minnesota on a break, just called to say hello. What's your sister up to?"

"She's actually thinking about taking some time off work, come up for a visit."

"It's been a long time." Rosie paused, thought about it. "At least four years," she remembered, "maybe more." Her memory wasn't sure. "When's she coming?"

"Next weekend. Bringing the girls." Elsie smiled.

Rosie smiled too. "They're getting big."

"When was the last time you saw them?"

"When I went with Lester to the hospital. I stayed with them."

"You mean you babysat for her." Elsie remembered how it was when she visited her sister, left alone with the girls while Theresa worked.

"I spent lots of time with my granddaughters." Rosie's answer was definite, final.

Elsie respected her mother's tone, accepted the bare truth of the statement. "Well, it'll be good to see them again." She acquiesced, then changed the subject. "How's Lester?"

"Not good."

"Going back to see him?"

"Maybe." Rosie thought for a second. "Yeah, maybe I'll go back with Theresa." She wasn't sure. Something was coming, she listened for it, then turned to Elsie, "Maybe you should go and clean up the house. I think Ben might be coming home today."

~

"No big deal." Ben examined the truck. "Nobody was hurt?" He looked to Benji.

"No, like I said, we were both at the tree." Benji did not want to be here. He wanted to be anywhere else, but he stood straight. "I am really sorry, Dad." He said the words, words he'd rehearsed over and over. They didn't come out the way he thought they would, the way he practised them. These words were filled with hurt, the practiced words were empty, probably why he tried over and over to make them right. Standing here in front of his father, beside the smashed truck, the son, the son who tried to do good, here the son spoke from the heart and the words came out naked, honest.

"No big deal, we'll get another one." Ben heard more than the words, he heard the meaning.

"And the boat dad, I got the parts for the motor. Red said he'd help put them in."

Ben shrugged. "Lots of time for that." He looked around, spring was a long way off. "How have you made out?"

"What with?"

"Everything else."

Benji thought for a second, spun his thoughts through time back toward Ben's arrest. "Elsie?" he asked thinking of the important things.

"Sure, how're things with Elsie?"

"Good, things are good with Elsie, and Rachel, and Rosie, and Red. Everything has been good, Dad."

"Good." There was nothing more to say. "Let's go eat some of that moose you shot."

"I didn't shoot it. Red shot it."

"Don't matter, let's go eat it." Ben's hunger was for more than meat, he wanted to be inside with his son, with Rosie, with Rachel, with Elsie, with Red, with Lorraine, with Monica, with people, with laughter.

~

One of the reasons, maybe the main reason, that Theresa avoided coming back to Moccasin Lake was because here she often ran into people who recognized her from work, from the other side of the reinforced glass. She was never sure how to make the adjustment from institutional to social. The contact often ended in uncomfortable silence, sometimes bitter silence.

Rosie was happy to have both her daughters in the house, and her three granddaughters. They filled it with sounds, little girls squealing, shrieking. She had forgotten that little girls made that sound at every surprise, at dogs, at babies, at each other. It was a warm sound. She was happy to hear her daughter's visit, the chatter and laughter, to hear Theresa remind her girls to keep the volume down, just a little, so that adults could hear themselves think. When Rachel was not trying to climb onto every lap, especially her grandma's, she was chasing her cousins who were happy to be caught, to pick her up and carry her, feet dangling, to kiss her, give her baby smooches. "She's so heavy, Mom." And plop her down.

It should all be perfect. Ben was home next door. There was fresh meat in the house. Winter was not harsh, the way she remembered it could be. Yet something nagged at her, some old dark dread she could not name. Dougie should be here, then it would be perfect.

She fell silent, looked often into her teacup that she held in both hands, listened to her daughters visit, Theresa's serious voice.

"I didn't know you were living with his son."

"About seven months now."

"What's he like? The truth now, you're talking to your big sister here."

"Like his dad — " She paused, thought about it — modified it. "Almost."

"How's that?"

"Well, he's a thinker, likes to think things out, and he does. He's learning how to live here. Like going hunting, and he's had a net in for most of the winter until Mom told him she was getting tired of eating fish."

"How long have you and Ben been friends?" Theresa drew her mother back into the visit.

"Forever," Rosie came back slowly.

"You never talked about him. I had no idea who he was when they brought him in."

"If you had come home more." Rosie immediately wished she had not said it. "It's okay, my girl, I'm happy you're home." She took the sting out of the words as best she could, touched her daughter's arm, soothed the flesh with her fingers. "Ben and I were friends when we were kids, then he moved back about three years ago."

"Yeah, I got that much. But why didn't you ever talk about him?" Theresa was unstung. "You talked about absolutely everything else over the years."

"Must've missed some things." Rosie did not want to talk about pictures of a pedophiliac priest, not then, not now.

"What's with you Mom?" Elsie wasn't sure how to take an untalkative mother.

"Tired, I guess," Rosie lied.

~

Ben lay on his bed, his own bed, for the first time in almost five months. It felt good, sleep was looking for him, circling the cabin, drawing on his will to stay awake. He went to his routine place, his prayer before leaving the world, the place where he said thank you. But first he remembered the day, the thing he was giving thanks for, from waking up on Monica's couch, to the ride home and the welcome. Poor Benji, he felt so bad about the damage to the truck and the boat. Elsie, was obviously uncomfortable with Ben being home again. It had been her house, her nest; now she wasn't sure. Something needed to be done. She and Benji were living as man and wife in a one-room house with an old man. Maybe a partition to give privacy. He let it go. That was for tomorrow.

He remembered Rosie's laugh, loud, from the belly. That in itself was worth coming home for. But, he heard something else in the sound. The laugh was the same. He let it repeat itself in his mind, let it fill him again. Rosie laughed easily, always, but today it sounded like she was trying, even forcing the laugh.

Ben let himself move forward, remembered Theresa, that was her name. She became more of a human with a name. And she was Rosie's daughter, a relative of sorts. Ben remembered Theresa's face when she first recognized him, a will not to show emotion, or surprise, or to even acknowledge the recognition. "Nice to meet you, sir." She stretched out her hand to him when her mother introduced them. No need for anyone other than them to know they had met before, had a history together. It was best that they start a new relationship, a human relationship away from concrete, cinderblock, and reinforced glass. He remembered the feel of her hand, strong in his, and warm. Here, among relatives, they could be persons, they could be the person their hearts chose to be, not the person dictated by the uniform or the orange coveralls.

He remembered Monica, the long visit on the drive back north. Monica wanted so much to be academic, to discuss ideas. Mostly he listened, let her create paradigms, problems within the paradigm, and propose solutions. He was not convinced. His heart was not in the discussion. He played along, enjoyed the sound of a human voice for the sake of the sound. He remembered the hug she gave him before she left, felt her arms around him again, noted that he was hugged last, after she hugged her son and her daughter-in-law, not quick, polite, proper little hugs. Monica's hugs were long, endearing. She was learning.

Sleep pulled at Ben. He whispered into the dark "Thank you for today, Grandfather." Pulled the blankets a little higher, shifted the pillow so that it cushioned his head, eased the ache there, and let himself drift away.

~

Dougie liked this time of day, wondered if he got it from his mother or his father. His father probably. He remembered him on the farm, in the good days, before Darren, up early, before the sun, at first light, out on the tractor, coming home for breakfast after he put in a couple of hours of work. His father knew something about work, something about sunrises, something about the land and how it breathed again at first light, a long, deep inhalation. Dougie was not on a tractor or even in his truck. He stood in front of the little South Dakota nowhere motel with a coffee brewed moments before in his room. Good coffee, strong, black, sweet, the wonder of a simple French press and an electric kettle.

He watched the eastern sky begin to redden, enjoyed the bitter, nutty, flavour of his coffee. There was no wind. Dougie remembered his father once saying, "Twelve days a year the wind doesn't blow on the prairie, maybe today will be one of them." Dougie concurred. Maybe today would be one of them. Maybe today the dust would not blow black across the earth.

It was still properly winter, there should be snow. Maybe there was. Maybe come spring one of those black mounds would melt, turn to mud instead of slush, maybe they would call it mush. Maybe there would be no spring, can there be spring if there was no real winter? Maybe the earth would stay black, never bloom again.

He thought of home, of his mother up at Moccasin Lake. There was snow up there, lots of it. When spring came, that country would green up. Grouse should be in the poplars about now, eating the forming leaf buds. Dougie remembered hunting this time of year, him and Darren sharing a .22. He'd been thinking a lot about family recently, just homesick, part of the job, part of what he did. The job was going well. His men were still asleep, each with their own motel room. They would eat breakfast together in the restaurant then head out to the pipeline.

He felt someone beside him. He did not have to turn to see that no one was there. It was Darren. He knew. It didn't feel scary, or awful. It felt okay. It felt right to have his brother beside him. "In May," Dougie spoke to the presence. "In May, I will come visit you again, when it's time to plant."

"Where did you get the coffee?"

Dougie turned to meet the voice. It was a slow voice that spaced words, forced each word to follow the last.

"In my room, would you like a cup?" Dougie indicated the door behind him.

"You're a Canadian." The slow voice said.

"Yeah, eh." Dougie smiled at his own joke.

The man turned, walked back the way he came, four doors down the line of motel doors and went into his room.

"His problem." Dougie spoke to his cup. It was nearly empty and getting cold. Didn't matter, there was a carafe in his room. If the American didn't want his coffee because he was Canadian, then he would drink it by himself.

The presence that had been Darren was gone. Dougie felt very alone under a large prairie sky.

⌒

The light woke Ben. He dressed quietly, let Benji, Elsie, and Rachel sleep. Outside the world was quiet. He could hear his own breathing, drawing in cold air, warming it, releasing it in a soft white mist back again. He looked toward the stars, dim now that the eastern sky was beginning to brighten. "Thank you for today." He spoke toward the specks of overhead light, somewhere up there his ancestors were watching. His boots crunched in the snow, loud in the absolute quiet of early morning as he started out on a walk, a pilgrimage, a blend of exercise, prayer, and meditation.

A mile down the empty, ice-packed road, Ben stopped, looked at the house, the house with the lights that reflected off the snow. Someone else was awake. He forced his mind to remember, clicked through names of neighbours, until he came to Leroy. That was Leroy's house. Ben had not talked to Leroy since the funeral, stood beside him at the gravesite as Elroy's casket was lowered, and covered.

"I was hoping someone would come visit me today." Leroy was moving much slower than when Ben had last seen him.

Leroy's coffee was weaker than what Ben preferred. Ben let the first liquid of the day fill his mouth, hot, watery, smooth with a hint of sweet.

"So, I heard they drilled a hole in your head to let in some light."

Ben did not respond, just smiled, relaxed into the armchair, tasted the coffee again. He remembered how to take teasing.

The old man was doing him a favour, doing something good for Ben, helping him to laugh at his misfortune. It needed to be laughed at.

"I heard they used a number 12 Robinson."

"No, it was only an eight, maybe even a six."

"That's how it goes, people add on. Just wait, pretty soon it's going to be a lag bolt." Leroy's smile held a hint of mischief.

"I'm sure if you have anything to do with it, it will have gone in one side and come out the other."

Leroy laughed, a little chuckle laugh. "Now that would be a story worth telling." He was comfortable now that laughter had chased away the tension. "So why were they pissed off at you about in the first place?"

"Oh, I had a gun I wasn't supposed to have."

"What kind of gun?" Leroy exercised the privilege of bluntness that comes with age.

"M-37 assault rifle."

"What the hell did you want with one of those? Were you going to war, or what?"

"No, I just got scared. I was getting tangled up with the resistance and, well, things were getting scary."

"So, you went looking for trouble and you found it."

"Something like that."

"You know better." Leroy exercised the other privilege of age, the right to scold. "Didn't your dad teach you anything? I used to work with him, out in the pulp camps, long time ago when there was still trees worth cutting. There was a man, would never go looking for it. Us Indians Ben, we got enough trouble every day. Don't have to go find it." It was said, done, Leroy did not have to say anymore.

Ben felt a little smaller, as though the armchair had grown. Like the teasing, this scolding was meant to help him, help him feel humility, help him to be human. He remembered to be appreciative. "Thank you, Uncle." He kept his head down, focused on the darkness inside his cup.

"Okay then, enough of that. How's your boy?"

"Benji? Benji's doing good." Ben looked up.

"You are a lucky man, Ben Robe. I was worried about you for a while, not having any children. Then out of the blue you have a son. What a blessing, someone for you to pass along all those things your dad taught you."

"Yeah, it's good." Ben agreed fully.

"You know, maybe it's just age or something, but I don't think so, it's something more. I've been thinking about all the people that have gone ahead of us. Your dad, my dad, my mom, my sisters." Leroy paused, then said what he wanted to say, said it as simple matter of fact. "Elroy was here this morning."

"Yeah." Ben agreed with him, acknowledged what he said, not patronizing. If Elroy was here, Ben knew it was for a reason.

"I guess I won't be here long." Leroy stated the reason. "I don't know how many times I've been told that when it's time to go, one of your relatives will come and get you."

"Yeah." Ben agreed. "What did Elroy have to say?"

"He never said anything, just walked in, smiled at me, and sat in that chair you're in, sort of waiting for me."

Ben was suddenly acutely aware of the chair, its shape, how it wrapped itself around him. He forced down an impulse to stand up.

Leroy smiled at Ben's discomfort. "You don't have to be afraid of Elroy. He always liked you."

"I liked him too." Ben made peace with his situation.

"You know, I'm half a mind to go for a walk. Just go out and find a big old spruce tree and sit down and wait like they used to do. You know they tell stories about long ago, old people went out to die. They said it was because those old people didn't want to be a burden, as if everything was really bad for us, like we were always starving. I don't think so. I think those old people just wanted to go some place quiet, sit down, relax, let what happen what was going to happen. That's what I think."

"I think you might be right."

"Don't think about it too much my young friend. Not like me, I think this is my last winter; North Wind is going to come get me, take me home. You . . . " Leroy nodded toward Ben . . . "You got lots of time. Your job is to remember all the good things. Like the old people did for us when we were young. When times were tough, your grandma or grandpa would start talking about when they were growing up. How it was. They never told us stories about starvation or freezing. They told us about how good it used to be. That's your job now. Remember how it was, so that the young people have some hope. Remember how the world was, how the trees grew, how there used to be big fish in the lake, how people were decent to each other. Now you got a hole in your head to let in some light so that you can see your way around in there. You'll be all right." Leroy sat back, relaxed. "Yeah, you'll be all right, Ben."

At first Ben thought the old man was just talking the way he talked all his life, loud, in your face, always the one to step forward, take a position and defend it, but the more he listened the more he realized Leroy was talking in a rush. He was speaking as though he might never speak again.

He watched the old man on the couch, flannel pyjamas that might have fit better even a few months ago, now hung on his thin frame. He seemed to be shrinking, fading as he spoke. Ben tried to focus, wondered whether what he was seeing was real or a product of his damaged brain.

"You got money, Ben." It wasn't a question. It was a statement.

"Some."

"A little more than some I think."

"I've got enough."

"That's going to be the hard part. Like I told you, you're going to be all right. But that money you got. That's going to be your challenge. You got to figure out how you're going to do some good with that. Money has always been hard for Indian people."

The old voice dimmed. Ben leaned forward to hear. He missed a few sentences, something about residential school money.

"You, figure it out. I still believe it can be done."

"I thought about giving it to the resistance."

"*Resistance!*" The old man came back to life. If he had a table he would have pounded it. "Resistance. You ever go moose hunting with a stick? You're just trying to throw it away, give it to someone else to worry about. No. It's yours. You figure out how to use it. Resistance is just going to cause a whole bunch more misery. Who said 'an eye for an eye makes the whole world blind'?"

"Gandhi."

"Yeah, him. We need another one like him. Think you're man enough?" Leroy raised his chin higher, pointed with it toward Ben.

"He walked to the ocean to make salt and kicked the English out of India." Ben thought about the old movie, remembered images of dusty feet, and men beaten with bamboo rods.

"Think about it. You can't ever buy enough guns and bombs. I know you have money, but can you buy even one fighter jet, can you put a satellite into outer space, drop bombs from up there on Washington?"

Ben remained silent, accepted the truth of the old man's words. His head began to throb, little bubbles of pain, a pulsating ache. He consciously relaxed, let his shoulders sag, and breathed, slow, deliberate deep inhalations, and controlled release.

"Did it change you?"

"Did what change me?"

"That screw in your head."

"No." Ben answered quickly. He thought about it. It hadn't changed him, he was the same Ben, the same convictions. Then he became acutely aware of the numbness that ran down his left side. "Yeah, a bit." He changed his answer. He was a changed man. He was slowed down physically. Mentally he was as sharp as ever. He thought about that too. His mind was sharp but it wasn't as ever. The fog was gone. That haze that accumulated with age had dissipated. The mist in his thinking that he became so accustomed to, or perhaps because he had no reference to anything other, that he perceived it as normal wasn't there anymore. His thinking was crystallized.

"Yeah, Uncle. It has changed me."

"Tell me about it."

Ben was about to tell Leroy about the numbness and the mental acuity, but when he opened his mouth, his answer surprised him. "I used to be afraid."

"Of what?" the old man still had strength in his voice. A bit of power.

"I wasn't afraid of death, well not much, it wasn't the dying part that scared me. When I first found out I was in trouble with HS, I was really scared they were going to torture me."

"And they did."

"That's right. And I'm not afraid of it anymore."

"You survived it."

"I survived it." Ben and Leroy were on the same page, nodding toward each other as they spoke, echoing.

Leroy carried it forward. "It was bad."

Ben nodded.

"Hurt like hell."

"Oh, Yeah." Ben remembered.

"But now you're okay with it. Not with the torture. I mean you're okay with the fear of it. You're not going to go and buy another rifle and try to take on the whole American army by yourself again."

"No, you're right, Uncle. I'm way past that."

"Good. But you're still afraid of death."

Ben had no response to Leroy's direct statement. He couldn't deny it. But, he couldn't quite accept it either. Fear of death — wasn't everyone afraid of death?

"You stay with me today." Leroy broke the growing silence.

"You want me to?"

"Yeah," the old man nodded. "Stay with me. I don't want to be alone, but I don't want a whole bunch of people around. My granddaughter is going to come in a few hours and make lunch. We'll eat together. Then she'll go back to her family. It'll be all right."

"I'll stay."

"All day?"

"If that's what you want."

"It's what I want. You know what, I think it's time for a nap. Think I'm gonna lay down on this couch for awhile, close my eyes for a little bit. You're gonna stay?"

"I'm gonna stay."

The old man stretched out his long, thin body, pulled down a Pendleton blanket from the back of the couch and wrapped himself in it. He struggled to get it right, let out a little groan as he tried to get it around broad shoulders. Ben noted the feebleness, reached over from where he sat and tucked it around the callused, bony feet; wondered how many miles they had walked. Leroy twisted around, straightened the pillow so that it fit better under his head, closed his eyes, and sagged into a comfortable sleep.

~

The sharp, rugged Argentinean Andes Mountains faced a dull blue sky. Clear, cold wind, the always wind of this place tugged at the flimsy satellite dish in Stan Jolly's hand. He set it down, found a flat rock nearby and leaned it against the base. He needed it to point north, toward the equator, toward satellite WV3114.

There was enough power in the platform, the battery checked at 68, but with the sun out, it would be a good time to use the solar panel. Using more rocks to stabilize it, Stan aimed the concave black dish generally toward the west. Precision was not necessary. This solar dish was designed based on the sunflower. It knew to follow the sun in its arc across the sky, always in direct sunlight, a technical solution borrowed from the botany of a plant that learned millennia ago to harness solar power.

Ready, he keyed the computer, waited for connection, entered the password that was written only in his memory.

His program. It was his program now, he was the only person remaining who knew of it, the rejected program, perfectly adequate, simple, rejected by HS for a more complicated security program, because for some decision maker, complex equated with better. The program Stan used, this rejected program, once existed on a single disc, a disc left on his desk when he still worked as the Canadian Liaison on Security and Trade. He could not say for certain that the program was given to him, or that it was deliberately left for him to pick up and use, all he could honestly say was that he suspected it was left by the program writer out of frustration at having his program rejected, feeling rejected. The program now only existed in the memory of Stan's platform, labelled Space Invaders and filed fourth on a list of a half-dozen games.

Stan always worried at this point, when he connected to the satellite, entered his password. Would the system suspect him, randomly select him for detailed protocol assessment, search for his uplink position? It didn't. Stan, as ever, was allowed in. He scanned through files of communications, searched for friend's names, scrolled down a list of the last 24 hours, found Monica Bird, stopped and read:

"The bunker contains seven-hundred-and-fifty kilograms of U238 unprocessed Yellowcake uranium. Operative Monica Bird attends regular to bunker."

Stan clicked up the communication trail to the next message.

"Sensors indicate slight elevation in radiation at and near house at civil address 3112 Avenue H North, Saskatoon, Saskatchewan, Second Division."

He clicked up one more, the latest communication, minutes old, held his breath as he read:

"Thunder Bolt Satellite directed to position. Wait for confirmation operative is in bunker before dropping. Ground surveillance directed to positive identification of operative. Gentlemen, we want to be absolutely certain she is in there before we drop."

Why? The question crawled into Stan's mind. Why a Bolt from Heaven? Why not just shoot her? There were no logical rational answers. This wasn't calculated. Someone decided this way rather than another way. The decision was probably based on nothing more than someone wanted to play with the big toys of war.

The important question was, who turned? Someone turned. Stan frantically searched through the trail of communications, senders, receivers, names — he needed the name, the name of the informer, the enemy within. He raced against his own addition to the program. It was going to automatically disconnect him at one-minute fifty-nine point nine seconds, just before the two-minute mark when the system would perform another security check. He thought of downloading the entire file and reading it later, but a large download would trigger the security program. Too risky. Or was it too risky to save a friend? Seconds clicked, Stan experienced an internal battle between rationality and emotion, expose the informer or risk exposing himself. He heard words coming from his mouth, a prayer, "please, please, please." His fingers clicked through the list, images appeared on the screen and disappeared in a blur as he searched for a name.

Then, there it was, not in the sender's box; halfway through a message he caught the words, not capitalized, "b.chance". Betsy Chance. Betsy Chance. The name echoed in Stan's mind. Betsy betrayed Monica.

The message froze to the screen, he was disconnected from the satellite. He read the message again this time in its entirety. It was a longer message with several points from someone using the name RaynCloud, to HS Second Division, a generic address. He reread the important phrase "confirmed data with original b.chance. confirmed safe passage. All payments made."

Stan fought the wind against the thin dish again, rearranged rocks to support it, used the built-in spectrum analyzer to find the new satellite, the civilian satellite, connected and began sending emails. Now he was the Canadian on vacation, the kayaker, the mountain climber. He stopped and blew on his fingers to warm them, unaware whether it was the keyboard that was cold or the message he was sending.

～

Abraham Isaac Friesen knew he spent too much time on the computer, knew he spent too much time indoors. He should be outside, even in winter, out on the land, on the bare prairie, watching the sky for weather. But he was a landless man now, city bound, hiding. They gave his land, his farm, to a retired Homeland Security colonel. What would a warmonger know of land? Something to drop bombs on, tear up with tracks and tires, dig trenches in. Land is holy. Soil is life giving. Sift the dirt through your fingers at the beginning of a day, feel the moisture, clumpy; or feel the dry, dusty; hold it to your nose, inhale the smell, fill your body with the richness.

Abe sensed a familiar wind at the same time the screen informed him that another message had been sent to the Spam folder. He clicked the icon. The message was from 'JACK', all capital letters, not the usual 'jack sprat' or even 'Jackie Blue'. Abe wondered at the boldness. He read through the garble until he found the word 'THAT', also capitalized. He read the message only once before he sprinted his large frame to the door, remembered parka and boots. He was going out. Out into the new dangerous world where he might be found. He was going to find Monica.

Maybe they were watching, probably not. There were seven-billion people on the planet, Abe reasoned — even with technology, they would need seven-billion people at seven-billion monitors to watch all of the people all of the time. He wasn't afraid of the sky.

~

Dougie knocked on the door to Wesley's room, a loud pounding knock. Wesley was one of those who was difficult to wake in the morning, one of those that stumbled around groggy for the first hour of the day, grouchy, uncommunicative. Dougie had seen him close his eyes between mouthfuls of breakfast, pulled back to the sleep world, the dream world. Every morning, every transition, was difficult for Wesley. It took time for him to shift from that world to this.

But once his eyes were open, once he was into the day, into the job, Wesley stayed with it, completely into the work. Wesley focused on whatever was in front of his eyes, whether it was the work of welding pipes together or the inside of his eyelids and stayed with it. He ignored the world around him as he worked, didn't feel the cold or care about the wind. Dougie figured you could drop a bomb beside Wesley while he worked and as long as it did not knock him off his stool, he would keep working. He was a good employee.

Dougie pounded on the door again, louder, harder, rattled the door in its frame. He stopped, listened, heard a groan, and someone moving. He pounded again. Once Wesley was moving, you had to keep him moving or the bed would call him back.

"Canadian."

Dougie turned at the voice behind him.

Dean held the big handgun in both hands, held it up and out, arms straight — pointed the barrel in Dougie's face.

"My son's name was Ricky, Richard James Fisher, he was only twenty-years-old."

He wants to make a speech, Dougie realized. He wanted to listen, pay attention, hear the man out, but the black spot, the hole surrounded by blue steel stuck in front of his face grew and pulled Dougie into it.

'Is this what Darren saw?' Dougie wondered. 'This black, is this the last thing he saw? Did he look into it, go into it?'

Dean Fisher was talking, speechifying, slow deliberate words, words said over and over again in his mind, rehearsed, now vocalized, freed, spoken. Dougie did not hear the words, he was in the cab of his father's truck with his older brother. He was holding the gun with the big black hole.

"Don't fool around with that. It might be loaded."

"Don't be stupid, Dad would never leave a gun loaded."

"Don't fool around with that. It might be loaded."

"Don't be stupid, Dad would never leave a gun loaded."

"Don't fool around with that."

"Don't fool around with that."

~

Rosie came out of the bedroom, down the hall to the kitchen where her daughters were visiting. She hadn't slept well; tossed often, or simply lay there with her eyes open. The girls were giggling as she entered, sharing a corner of the table, heads together over cups of coffee. Rosie didn't join in. That was the first indication to Theresa and Elsie that something was wrong. They knew it was serious when Rosie said almost angrily, "Someone should go out there and chase away that woodpecker."

The girls looked at each other before both turned to look toward the window. The bird's rat-a-tat barely penetrated the winterized house, audible only now while they held their breath. It was halfway up a partially dead black spruce a few metres beyond the double glass panes, ignoring them, its back turned, intent on the rough flaked bark and whatever might be beneath.

"How long has it been hanging around?" a newly serious Theresa asked.

"Yesterday morning." Rosie turned on the stove to heat water for tea, stood there at a different angle and watched the black-and-white bird walk up the trunk a couple steps before it hammered a new hole.

No one was going out to chase it away. That would not do any good. Everyone knew that. The woodpecker was simply a messenger, or perhaps a mourner, come to tell them of the impending loss, or to be with them at the time of their suffering.

Eight-year-old Dorothy figured it out, saw her mother, her grandmother, and her aunt silently, fearfully staring out the window, saw the bird, knew from the adult's expressions or lack of expression that this was serious. "Get the hell out of here!" she yelled and banged against the glass. "My Grandma doesn't want you to come around no more."

The bird turned as it dropped from the tree, spread its wings and in a flurry of flapping gained a bit of altitude before it was out of sight.

"Watch your language young lady." Theresa's scolding didn't have any edge to it.

"It's okay, my girl." Rosie felt relief at the little girl's action, something lifted, maybe only for a while, but in this moment it was a good feeling. She readied the teapot, brought down a package of cookies from the cupboard and joined her daughters at the table to wait for the water to boil.

"Here, my girl, cookies for breakfast," she called Dorothy to her lap.

~

Elsie, Theresa, Darren, and their mom were with Dougie, a flat tire, no spare, on a dirt road in the winter. "Here Dougie, you wear my mitts. I have warm pockets," Theresa the Saint's pockets were not any warmer than his.

"Keep your knife at twenty degrees to the stone," his father showed him, pulled the skinning knife across the new Arkansas stone.

Elsie squealing, her arms so tight around his neck that he had trouble breathing as he ran, his little sister clamped to his back, spindly arms and spindly legs and shrieking in his ear.

"My son. You took my son. That was all I had. You took all that I had." Dean Fisher's voice came from behind the black hole, brought Dougie back to the motel on the edge of a little prairie town, to the door, to the morning. "He had a mother, a good mother . . . "

Dougie looked into the black hole and left again. He was with his mother. Rosie hugging him. "You have to be strong now, my boy," whispering into his ear, "don't let this ruin things for you. Darren was going to have a good life. You have to live it for him now. Make sure that it's good."

This was going to be the end of that good life. The crying American was going to pull the trigger any second and Dougie was going to be with Darren. Would anyone come and put flowers on his grave, the way he put flowers on Darren's grave every May 11th. One day each year he let himself feel sorrow, made a pilgrimage to that little cemetery, cleaned up around the mound that marked where they put his brother's body, sat for a while and told him about the things that happened in the last year. "I have another daughter. Mom is still in Moccasin Lake. Theresa has a new job."

The door to the motel room opened. "I'm up," Wesley sighed. He didn't open his eyes completely until Dean shifted the handgun away from Dougie and pointed it directly at him. "What the . . . " was all he had time to say before Dougie hit Dean. His fist arced in a roundhouse swing that ended in a solid collision just below Dean's left ear, crumpled him into silence on the cement walkway. Dougie kicked the handgun away; felt a moment of hate as his boot connected with it.

~

Ben waited. He sat in the black leather armchair with his thoughts. What brought him to the old man's house this morning? It really didn't matter which forces were at play; ancestors talking, tugging, he was where he should be.

The room slowly lit as the sun cleared the horizon, found the east windows. Ben pulled himself from the armchair, turned off the light. While he was up, he made another pot of coffee, a little stronger than the last, stood around the kitchen for a while, reading the things magnetized to the fridge door, waiting for the brewer to finish its work. When it was done, he took his cup back into the living room, quietly finding the armchair again, and waited.

Midmorning Leroy stirred, pulled himself determinedly into a sitting position, forced old muscles to do his bidding. "How's it over here?" he asked.

"Quiet."

"Same over there, lots of people just waiting around." He scratched an itch at the side of his neck. "There's something on that cabinet," he pointed with his chin toward an oak and glass cupboard.

Ben stood and walked over, looking.

"It's a card, should have flowers on it."

Ben moved things around, a birthday card, held it up.

"That's not it. It's just a card, doesn't open up."

He moved a few more things; a power bill, a little book of Saskatchewan birds, found a yellowed card printed on one side, began to read. "I haven't seen this in quite a while."

"That's it. Bring it over."

Ben handed Leroy the card.

"Yeah, this is it," Leroy read the first few lines. "This is the truth. Want truth, Ben? Right here," he shook the card in Ben's direction. "I met the person who brought this." He handed it to Ben.

Ben leaned back, turned the paper toward the light and read it through. Leroy waited for him to finish, to lower it. "Me too," the old man sagged on the couch.

"You too, what?"

"I was expecting something in Cree, maybe a song, a death song or something. Then I meet this person. Can't tell if it's a man or woman over there, and they tell me that there is the truth, brought it for everybody, that's why it's in English."

Ben looked at the card again, read it in new light. "Most people have forgotten this."

"Then it's up to you to remember." Leroy noted Ben's expression. "What? Don't think you can?"

"Well, my memory isn't what it used to be."

"That's because you don't exercise it. When was the last time you memorized something?"

Ben couldn't remember, shook his head.

"Memory is just like anything else. Gotta exercise it or it gets lazy. Used to be in school they made us memorize all kinds of stuff; the times table, days in history, when Columbus came here, poems. When was the last time you recited a poem to a woman, Ben?" Leroy smiled.

"It's been a very long time, if ever. I don't remember."

They both laughed.

"What's the use of having a life if you don't remember it? You memorize that." He indicated the card in Ben's hand. "It'll be good exercise for you." Leroy slouched back down, wrestled a moment with the pillow again and again closed his eyes.

Ben stayed in the leather armchair and waited, but now he had something to keep his mind busy. He read the card over and over, stopped and stared out the window, his lips involuntarily moving over words forced through a resisting neuron net.

At eleven-thirty, Leroy's granddaughter came over and made lunch, heated a can of soup and put together a plate of sandwiches. "For when he wakes up," she was putting her coat back on. "He sleeps lots now, it's good he has some company. Tell him I'll be back to make him supper," and she was out the door, back to her own young life and the things that were important to her.

⁓

Leroy woke once more that day, early afternoon he stirred, this time he didn't try to sit up, looked around the room, gave Ben a weak smile. "You'll be all right," he assured, "you'll do good. Know how I know?" There was a hint of mischief in his voice.

Ben leaned forward for the answer.

"There's a little guy standing beside you," Leroy almost whispered.

Ben looked.

"The other side. Can't see him, can you?" Leroy let his eyelids fall.

"No."

"I didn't think so."

"Who is he?"

"I don't know, maybe he's your grandson." Leroy took a breath. "Keeps looking up at you," he let the breath go, "like he's trying to decide. Do I want you for my grandpa or what?" He sagged deeper into the couch, shuddered and drew in a breath that rasped deep in his chest. Ben leaned forward, listened. Leroy's breathing was irregular, noisy. Ben got up, limped over and sat on the floor beside the couch. But, Leroy had no more words for him. He stopped breathing. Ben thought maybe this was the end when Leroy drew in another rasping gasp, let it out, opened his eyes staring into nothingness, his mouth moving around voiceless words. The end was without any twitch or movement. The old man drew one last shallow breath and when he let it out, he left with it.

～

Lester made it to the funeral. He looked sickly but he was standing. Rosie stood with her daughters and granddaughters. Ben was an honorary pallbearer. He was expected to be up close to the grave, just back of the bishop who was taking bishop's privilege to make a long speech before they lowered the ornate casket into the ground. Ben looked over at Rosie, remembered what she said last night at the wake. "I always wanted to have a child with you, Ben. But, we're going to have something better, we're going to have a grandchild together." He thought about Benji's mother. How would Monica take being a grandmother. He hoped she would take it well.

The bishop finished speaking, stepped back from the grave and aside to let Ben come forward.

Ben stood at the edge of the sandy hole. He spoke softly. Even people close by had trouble hearing him as he recited the faded words on the yellow card in his shirt pocket. He still did not completely trust his memory. "Go placidly amid the noise and haste, and remember what peace there may be in silence. As far as possible without surrender be on good terms with all persons. Speak your truth quietly and clearly; and listen to others, even the dull and the ignorant; they too have their story." Ben was aware of his voice and how it carried over the snow-covered ground and was swallowed up by the trees. He put more volume to it, "Avoid loud and aggressive persons, they are vexatious to the spirit . . . " Ben's gaze fell from the large gathering of people down to the casket. He recited as much to Leroy as to them. "Take kindly the counsel of the years, gracefully surrendering the things of youth. Nurture strength of spirit to shield you in sudden misfortune. But do not distress yourself with imaginings. Many fears are born of fatigue and loneliness"

∼

Betsy stood straight, faced her end, she would not go whimpering and crying. There was no out from here. Everything catches up to you in time, and Betsy's time had come. She knew it was coming, had known it for years, had made friends with it over and over again. "I only followed council's instructions," she answered again.

"You set up the thing with Ed Trembley." Monica held the weight of the pistol in the large fatigue jacket pocket.

"On council's instructions."

Abe Friesen felt the rough bark of the "walking" stick in his right hand, remembered the night he crept back to his farm to cut it down from one of the maples, a memento from the land, the land that was to have kept him in his old age. "You weren't at the gathering of thinkers," he accused.

Betsy did not answer, stood silent.

Abe waited, lifted the walking stick from the floor, held it in both hands.

"You knew the risks." Only her eyes and her mouth moved as she spoke, her eyes on the heavy length of branch in Abe's hand.

"I lost my farm. I went to prison."

"And I got you out."

Abe felt the urge to swing the maple branch, to smash, to hurt.

"How did you do that, Betsy?" Monica stepped slightly closer, between Abe and the woman who had once been her friend. "How was it that you could negotiate with the bastards? Tell me that."

"I think you figured it out."

Monica had her answer. "Yeah, we figured it out, figured out why you weren't in the house in Lac La Biche."

The accusation hit like a punch to Betsy's stomach. She involuntarily stepped back one full step.

Monica knew the force of her words from the sudden glare in Betsy's eyes. "We made you a hero because of that. The survivor of Lac La Biche is just a bitch."

Betsy had no answer, no explanation, no rationalization. She had walked away from the house with the men who laughed and joked and teased, young men who wanted to be revolutionary heroes. She had walked away, and in all the next years she kept walking back. The story about the falling star in the daylight and the vaporized hole was just a story. She sat in the restaurant after the agent left. Sat and drank coffee and waited until the blast four blocks away rattled the windows. Then she simply drove off and never looked back, never even ordered the chicken she volunteered to go get.

Now Betsy was walking into 3112 Avenue H North. Monica and Abe did not have to watch, did not have to make sure she didn't try to run. Betsy had nowhere to go. It wasn't that Abe and Monica had forced her to come here. She had volunteered. Betsy put the idea forward, offered an ultimate solution. It wasn't an act of honour so much as a declaration of *fuck it all. Fuck everything. Lets bring this fuckin' show to an end. Get it done. I'll show you bastards how it's done.*

Monica's coat fit Betsy a little too tight and the scarf smelled of her perfume. The two men who sat in the running car across the street were obvious, bold, sure. Betsy felt an urge to wave, to tell them, "Okay, call on your brimstone, bring on your heaven, bring on your hell." She didn't. She turned in at the gate, walked calmly to the house and used Monica's key to open the door. She took off the coat, dropped it on the floor, dropped the scarf and sat down on the pile to wait. She heard the sound of the car across the street drive away.

"Hey Freddy, hey Joe, how are you guys? I'll be with you in a minute." She may have spoken to the empty room at 3112

Avenue H North, Saskatoon, but she was back in the house in Lac La Biche and her friends, her true friends, were with her again.

~

"A dog sled?" Red wasn't at all expecting this phone call. And he certainly wasn't expecting that the person asking him to build a dog sled would be Ben Robe. "I could make you one, or I could give you the one in my shed."

"What's in your shed?"

"Oh, about a ten-foot toboggan, the canvas might be a bit rotten, but I've tried to keep it dry."

An hour later, Ben and Benji helped Red slide a solid oak toboggan down from the rafters of his shed, over piles of "stuff" and out into the snow. "It was my Dad's," Red explained. He grabbed the canvas carryall in both hands and tugged, hard. The canvas did not tear. "Well it didn't rot. It's only been up there for about thirty years."

"You've done a good job in taking care of it." Ben stood at the back of the toboggan, gloved hands on the handles. It felt right, felt like something normal, real, something with history, from a time when things were better.

"See the rubber there," Red pointed. "On the handles. My dad put that there. He cut an old inner tube into strips. Used to tie everything with that stuff."

Ben gripped the handle harder, it had a good feel to it.

"My Dad had lots of tricks like that. If you tie something with rubber, it isn't coming undone, and ice doesn't stick to it."

"I imagine it would be warm as well." Ben's hands had not left the handle.

"I suppose you are going to want harness too." Red turned back toward the shed. A moment later and he threw a bundle of harness and gang lines into the toboggan carryall.

Benji knelt to check them out, to tug at nylon harness, to open a brass snap, feel the pressure of its spring, note that it wasn't corroded or stiff. "What made you keep all this stuff?" He looked up toward Red.

"I didn't keep it." Red's smile widened ever so slightly. "I just never bothered to throw it away."

～

A child once played on this floor, crawled around on the hardwood, hands and knees slipping on the shine; not hers, not Betsy's; Betsy never had any children. She ran her hand across the wood grain, stroking, perhaps even caressing — something from this world, solid, tactile before the moment of vapourization, before she crossed over to another world.

She imagined someone somewhere, perhaps he even looked like Ernie, perhaps it was Ernie himself at the controls, guiding a satellite, adjusting, lining up, perhaps there were even cross-hairs, and Google Earth type zoom, and he would put the satellite directly above her and drop a tungsten rod that would heat up in the atmosphere until it was pure vapour, then it would hit the house, and Betsy and the house and the hardwood floor would all be vapour, would all be ghosts.

Didn't Ernie say that they were not using tungsten anymore, too expensive, they were using spent uranium? Just Betsy's luck eh, hit with an old fuel rod from a nuclear reactor because someone didn't want to pay the storage costs. That would be more like it — more fitting with the way the rest of Betsy's life had gone, or hadn't gone.

Fuckin' Ernie. What an asshole. At first she'd thought —
and that was decades ago now — at first she'd thought he was
maybe like a Hell's Angels guy or something; getting her to
move stuff, a little something from here to there; something
exciting, something with a bit of thrill to it. What's a few guns
from Ottawa to Edmonton? Then Ernie wanted her to become
friends with people who were going to protest at the G-20
meetings, just find out what they were up to, go along, become
one of them. *"Hell, Betsy, even go to the protest, have a little
fun. If you happen to get arrested I'll cover your ass."* Fuckin'
Ernie.

There' was no quitting when Ernie had his hands on you.
You didn't bow out on Ernie, Fuck no. There was only one
out — only one exit — and this was it; the hard way out, the
permanent fuckin' door slam.

At least it would be quick. Betsy put her palms to the floor,
pressed down, held her breath. What was taking so fuckin'
long? Let's get this done.

And Monica; what a silly bitch Monica was anyway, with
her ideals, her fuckin' high ideals, her perfect world, perfect
ecological order, perfect utopian crap. Crap; that's all it was,
fuckin' crap. The world would never be the way Monica
wanted it to be; there were too many Ernies, too many people
who needed you to do what they said. And if you didn't, if you
doubted, you never did anything ever again, and if your family
was lucky they found your body on the side of the highway
and your family had something to bury, if you were lucky.

What a fuckin' life. The hardwood wasn't slippery shiny
anymore; it was sticky, sweaty and sticky and she wiped her
hands on her pants, and the sweat showed on the floor, a
smear, a dull smear on the gold-grained wood. Was that it?
Was that all her life was going to amount to, a fuckin' smear

on a beautiful floor where a baby once learned to crawl, and maybe even learned to walk?

She imagined a baby, a boy baby, crawling across the floor toward her, her imagination so vivid in this ultimate moment that she could almost see the child, her child, her child that never was. As soon as she began to feel, to experience an emotion other than anger; as soon as she started to open herself to the imagined child, Monica came unbeckoned and picked up the child from the floor and held it to her breast.

Fuck this.

Betsy hit the back door to 3112 Avenue H North at a dead run, across the backyard, through the place where someone once had a garden, and hurdled the back fence. At the alley she turned right, turned north, and ran as hard as her legs would carry her. At the house, just before the alley met the street, someone had left their car running, backed it out of the garage, left it in the driveway to warm up for a minute. Betsy didn't have a coat or even shoes and now maybe there was a God, maybe there was life after Ernie. The car doors were not locked.

~

Abe wasn't watching, he had turned away, just a glance down the snow-rutted street. Monica was watching. There was nothing that represented a falling star in the daylight. One second the house across the street was the same house that Monica had spent days and weeks confined to; it was the same house she had just watched her best friend walk bravely into, walk bravely to her end — and in the same second the house disappeared, replaced by a flash. It was very fortunate for Abe that he wasn't watching. The flash lasted through the end of that second and through the next second and part way through the second that followed that, but the brilliant flare in Monica's eyes did not end after the house was replaced by a glass-lined hole.

The flash continued, painfully, as though someone had thrown sand into her eyes, blinking hurt and did not dim the bright blue that Monica continued to see. Even though tears continuously poured from her eyes, they felt paper dry as she blinked and rubbed and desperately tried to relieve the pain. She considered using snow, but without sight was not sure she would select a handful clean enough to rub into the sockets and put out the fire that continued to burn there.

Monica clung to Abe — one hand with a desperate grip of his parka, the other constantly wiping at her face — as they both stumbled down a sidewalk that desperately needed the attention of a snow shovel.

Abe's growing belief that Monica might be faking her injury came from his own experience with welder's flash. Yeah, it hurt, your eyes watered, felt like there was sand in them, but you could still see. It wasn't until he had Monica back in his basement apartment, seated in the leather armchair, and he couldn't undo the zipper on his parka that he realized maybe her eye injury was serious. The nylon zipper, designed for cold weather, was melted together and would not open.

~

"They're getting it. They're trying to figure it out." Ben untangled a dog from harness and gangline as Red looked on. "They mostly got it right." With the dog free, Ben headed back to the sleigh. "What I really need is a leader."

"How about the mom?" Red offered.

"Tried that, she won't stay on the trail, keeps trying to take us through the bush after any rabbit or squirrel or grouse that happens to catch her attention."

"Hunter." Red summed it up in one word.

"Hunter," Ben agreed. "One of these six has to be the natural leader." He indicated the team in front of him. "I just have to find out which one."

"How you going to do that?" Red held the lead dog by the collar, kept the team in somewhat of a line as Ben got back on the sleigh.

"Just have to keep trying — let them go."

Red stepped away from the dogs and they responded to Ben's "*Hike!*" by bursting into a sprint down the trail in a mix of puppy excitement and natural instinct. Ben held firmly to the sleigh handles. The team was a bit faster than he had anticipated and without his normal balance was having difficulty staying on the sled.

Red liked what he saw, liked the line of dogs and sight of his dad's sleigh and Ben determined to make a litter of puppies into a team. He liked the idea of it even more when the snow machine didn't start and he had to pump the primer again and again and pull on the starter cord again and again and again, until the engine sputtered, caught, ran rough for a few seconds before Red set off to follow Ben, thinking two-stroke engines were never designed to run on alcohol.

$$\sim$$

"Fuckin' Monica." Betsy turned the car toward the pile of snow that marked the side of the street. "*Bitch!*" she screamed into the still frosted windshield. The heater was doing its best, but the engine wasn't warm enough yet and Betsy had the heat control set to the floor, toward her feet. As soon as she had the car in park, she immediately pulled her icy foot from the brake pedal. At first she just lifted it, like a shorthaired dog standing on the step whining to be let back inside, one paw in the air and then another. "Fuckin' Monica." This time the words were more resigned — and more determined.

She vigourously rubbed a foot rested on her right knee, brushed the snow from the wet cotton sock, switched and rubbed the other foot. Her body vibrated with more than cold, more than the pain of fresh frostbite; she clawed a frozen chunk of snow from the heel of her right foot, fingernails angrily into the stiff cotton. "Who the fuck does she think she is?" Betsy pulled off the wet sock and threw it on the passenger-side floor, cupped her toes with both hands and applied pressure, firm, steady, strong, breathed in, held the breath in her lungs a full long second. Her body slowed, stopped vibrating.

Betsy's anger calmed, settled into a simmer, a glowing red coal that spread its warmth and chill. "Her and her fuckin' ideals. Who does she think she is anyway with her fucked superior morality." She sat sideways on the seat, her back against the door. She banged her head against the glass, hard. "*Fuck Monica!*" she screamed into the empty car. "Fuck her and her Ben." She banged her head again, harder. "*Fuck Ben.*" She calmed, an idea forming, banged her head again, not so hard, "Yeah, fuck Ben."

~

Ben read slowly, carefully, enjoying the imaginary landscape of Yoknapatawpha County and the character Joe Christmas:

At last the noise and the alarms, the sound and fury of the hunt, dies away, dies out of his hearing. He was not in the cotton house when the man and the dogs passed, as the sheriff believed. He paused there only long enough to lace up the brogans: the black shoes, the black shoes smelling of Negro. They looked like they had been chopped out of iron ore with a dull axe. Looking down at the harsh, crude, clumsy shapelessness of them, he said "Hah" through his teeth. It seemed to him that he could see himself being hunted by white men at last into the black abyss which had been waiting, trying, for thirty years to drown him and into which now and at last he had actually entered, bearing now upon his ankles the definite and ineradicable gauge of its upward moving.

Benji disrupted the quiet afternoon, scraped a chair back and put his book on the table, "So, exactly what do you believe in?"

Ben laid Faulkner on his lap, his finger keeping his place at page 313. He noted the author of Benji's book: Russell, and answered accordingly. "I am beginning to believe in nothing." He nodded toward the red dust jacket with big white letters in front of Benji, "I suppose he would call me a nihilist."

"Really?" Benji looked closely at his father's face, looked for an explanation, looked for something that he might not have seen before. He couldn't find anything, it didn't make sense, didn't match with his understanding of Ben. "But, you pray."

Ben took greater notice of Benji's book, beyond the author, he noted the title; *Why I am Not a Christian.*

"I suspect your question is more religious than philosophical. Doesn't matter; it amounts to much the same thing." Ben put a bookmark in place of his finger, turned behind and placed the yellowed novel on the little stand against the wall; it would be a while until he returned to it. "What I meant when I said I didn't believe in anything was that I am not a liberal, not a socialist, not a conservative; I really believe, more now than ever before, if we ignore government, maybe it will go away."

"We'll just pretend it isn't there, just like that, and the Americans will go home?"

"Almost" Ben answered. "If we don't participate, they have no power. The only real power the Americans have is that we accept them."

Rosie perked up, tuned in to the conversation over at the table. The light coming through Ben's front window was almost white, most of it reflected from snow. Rosie didn't even pretend that the reason she was at Ben's was because of the light as she sewed beads to leather, making a little pair of moccasins for Rachel. She was here because everyone else was here, Ben and Benji at the table reading, Elsie on the computer and Rachel asleep. It had been quiet, peaceful quiet, family quiet, a collection of people together, comfortable and safe with each other, comfortable with silence.

"I don't know about that." Benji rubbed his chin. "If we ignore the Americans they will just do whatever they want with no one to say they shouldn't. I think we should at least speak against tyranny."

"And what are you going to say?"

"How about, 'Go Home'."

"And do you think they will?"

"Maybe if enough of us shouted it."

"I doubt it." Ben settled into the conversation, prepared for a long, patient explanation. "If you and all your friends and all their friends start shouting at the Americans, all that will happen is that they will become more resolved to stay and show you they can't be pushed around. You will only escalate the conflict."

Benji sat and waited for the obvious more that was to come.

Ben continued. "When you fight someone, you make that someone stronger, conflict always does that. And, it is not the natural state of being. We are not always in a state of for-and-against. That's just a simple pattern of thinking. The world doesn't divide itself into dichotomies, left, right — good, evil — us, them — black, white."

"Well, I appreciate that everything isn't black and white, there are grey areas."

Ben cut Benji off. "No, not grey. That is still applying the principles of black and white, just mashing the two together. When people speak of the grey area, they are still caught in the dichotomy of opposing forces. There is more than black and white, a whole rainbow of choices. We have to be careful not to get stuck in these ideas"

Ben paused, thought through what he needed to say "We get stuck in ideas that out of oppositional forces we will arrive at truth. Look what happens when we apply that idea to anything; to law, to education, to religion. All we end up with is more conflict."

"But law works, don't you think? Two sides bring their dispute to a judge who decides based on the arguments put forward. It sure beats trial by combat."

"See, that's the thing. We've all been taught to believe that law works. It doesn't. The dispute isn't resolved by the judge. The judge just picks a winner and a loser, and it's a winner-take-all situation. Disputes are almost never only between two people, the whole community is affected by the conflict at some level, even if it is only an experience of rising tension. Law says there are always two sides to a story. Well, there are a whole lot more than two sides to anything, I don't know about everyone else, but my world is multi-dimensional."

Benji felt stung, as though the words were aimed at him. "What do you mean, you don't know about everyone else. Of course we aren't two-dimensional."

"But I don't know that." Ben spoke softer. "I don't know what others experience. I only have my own experiences to trust."

Rosie hoped Ben would get those ideas across to Benji; she was about to offer a prayer, a little something to those entities that were her constant companions, something to the effect of "give Ben the words he needs." But she thought better of it, it was best to let Ben find his own words, find his own way through to his son. Prayer was for important things, like health and happiness. It was always good practice to let the universe conspire to do whatever it was the universe conspired to do. It would give Ben what he wanted, the same as it perpetually gave her what she needed. Now if only Ben could show his son how to walk in the balance of all things. She threaded another half-dozen beads, shook them down to the leather, and continued her creation, glass, leather and thread; and good thoughts — these moccasins needed to have good thoughts put into them so that her granddaughter wouldn't trip.

Ben reached across the table and picked up the red-and-white book from in front of Benji. "This isn't so bad, I like the comparison between Christianity and Stalinism and Hitler, but it doesn't really get us anywhere. Attacking Christianity doesn't increase our understanding of where we are." He put it back down; "When you finish it maybe you would like something written without the confusion of philosophy. I can't remember who it was, someone once said that rationality was the flatulence around reason." And with that he went over to his little library of three bookshelves against the back wall where he kept only those treasures that were too important to abandon when he left academia. He searched for a few seconds before he found what he was looking for, returned and set the thin volume at Benji's elbow.

Late in the evening, after Rosie went home and after the supper dishes were done, when Elsie and Benji were alone momentarily, when the warmth of the log walls absorbed her words, Elsie asked, "So what was that book your dad gave you this afternoon?"

"Oh that. You know, I was sure he was going to give me something by Nietzsche." Benji went and got the book and brought it to her. "He said to read it after I finished Bertrand Russell, so I'm kinda skimming along to get it done."

Elsie examined the cover, "Doris Lessing, *Prisons We Choose to Live Inside*. I think I would like to read this." She turned it over to read the back jacket.

~

Monica cried. It was more than that her eyes watered from being burned; she lay in her bed, covers over her head and her face buried deeply into a pillow and cried. She was by herself; Abe left hours ago. He assured her, promised her that her sight would come back. "It's just severe welder's flash, hurts like hell for a few days, but you'll be all right. Just stay in the dark and I will be back now and then to check on you."

She hugged the pillow her face was buried into; squeezed hard, pulled it to her breast and let her tears pour. The worst part about being blind wasn't the pain, it wasn't even the fear; the fear that someone or something unseen was going to attack and you were defenceless in a world of white light. No, the worst part about being blind was this strange form of loneliness, unable to see people, forced to live inside of your head, alone.

She wondered if she might be crying for Betsy — probably not; Betsy was a traitor, a fake, a liar — if she was crying at all for Betsy, it was for the loss of a friend and that friend was lost before Betsy went into that house.

Perhaps she was crying for Ben, for the life companion, the husband that he had never become. She wasn't sure. She was filled with sorrow and despair that seemed to gurgle up from the deepest part of her soul as though she was mourning. She wondered if she was crying for a home, for a family, for Benji; all of those things that she had denied herself, given up for the resistance.

She sat up, sniffed loudly; wiped the wet away from her eyes with the sleeve of her blouse. Her eyes burned, but not with the same intensity as before. She strained to see something through the white glare, anything; and was rewarded with the dim silhouette image of Abe standing silently in the doorway.

$\sim$

"¿Señora, Quieres algo para desayunar?"

Kay smiled back at the young, nicely tanned waiter. "*Yo no hablo español,*" she did the best she could.

"Oh, Señora, I asked if you wanted breakfast with your coffee," without any hint of an accent.

"I'll wait, my husband will be down in a few minutes."

An easy wind came in from the Atlantic and brushed Kay's bare shoulders. Maybe she should have brought a shawl; yes a shawl would go nicely here at the sidewalk café. She could have sat inside, but it seemed that she had been inside all winter and when you are on vacation, well . . . you put up with a little chill in the morning. Here in Miramar, Argentina, it was summer, or rather late summer, early autumn. It wasn't cold, frozen Toronto where Kay and Stan Jolly kept their home, and it was definitely a lot warmer than mid-March on the Saskatchewan prairie and Kay's family's farm.

She liked it here. She could relax. The tension of home, the constant tension, the tension that was always there, so always there that it became normal and you didn't notice it, wasn't here. They left it behind, left the constant wariness; they stepped off the plane in the sunshine and it was no longer heavy on their minds, on their bodies, on their spirits. Here she was just a tourist, just a retired schoolteacher from Canada tourist, having a normal morning cup of coffee, at a normal outdoor restaurant, and Stan . . . well today he too would be the tourist. He would join a group of kayakers and explore the coast, a normal tourist thing to do, and Kay would maybe go down to the beach, more probably wander the streets looking into shops, not shopping, listen to people speaking Spanish just for the sound, have lunch somewhere, a nice sandwich, and later in the afternoon maybe a *yerbe mate*. She had become quite fond of the local drink, an infusion served in a gourd and drunk through a silver straw, and the known fact that it reduced cholesterol simply added to the pleasure. And it seemed to Kay that it helped with her arthritis, maybe she was imagining it, it might be the sunshine, or more probably it had to do with not living under constant stress; anyway the ache wasn't as intense as usual. It wasn't enough that she could go kayaking with her husband today, or mountain climbing with him last week, but it made life much more enjoyable.

A chair scraped and she looked up. "You finished posting?"

"It's done." Stan put the computer bag on the sidewalk beside the chair before sitting. "You have my absolute undivided attention until noon." He looked around for the waiter.

Kay touched his elbow across the table. "What was the result?"

He looked back toward her: "Inconclusive."

"Come on Stan, was it or wasn't it?"

"I honestly don't know."

"Well, what did you post?" she corrected herself, "what did That Jack post?"

"Only that the bolt from heaven was dropped on a house in Saskatoon. I didn't say anything about the barrel of yellowcake."

"Why not?" Kay's tone changed, Stan could be frustrating at times.

"Because we don't know for sure."

She stared at him for a long second, he was serious. She leaned forward, lowered her voice a little, "We know they dropped it on the house, we know there was a barrel of yellowcake uranium in the basement. Now, maybe no one has done any testing, but it seems only logical to me that Saskatoon is completely contaminated."

"Okay, then let's examine what we know for sure. When the bolt hit the house it was pure plasma. Tungsten melts at 3,422 degrees celcius, and uranium melts at 3,027 degrees, so we can assume that all of the uranium was vapourised."

Kay sat back. Stan had done his homework. She thought of something she had read not that long ago. "Remember Suzuki's *Sacred Balance*?"

Stan was looking for the waiter again, "Uh-huh."

"Remember that bit about Shapley I think his name was?

"No." Stan looked back at her.

"Well he said that if we calculate the amount of argon in a single breath, I can't remember how many atoms there are, but something like trillions and trillions and he calculated — and I do remember this — each breath we take has about four hundred thousand atoms that Gandhi once had in his lungs. And each breath we take has atoms that Jesus once had and atoms from Hitler and Stalin."

Stan thought about it for a moment. "It's worse than that. Even if the uranium was vapourized on impact, it would only be vapour until it cooled down again."

~

"Okay, so I've read Doris Lessing and I get it." Benji held the lead dog, Duchess, while Ben harnessed one of the full-grown puppies. "Don't belong to any organization, how simple."

"Right. If you *belong* to them, then they own you."

Benji thought for a moment about that play of words. "Yeah." He nodded his head, happy outdoors in the sunshine of early March, with a bit of warm wind coming from the southwest.

"It's also kinda like that dog you're holding there." Ben finished harnessing, attached a tug line, and stopped. "For most of the winter I've been telling her that haw means I want her to turn left and gee means I want her to turn right. She doesn't question it. She's been told it so many times consistently that it's become her truth. She probably believes me because I am the alpha male here. I am the one that brings the food. And her puppies." Ben waved a gloved hand at the other five dogs harnessed to the toboggan, "They believe that this is normal, perhaps even natural and necessary, look at them, they're anxious, they want to do this. It's like they're saying, come on already, let's go. I've only been running them a few months and already this is their absolute truth, they belong to this team." A dog jumped over its teammate. Ben gently put it back on its side of the gangline. "People get that way too, get to believing something is natural and necessary because that's all they ever experienced."

Benji joked, "So should I turn her loose?"

"Naw, she's too domesticated, wouldn't survive on her own yet. In time she could learn to go back to being wild and free, run with a pack because the pack was her family and not because the pack was a yellow dog pack or capitalist pack or conservative pack or a resistance pack." Ben stood on the back of the toboggan. "Okay, let her go."

Benji let go of Duchess's collar and stood aside. The team began to run all at the same time, a fast, long-legged lope, and as Ben went by, he leaned out and gave Benji a pat on the shoulder. "Be back in about a couple hours."

⁓

She could kill Monica, that would be easy, she knew where Monica lived, knew her habits, how she always used the elevator to get to the parking level of her apartment. It would be simple, Betsy would sit in a car near the elevator and wait — simple, easy and unsatisfactory. No, Monica deserved to die a fuck of a lot slower than that. It was simply a matter of principle. Betsy grinned at the idea, "Yeah, on principle, Now who was being principled — bitch?"

Her feet still hurt from the frostbite, and the new shoes didn't help. The pain fed her anger, she breathed in deep, exhaled with a surge through clenched teeth. She was going to fuck Monica the way Monica had never been fucked before, take away the one thing that that the bitch cherished the most. Betsy was going to kill Ben — kill the idea, kill the principle. Then she would come back and kill Monica too — and Abe — just for the fuck of it.

⁓

The early sun reflected off the sharp edge of an axe that hung by a strap attached to the dog sleigh, a tiny flare lost in the sparkle of sun on crystallized snow. The sleigh runners made a slicing sound behind the team that ran a familiar track along the edge of Moccasin Lake. Ben stepped down on the sleigh brake, and shouted a calm "whoa" that brought the team and the sleigh to a stop. Most of the seven dogs looked back over their shoulders as though to ask, "What's up, why'd we stop?"

Ben had no reason. The dogs had not run far and did not need a rest. The track across the lake was clear. No reason other than he wanted to, it felt right, just stop and enjoy the warmth of the sun on his face for a minute, to take off his gloves and grab a handful of snow just to feel it melt between his fingers and wipe the wet across his face, to walk up to the lead dog and scratch her behind the ear for a minute and tell her she's "a good dog, yeah, you're a good dog."

There wasn't much left of winter, the remainder of March, then most of April and the geese would come back and the lake would melt. The sun already gave a good warmth and stood higher in the southern sky; a pale blue completely cloudless sky. There to the south, just above the horizon, a black spot caught Ben's attention. He watched it, mildly curious, a raven probably; more than likely a raven. But ravens were still mating this time of year and there should be two of them.

The black spot became slightly larger. It was clearly a bird. Ben noted the flight pattern of flap and glide. Pelicans fly like that, so do eagles, as do ravens occasionally. It wasn't a pelican, too early, no open water. So, it was either a raven or an eagle. If it was an eagle it would be the first to migrate back, the first to return to their nesting grounds. Ben waited. Scratched the lead dog's ears absentmindedly for no other reason than she deserved kind treatment and for the feel of fur on his hand.

The eagle flew straight towards Ben and the team. He recognized its flight long before he could make out its white head and tail. As it passed directly overhead in a long glide, wings outstretched, it banked steeply to its left, made a circle as it descended and landed on the snow-covered lake a dozen metres from the back of the sleigh.

At first Ben was wary, looking around. This was not normal behaviour for an eagle. There was nothing here to attract it. It wasn't like a fisherman had left something out on the ice that an early eagle would be interested in, something to eat before the lake ice melted and it could fish for itself. It would be hungry though, it had come a long ways. He took a sack filled with chunks of frozen fish from the sleigh, snacks for the dogs, and tossed a few greasy pieces out towards the large bird.

It kept its distance. Ben dumped the sack. There wasn't a lot in it, something though, a bit, an offering. "Hey, Mikisew," he spoke softly, reverently, "Hey, Grandmother. You can see far, you can see the future, you can see the past. Thank you for coming back to us." He gave the sack a final shake for the last fish crumbs, pulled up on the sleigh brake. The dogs leaning into their harness, eager to run again, did not need to be told when the tension came off the gangline. They burst into a quick lope. Ben looked back, turned around on the sleigh so that he was facing backward and watched the eagle hop toward the offering he had left, accepting it.